# Sporting Blood

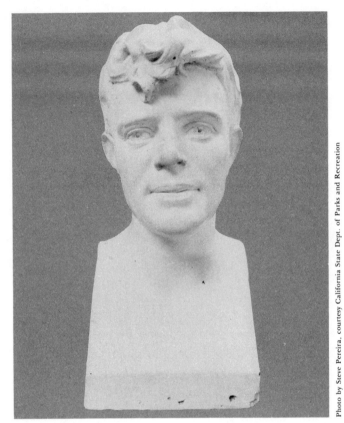

Bust by Finn Frolich

# Sporting Blood

Selections from
JACK LONDON'S
Greatest Sports Writing

Edited by Howard Lachtman

PRESIDIO PRESS

Copyright © 1981 by Howard Lachtman and The Estate of Irving Shepard.

Published by Presidio Press, 31 Pamaron Way, Novato, CA 94947

**Library of Congress Cataloging in Publication Data**

London, Jack 1876-1916.
  Sporting blood.

  Contents: A royal sport — A piece of steak — The
stone-fishing of Bora Bora — [etc.]
  1. Sports stories.  2.  Sports—Addresses, essays,
lectures.  I.  Lachtman, Howard, 1941-      .  II.  Title.
PS3523.O46A6  1981       818'.5209       81-4889
ISBN 0-89141-126-7                 AACR2

All selections in this volume reprinted by permission of
I. Milo Shepard, Executor of The Estate of Irving Shepard.

"Cross Country: King of the Road" (originally entitled
"Holding Her Down") is reprinted from *The Road*, Macmillan, 1907.

Unless otherwise noted all photographs by permission of the
Trust of Irving Shepard and courtesy of Russ Kingman.

Jacket design by Jon Goodchild
Book design by Vicki Martinez
Printed in the United States of America

For father George, golfer Al,
jogger Warren, fisherman Sal, and
"old sport" Earle

# Contents

# Introduction
## Jack London, American Sportsman

JACK LONDON WAS our first celebrity sportswriter. He brought to the subject a color and verve all his own, a personal style which distinguished him from writers of his time and later writers for whom he was either an influence or an inspiration. He was not as obsessed with sport as Hemingway, nor as pedagogic as Michener, nor as cerebral as George Plimpton, nor as nostalgic as the recent school of "sentimental sportswriting" — but then, he could not have been. He could only be what he was and what he remains: an American original.

The high apostle of adventurous living and writing in Ragtime America, London was the first to stake a claim on the sports world as a legitimate and worthwhile subject for writing, and the first to depict that world in the multiple forms (short story, novel, journalistic report, autobiographical essay) of his craft. He was also the first prominent American writer of the new century to win the popular accolade of sportsmen, and he won it fairly, on the basis of his spirited portrayal of the sports world and his equally enthusiastic participation in it.

"I boxed and fenced," London recalled about the exercise breaks he took from his writing stints, "walked on my hands, jumped high and broad, put the shot, tossed the caber, and went swimming." He also rode horseback and long-distance bicycle, sailed yachts and kites, and went surfing and target-shooting. During these activities, it occurred to him that some of his many-sided athletic and outdoor interests might

xi

make stimulating subjects for his writing. Once written, his sports reports and tales led some readers to assume that London was an accomplished athlete. It was easy to imagine, as London's fans did, that the excellence of the writer's athletic skills lent themselves naturally and fluently to prose exposition and description.

But this was not the case. A man of energy and diversity, London was certainly more of a "jack-of-all-sports" than a master of any one in particular. He was an average fencer and a competent rifle shot, a scrappy boxer and a powerful swimmer, a plucky horseman and an adept small-boat navigator; but he possessed neither unusual physical skills nor exceptional athletic talents, and the early onset of rheumatoid arthritis and other ailments wrote an untimely end to many of his more strenuous activities as an amateur athlete.

It was when he sat down at his desk and began to write, however, that Jack London became the complete professional. What put him into the record book was not his reputation as a sportsman, but rather his contribution as the founding father of modern American sportswriting.

Graduating from sports reporter to storyteller, London studied "the great game of life" wherever it was played, from urban arenas to arctic and tropic frontiers, from stadiums of sanctioned ferocity to distant outposts where the rules of the house (and of civilization) were only as good as the fist or revolver that backed them up. London knew. He had been there himself. He understood that competition and conflict were the essence of life as well as of fiction.

Having seen at firsthand what "the game" and the odds of the game were like, London was superbly equipped by temper and talent to introduce the world of sports to American writing. But he did not stop with an introduction. Experimenting with topics and themes, he mixed science and surfing, sociology and boxing, meditation and mountain-climbing, self-analysis and sailing. He found his subjects in the unlikeliest characters: a washed-up fighter, a malcontent at a bullfight, an athletic hobo's running battle with a train crew. No matter where he roved, and no matter in what vein he wrote, he enabled his reader to perceive that the same elements that dictated victory or defeat in games — skill, stamina, courage, daring, resourcefulness, imagination, strength, and luck — also made for success or failure in the contest of life.

This collection of stories and reports is intended to help the modern reader become better acquainted with Jack London himself. Behind the often misleading myth of London is the man as he was — and he was as wonderful a character as any writer could possibly invent. In this book, you will meet that active, articulate man at work and play. He is the restless adventurer seeking new experience. He is the robust reporter capturing the comedy and drama of men in competition. And he is the vigorous storyteller with a variety of subjects and styles at his command.

In London's company, you will travel the world, witness glorious games and pitiful ones, thrill to the romance of the sport, and feel the unbearable suspense of being unable to guess the outcome of a match in which your chosen favorite is up against the odds.

Although he makes the sights and sounds of long ago come to life, London has something more than lost worlds or old nostalgia to offer readers of today. Those interested in the history of sport will find him a lively historian, one who has the knack of taking us into his confidence and making us forget the years that divide his day from our own. For one who died in 1916, he is strangely undated, timelessly relevant to the human situation in any age. He is our contemporary, his actual age betrayed only by an occasional old-fashioned word or phrase.

No writer is perfect, and London's writing has its share of the mawkish and the muscular; but judged by his best, he earns the highest praise one can give any writer: he is consistently readable and habitually incapable of being dull. For those reasons, he is sometimes saluted as a storyteller's storyteller. More than one aspiring writer has profited from his three-dimensional style, the mixture of graphic realism and heroic romanticism, and the swift-paced momentum of a good tale well told.

London did not write with other writers in mind, however. He wrote for readers who wished to be entertained, taken away from life as it is and transported to life as it might be. As the sports stories show, he is a passport to adventure: fishing and hunting in the South Seas, boxing in California and Australia, sled racing and table-staking in the Klondike, surfing and mountaineering in Hawaii, and navigating from the fog-shrouded waters of San Francisco Bay to the cannibal-haunted inlets of the Solomon Islands.

London also wrote for readers who do not read purely for escape. Those whose special concern is the history and psychology of sport as a subject in modern American writing can find, in the following tales and reports, the matrix of a literary tradition. Before Jack London, the world of sports in American literature was largely limited to an occasional jumping frog, discreet canter, or polite game of whist. Sport was more useful as a figure of speech or tall tale; if described at all, it was apt to be remote from the writer's personal experience. After Jack London, and largely because of Jack London, sport became an established part of the writer's repertoire, a subject capable of reflecting the society of which it was a part or revealing the heart of the writer who viewed his own craft as a kind of athletic enterprise. London, who was twenty years old when Baron de Coubertin revived the modern Olympic games, understood why the ancient Greeks had wreathed the heads of champion writers.

We have grown so accustomed today to media sports events, to the electronic images and vocabulary ("instant replay," "color commentary," "satellite relay") they have spawned, that it is a little difficult to imagine how, in an era without radio or television, a writer had only himself and his words to offer a mass audience. Today, a sophisticated, knowledgeable, sports-minded public is eager to read about professional sports and amateur games; in London's day, a writer had to describe events which many of his writers might never witness (surfing was virtually unknown in America, for example, until London helped popularize it).

To those who relied on him to be their eyes and ears, London was a faithful reporter who delivered all the action and passion of life that he could capture on a page. He communicated the ecstasy of victory and the agony of defeat long before these emotions were "canned" on videotape and brought to you by your favorite beer or soap.

By living a life of adventure and relating it in living language, London made his world vividly and intensely real to his readers. The measure of his artistry is that his word pictures have not yet faded; their bold colors are still as bright and fresh as the day they were applied to the "canvas" of the writer's typing paper. The boxers and bullfighters, surfriders and thrillseekers, victors and survivors of our twentieth-century sports literature have their root in the tales of this writer who was unafraid to report what he had seen of life beyond the pale of his era's genteel and reluctant view of reality.

Although he liked to think of himself as a common man, London brought some uncommon skills to his profession. He was, first and foremost, a man of sporting blood and fighting spirit. He had an undeniable talent for depicting scenes of action, for portraying the struggle to compete and survive against ultimate challenges, and for delineating character shaped and strengthened by adversity. His talent was fueled by the personalities and themes which he drew from the world of sports. That world also engaged his humanitarian impulses as he attacked the exploitation of athletes, denounced the glorification of blood sport as public entertainment, championed the cause of underdogs who defied the venality of the sports mob, and satirized sports fans who demanded victory at any cost. It is because these problems continue to plague the sports world that London's stories retain their power to make us aware of the human issues underlying the spectacle of athletic competition.

A writer who opened the press box doors of modern sports journalism and the doors of the house of sports fiction, Jack London continues to pioneer, to break new ground and open fresh vistas for any reader eager to enjoy the zest of his physical and intellectual explorations. It is the same for those who come to his writing for the first or fiftieth time. What is the secret of this timeless appeal?

The power of London's pen grips us not simply because it is blunt, but also because it is sympathetic, capable of fine shadings and a poetry that is part of the power. He can make us experience what it is like to stay afloat in the curl of a wave, to stay conscious in a brutal prizefight, or to stay alive on the red sands of a bullring. He can make *our* hand the one that lashes the racing team, steers the small boat on a perilous sea, or turns up the fateful card on which a man's life depends. Without our quite knowing how it has happened, we find ourselves involved in the story, participants in the plot, readers who have become characters.

But there is another reason for London's appeal. The sum of this book may be greater than its parts, for the end of its reading experience is closer contact with a man who might be described as an experience in his own right. All of the selections reflect the mercurial sparkle of London's personality, the urgency of his need to reach out to his reader and his willingness to run actual and imaginative risks to do so, and the astonishing ease with which he enables us to become his imaginative collaborators in the arena of high adventure.

Read the following fictions and reports and you will meet an extraordinary sportsman, sharing all the excitement Jack London must have felt in setting down on paper his visions of human courage and endurance. For here is a spectrum of London's own Olympian spirit, a reflection of a passionate and persuasive writer who embraced the life of sport and the sport of life.

Stockton, California
July 28, 1980

1 JACK LONDON WAS neither the first American
author to describe surfing nor the first to attempt
to ride a wave. Herman Melville had defined "the
heathen sport" in his novel *Omoo* (1849), and Mark
Twain had actually tried to ride a surfboard to shore
(with disastrous result) in 1867. But it was left to London,
a visitor to Hawaii in 1907, to try his skill at coupling the
poetics and the mechanics of surfing. The result, in "A
Royal Sport," is an essay of photographic clarity and
color in which the writer's mastery of the language parallels his control of the surfboard beneath him. The means
of London's physical and imaginative propulsion, the
board is as much a metaphoric as an aquatic vehicle.

Despite London's celebration of self-achievement, "A
Royal Sport" is not a self-centered study. The easy and
intimate tone of his adventure in the Hawaiian surf cre-
ates an instant bond between writer and reader. London
makes his reader more of a participant in the event than a
passive spectator of it. Therein lies the secret of his report's peculiar charm. We might ourselves be the "godlike" rider on the board who harnesses the ocean for his
leap to shore. If I can do it, London seems to imply, why
not you? Nothing is impossible. The illusion is as compelling as it is complete.

"A Royal Sport" was written to aid Jack London's one-
man campaign on behalf of "the sport of Hawaiian
kings." London helped to create a new awareness and
popular interest in surfing at a time when it was in some
danger of dying out. His success in reviving the perishing

sport recalls the similarly strenuous effort by which, at nearly the same time, Theodore Roosevelt was busily saving American college football from extinction. But perhaps the lasting interest of London's surfboard adventure is the way in which it reveals the writer working at his personal peril to perfect his impersonal craft.

*"A Royal Sport" is reprinted from*
The Cruise of the Snark.
*Copyright 1911 by The Macmillan Company;*
*renewed 1939 by Charmian K. London.*

# A Royal Sport

THAT IS WHAT it is, a royal sport for the natural kings of earth. The grass grows right down to the water at Waikiki Beach, and within fifty feet of the everlasting sea. The trees also grow down to the salty edge of things, and one sits in their shade and looks seaward at a majestic surf thundering in on the beach to one's very feet. Half a mile out, where is the reef, the white-headed combers thrust suddenly skyward out of the placid turquoise-blue and come rolling in to shore. One after another they come, a mile long, with smoking crests, the white battalions of the infinite army of the sea. And one sits and listens to the perpetual roar, and watches the unending procession, and feels tiny and fragile before this tremendous force expressing itself in fury and foam and sound. Indeed, one feels microscopically small, and the thought that one may wrestle with this sea raises in one's imagination a thrill of apprehension, almost of fear. Why, they are a mile long, these bull-mouthed monsters, and they weigh a thousand tons, and they charge in to shore faster than a man can run. What chance? No chance at all, is the verdict of the shrinking ego; and one sits, and looks, and listens, and thinks the grass and the shade are a pretty good place in which to be.

And suddenly, out there where a big smoker lifts skyward, rising like a sea-god from out of the welter of spume and churning white, on the giddy, toppling, overhanging and downfalling, precarious crest appears the dark head of a man. Swiftly he rises through the rushing white. His black

shoulders, his chest, his loins, his limbs — all is abruptly projected on one's vision. Where but the moment before was
only the wide desolation and invincible roar, is now a man,
erect, full-statured, not struggling frantically in that wild
movement, not buried and crushed and buffeted by those
mighty monsters, but standing above them all, calm and
superb, poised on the giddy summit, his feet buried in the
churning foam, the salt smoke rising to his knees, and all the
rest of him in the free air and flashing sunlight, and he is
flying through the air, flying forward, flying fast as the surge
on which he stands. He is a Mercury — a brown Mercury. His
heels are winged, and in them is the swiftness of the sea. In
truth, from out of the sea he has leaped upon the back of the
sea, and he is riding the sea that roars and bellows and cannot shake him from its back. But no frantic outreaching and
balancing is his. He is impassive, motionless as a statue
carved suddenly by some miracle out of the sea's depth from
which he rose. And straight on toward shore he flies on his
winged heels and the white crest of the breaker. There is a
wild burst of foam, a long tumultuous rushing sound as the
breaker falls futile and spent on the beach at your feet; and
there, at your feet steps calmly ashore a Kanaka, burnt
golden and brown by the tropic sun. Several minutes ago he
was a speck a quarter of a mile away. He has "bitted the
bull-mouthed breaker" and ridden it in, and the pride in the
feat shows in the carriage of his magnificent body as he
glances for a moment carelessly at you who sit in the shade
of the shore. He is a Kanaka — and more, he is a man, a
member of the kingly species that has mastered matter and
the brutes and lorded it over creation.

And one sits and thinks of Tristram's last wrestle with the
sea on that fatal morning; and one thinks further, to the fact
that Kanaka has done what Tristram never did, and that he
knows a joy of the sea that Tristram never knew. And still

further one thinks. It is all very well, sitting here in the cool shade of the beach, but you are a man, one of the kingly species, and what that Kanaka can do, you can do yourself. Go to. Strip off your clothes that are a nuisance in this mellow clime. Get in and wrestle with the sea; wing your heels with the skill and power that reside in you; bit the sea's breakers, master them, and ride upon their backs as a king should.

And that is how it came about that I tackled surf-riding. And now that I have tackled it, more than ever do I hold it to be a royal sport. But first let me explain the physics of it. A wave is a communicated agitation. The water that composes the body of a wave does not move. If it did, when a stone is thrown into a pond and the ripples spread away in an ever widening circle, there would appear at the centre an ever increasing hole. No, the water that composes the body of a wave is stationary. Thus, you may watch a particular portion of the ocean's surface and you will see the same water rise and fall a thousand times to the agitation communicated by a thousand successive waves. Now imagine this communicated agitation moving shoreward. As the bottom shoals, the lower portion of the wave strikes land first and is stopped. But water is fluid, and the upper portion has not struck anything, wherefore it keeps on communicating its agitation, keeps on going. And when the top of the wave keeps on going, while the bottom of it lags behind, something is bound to happen. The bottom of the wave drops out from under and the top of the wave falls over, forward, and down, curling and cresting and roaring as it does so. It is the bottom of a wave striking against the top of the land that is the cause of all surfs.

But the transformation from a smooth undulation to a breaker is not abrupt except where the bottom shoals abruptly. Say the bottom shoals gradually for from quarter of a mile to a mile, then an equal distance will be occupied by the transformation. Such a bottom is that off the beach of Waikiki, and it produces a splendid surf-riding surf. One leaps upon the back of a breaker just as it begins to break, and stays on it as it continues to break all the way in to shore.

And now to the particular physics of surf-riding. Get out on a flat board, six feet long, two feet wide, and roughly oval in shape. Lie down upon it like a small boy on a coaster and paddle with your hands out to deep water, where the waves begin to crest. Lie out there quietly on the board. Sea after sea breaks before, behind, and under and over you, and rushes in to shore, leaving you behind. When a wave crests, it gets steeper. Imagine yourself, on your board, on the face of that steep slope. If it stood still, you would slide down just as a boy slides down a hill on his coaster. "But," you object, "the wave doesn't stand still." Very true, but the water composing the wave stands still, and there you have the secret. If ever you start sliding down the face of that wave, you'll keep on sliding and you'll never reach the bottom. Please don't laugh. The face of that wave may be only six feet, yet you can slide down it a quarter of a mile, or half a mile, and not reach the bottom. For, see, since a wave is only a communicated agitation or impetus, and since the water that composes a wave is changing every instant, new water is rising into the wave as fast as the wave travels. You slide down this new water, and yet remain in your old position on the wave, sliding down the still newer water that is rising and forming the wave. You slide precisely as fast as the wave travels. If it travels fifteen miles an hour, you slide fifteen miles an hour. Between you and shore stretches a quarter of mile of water. As the wave travels, this water obligingly heaps itself into the wave, gravity does the rest, and down you go, sliding the whole length of it. If you still cherish the notion, while sliding, that the water is moving with you, thrust your arms into it and attempt to paddle; you will find that you have to be remarkably quick to get a stroke, for that water is dropping astern just as fast as you are rushing ahead.

And now for another phase of the physics of surf-riding. All rules have their exceptions. It is true that the water in a wave does not travel forward. But there is what may be called the send of the sea. The water in the overtoppling crest does move forward, as you will speedily realize if you are slapped in the face by it, or if you are caught under it and are pounded by one mighty blow down under the surface panting and gasping for half a minute. The water in the top of a wave rests upon the water in the bottom of the wave. But when the bottom of the wave strikes the land, it stops, while the top goes on. It no longer has the bottom of the wave to hold it up. Where was solid water beneath it, is now air, and for the first time it feels the grip of gravity, and down it falls, at the same time being torn asunder from the lagging bottom of the wave and flung forward. And it is because of this that riding a surf-board is something more than a mere placid sliding down a hill. In truth, one is caught up and hurled shoreward as by some Titan's hand.

I deserted the cool shade, put on a swimming suit, and got hold of a surf-board. It was too small a board. But I didn't know, and nobody told me. I joined some little Kanaka boys in shallow water, where the breakers were well spent and small — a regular kindergarten school. I watched the little Kanaka boys. When a likely-looking breaker came along, they flopped upon their stomachs on their boards, kicked like mad with their feet, and rode the breaker in to the beach. I tried to emulate them. I watched them, tried to do everything that they did, and failed utterly. The breaker swept past, and I was not on it. I tried again and again. I kicked twice as madly as they did, and failed. Half a dozen would be around. We would all leap on our boards in front of a good breaker. Away our feet would churn like the stern-wheels of river steamboats, and away the little rascals would scoot while I remained in disgrace behind.

I tried for a solid hour, and not one wave could I persuade to boost me shoreward. And then arrived a friend, `Alexander Hume Ford, a globe trotter by profession, bent ever on the pursuit of sensation. And he had found it at Waikiki. Heading for Australia, he had stopped off for a week to find out if there were any thrills in surf-riding, and he had become wedded to it. He had been at it every day for a month and could not yet see any symptoms of the fascination lessening on him. He spoke with authority.

"Get off that board," he said. "Chuck it away at once. Look at the way you're trying to ride it. If ever the nose of that board hits bottom, you'll be disembowelled. Here, take my board. It's a man's size."

I am always humble when confronted by knowledge. Ford knew. He showed me how properly to mount his board. Then he waited for a good breaker, gave me a shove at the right moment, and started me in. Ah, delicious moment when I felt that breaker grip and fling me. On I dashed, a hundred and fifty feet, and subsided with the breaker on the sand. From that moment I was lost. I waded back to Ford with his board. It was a large one, several inches thick, and weighed all of seventy-five pounds. He gave me advice, much of it. He had had no one to teach him, and all that he had laboriously learned in several weeks he communicated to me in half an hour. I really learned by proxy. And inside of half an hour I was able to start myself and ride in. I did it time after time, and Ford applauded and advised. For instance, he told me to get just so far forward on the board and no farther. But I must have got some farther, for as I came charging in to land, that miserable board poked its nose down to bottom, stopped abruptly, and turned a somersault, at the same time violently severing our relations. I was tossed through the air like a chip and buried ignominiously under the downfalling breaker. And I realized that if it hadn't been for Ford, I'd have been disembowelled. That particular risk is part of the sport, Ford says. Maybe he'll have it happen to him before he leaves Waikiki, and then, I feel confident, his yearning for sensation will be satisfied for a time.

When all is said and done, it is my steadfast belief that homicide is worse than suicide, especially if, in the former case, it is a woman. Ford saved me from being a homicide. "Imagine your legs are a rudder," he said. "Hold them close together, and steer with them." A few minutes later I came charging in on a comber. As I neared the beach, there, in the water, up to her waist, dead in front of me, appeared a woman. How was I to stop that comber on whose back I was? It looked like a dead woman. The board weighed seventy-five pounds, I weighed a hundred and sixty-five. The added weight had a velocity of fifteen miles per hour. The board and I constituted a projectile. I leave it to the physicists to figure out the force of the impact upon that poor, tender woman. And then I remembered my guardian angel, Ford. "Steer with your legs!" rang through my brain. I steered with my legs, I steered sharply, abruptly, with all my legs and with all my might. The board sheered around broadside on the crest. Many things happened simultaneously. The wave gave me a passing buffet, a light tap as the taps of waves go, but a tap sufficient to knock me off the board and smash me down through the rushing water to bottom, with which I came in violent collision and upon which I was rolled over and over. I got my head out for a breath of air and then gained my feet. There stood the woman before me. I felt like a hero. I had saved her life. And she laughed at me. It was not hysteria. She had never dreamed of her danger. Anyway, I solaced myself, it was not I but Ford that saved her, and I didn't have to feel like a hero. And besides, that leg-steering was great. In a few minutes more of practice I was able to thread my way in and out past several bathers and to remain on top my breaker instead of going under it.

"To-morrow," Ford said, "I am going to take you out into the blue water."

I looked seaward where he pointed, and saw the great smoking combers that made the breakers I had been riding look like ripples. I don't know what I might have said had I not recollected just then that I was one of a kingly species. So all that I did say was, "All right, I'll tackle them to-morrow."

The water that rolls in on Waikiki Beach is just the same as the water that laves the shores of all the Hawaiian Islands; and in ways, especially from the swimmer's standpoint, it is wonderful water. It is cool enough to be comfortable, while it is warm enough to permit a swimmer to stay in all day without experiencing a chill. Under the sun or the stars, at high noon or at midnight, in midwinter or in midsummer, it does not matter when, it is always the same temperature — not too warm, not too cold, just right. It is wonderful water, salt as old ocean itself, pure and crystal-clear. When the nature of the water is considered, it is not so remarkable after all that the Kanakas are one of the most expert of swimming races.

So it was, next morning, when Ford came along, that I plunged into the wonderful water for a swim of indeterminate length. Astride of our surf-boards, or, rather, flat down upon them on our stomachs, we paddled out through the kindergarten where the little Kanaka boys were at play. Soon we were out in deep water where the big smokers came roaring in. The mere struggle with them, facing them and paddling seaward over them and through them, was sport enough in itself. One had to have his wits about him, for it was a battle in which mighty blows were struck, on one side, and in which cunning was used on the other side — a struggle between insensate force and intelligence. I soon learned a bit. When a breaker curled over my head, for a swift instant I could see the light of day through its emerald body; then down would go my head, and I would clutch the board with all my strength. Then would come the blow, and to the on-looker on shore I would be blotted out. In reality the board and I have passed through the crest and emerged in the respite of the other side. I should not recommend those smashing blows to an invalid or delicate person. There is weight behind them, and the impact of the driven water is like a sand-blast. Sometimes one passes through half a dozen combers in quick succession, and it is just about that time that he is liable to discover new merits in the stable land and new reasons for being on shore.

Out there in the midst of such a succession of big smoky ones, a third man was added to our party, one Freeth. Shak-ing the water from my eyes as I emerged from one wave and peered ahead to see what the next one looked like, I saw him tearing in on the back of it, standing upright on his board, carelessly poised, a young god bronzed with sunburn. We went through the wave on the back of which he rode. Ford called to him. He turned an airspring from his wave, rescued his board from its maw, paddled over to us and joined Ford in showing me things. One thing I learned in particular from Freeth, namely, how to encounter the occasional breaker of exceptional size that rolled in. Such breakers were really ferocious, and it was unsafe to meet them on top of the board. But Freeth showed me, so that whenever I saw one of that caliber rolling down on me, I slid off the rear end of the board and dropped down beneath the surface, my arms over my head and holding the board. Thus, if the wave ripped the board out of my hands and tried to strike me with it (a common trick of such waves), there would be a cushion of water a foot or more in depth, between my head and the blow. When the wave passed, I climbed upon the board and paddled on. Many men have been terribly injured, I learn, by being struck by their boards.

The whole method of surf-riding and surf-fighting, I learned, is one of non-resistance. Dodge the blow that is struck at you. Dive through the wave that is trying to slap you in the face. Sink down, feet first, deep under the surface, and let the big smoker that is trying to smash you go by far overhead. Never be rigid. Relax. Yield yourself to the waters that are ripping and tearing at you. When the undertow catches you and drags you seaward along the bottom, don't struggle against it. If you do, you are liable to be drowned, for it is stronger than you. Yield yourself to that undertow. Swim with it, not against it, and you will find the pressure removed. And, swimming with it, fooling it so that it does not hold you, swim upward at the same time. It will be no trouble at all to reach the surface.

The man who wants to learn surf-riding must be a strong swimmer, and he must be used to going under the water. After that, fair strength and common-sense are all that is required. The force of the big comber is rather unexpected. There are mix-ups in which board and rider are torn apart and separated by several hundred feet. The surf-rider must take care of himself. No matter how many riders swim out with him, he cannot depend upon any of them for aid. The fancied security I had in the presence of Ford and Freeth made me forget that it was my first swim out in deep water among the big ones. I recollected, however, and rather suddenly, for a big wave came in, and away went the two men on its back all the way to shore. I could have been drowned a dozen different ways before they go back to me.

One slides down the face of a breaker on his surf-board, but he has to get started to sliding. Board and rider must be moving shoreward at a good rate before the wave overtakes them. When you see the wave coming that you want to ride in, you turn tail to it and paddle shoreward with all your strength, using what is called the windmill stroke. This is a sort of spurt performed immediately in front of the wave. If the board is going fast enough, the wave accelerates it, and the board begins its quarter-of-a-mile slide.

I shall never forget the first big wave I caught out there in the deep water. I saw it coming, turned my back on it and paddled for dear life. Faster and faster my board went, till it seemed my arms would drop off. What was happening behind me I could not tell. One cannot look behind and paddle the windmill stroke. I heard the crest of the wave hissing and churning, and then my board was lifted and flung forward. I scarcely knew what happened the first half-minute. Though I kept my eyes open, I could not see anything, for I was buried in the rushing white of the crest. But I did not mind. I was chiefly conscious of ecstatic bliss at having caught the wave. At the end of the half-minute, however, I began to see things, and to breathe. I saw that three feet of the nose of my board was clear out of water and riding on the air. I shifted my weight forward, and made the nose come down. Then I lay, quite at rest in the midst of the wild movement, and watched the shore and the bathers on the beach grow distinct. I didn't cover quite a quarter of a mile on that wave, because, to prevent the board from diving, I shifted my weight back, but shifted it too far and fell down the rear slope of the wave.

It was my second day at surf-riding, and I was quite proud of myself. I stayed out there four hours, and when it was over, I was resolved that on the morrow I'd come in standing up. But that resolution paved a distant place. On the morrow I was in bed. I was not sick, but I was very unhappy, and I was in bed. When describing the wonderful water of Hawaii I forgot to describe the wonderful sun of Hawaii. It is a tropic sun, and, furthermore, in the first part of June, it is an overhead sun. It is also an insidious, deceitful sun. For the first time in my life I was sunburned unawares. My arms, shoulders, and back had been burned many times in the past and were tough; but not so my legs. And for four hours I had exposed the tender backs of my legs, at right-angles, to that perpendicular Hawaiian sun. It was not until after I got ashore that I discovered the sun had touched me. Sunburn at first is merely warm; after that it grows intense and the blisters come out. Also, the joints, where the skin wrinkles, refuse to bend. That is why I spent the next day in bed. I couldn't walk. And that is why, to-day, I am writing this in bed. It is easier to than not to. But to-morrow, ah, to-morrow, I shall be out in that wonderful water, and I shall come in standing up, even as Ford and Freeth. And if I fail to-morrow, I shall do it the next day, or the next. Upon one thing I am resolved: the *Snark* shall not sail from Honolulu until I, too, wing my heels with the swiftness of the sea, and become a sunburned, skin-peeling Mercury.

**2** "A PIECE OF STEAK" is a story that powerfully exemplifies its author's gift for fusing narrative action and human interest. London's account of the battered but resilient old pug who seeks to win one last fight is an unforgettable "main event," told with a cumulative and almost unbearable suspense.

Who will win — the old veteran who must rely on cunning and cautious skill, or the challenger who has little to offer save youth and raw strength? The implications of this battle go far beyond the square ring. The result is a vivid lesson in the law of life.

The scene of this masterly told tale is Australia. There, in 1908, Jack London had reported the Tommy Burns–Jack Johnson title bout and predicted greatness for the black champion. Two years later, in Reno, Nevada, London was again at ringside when Johnson stepped smiling through the ropes into the fight of the century with the so-called "great white hope," Jim Jeffries. As the following story shows, however, it was not only with champions that Jack London was concerned.

A closely observed study in professional violence, "A Piece of Steak" is also, as its unexpected (but thoroughly prepared) denouement shows, a poignant drama of retribution. Along with Conan Doyle's "The Croxley Master," Lardner's "Champion," and Hemingway's "Fifty Grand," this is one of the very greatest boxing tales in the literature of the sport.

*"A Piece of Steak" is reprinted from* When God Laughs and Other Stories. *Copyright 1911 by The Macmillan Company; renewed 1939 by Charmian K. London.*

# A Piece of Steak

WITH THE LAST morsel of bread Tom King wiped his plate clean of the last particle of flour gravy and chewed the resulting mouthful in a slow and meditative way. When he arose from the table, he was oppressed by the feeling that he was distinctly hungry. Yet he alone had eaten. The two children in the other room had been sent early to bed in order that in sleep they might forget they had gone supperless. His wife had touched nothing, and had sat silently and watched him with solicitous eyes. She was a thin, worn woman of the working class, though signs of an earlier prettiness were not wanting in her face. The flour for the gravy she had borrowed from the neighbour across the hall. The last two ha'pennies had gone to buy the bread.

He sat down by the window on a rickety chair that protested under his weight, and quite mechanically he put his pipe in his mouth and dipped into the side pocket of his coat. The absence of any tobacco made him aware of his action, and with a scowl for his forgetfulness he put the pipe away. His movements were slow, almost hulking, as though he were burdened by the heavy weight of his muscles. He was a solid-bodied, stolid-looking man, and his appearance did not suffer from being over-prepossessing. His rough clothes were old and slouchy. The uppers of his shoes were too weak to carry the heavy resoling that was itself of no recent date. And his cotton shirt, a cheap, two-shilling affair, showed a frayed collar and ineradicable paint stains.

But it was Tom King's face that advertised him unmistakably for what he was. It was the face of a typical prize fighter; of one who had put in long years of service in the squared ring, and, by that means, developed and emphasized all the marks of the fighting beast. It was distinctly a lowering countenance, and, that no feature of it might escape notice, it was clean-shaven. The lips were shapeless and constituted a mouth harsh to excess, that was like a gash in his face. The jaw was aggressive, brutal, heavy. The eyes, slow of movement and heavy-lidded, were almost expressionless under the shaggy, indrawn brows. Sheer animal that he was, the eyes were the most animal-like feature about him. The forehead slanted quickly back to the hair, which, clipped close, showed every bump of a villainous-looking head. A nose, twice broken and moulded variously by countless blows, and a cauliflower ear, permanently swollen and distorted to twice its size, completed his adornment, while the beard, fresh-shaven as it was, sprouted in the skin and gave the face a blue-black stain.

Altogether, it was the face of a man to be afraid of in a dark alley or lonely place. And yet Tom King was not a criminal, nor had he ever done anything criminal. Outside of brawls, common to his walk in life, he had harmed no one. Nor had he ever been known to pick a quarrel. He was a professional, and all the fighting brutishness of him was reserved for his professional appearances. Outside the ring he was slow-going, easy-natured, and, in his younger days, when money was flush, too open-handed for his own good. He bore no grudges and had few enemies. Fighting was a business with him. In the ring he struck to hurt, struck to maim, struck to destroy; but there was no animus in it. It was a plain business proposition. Audiences assembled and paid for the spectacle of men knocking each other out. The winner took the big end of the purse. When Tom King faced the Woolloomoolloo Gouger, twenty years before, he knew that the Gouger's jaw was only four months healed after having been broken in a Newcastle bout. And he had played for that jaw and broken it again in the ninth round, not because he bore the Gouger any ill will, but because that was the surest way to put the Gouger out and win the big end of the purse. Nor had the Gouger borne him any ill will for it. It was the game, and both knew the game and played it.

Tom King had never been a talker, and he sat by the window, morosely silent, staring at his hands. The veins stood out on the backs of the hands, large and swollen; and the knuckles, smashed and battered and malformed, testified to the use to which they had been put. He had never heard that a man's life was the life of his arteries, but well he knew the meaning of those big, upstanding veins. His heart had pumped too much blood through them at top pressure. They no longer did the work. He had stretched the elasticity out of them, and with their distension had passed his endurance. He tired easily now. No longer could he do a fast twenty rounds, hammer and tongs, fight, fight, fight, from gong to gong, with fierce rally on top of fierce rally, beaten to the ropes and in turn beating his opponent to the ropes, and rallying fiercest and fastest of all in that last, twentieth round, with the house on its feet and yelling, himself rushing, striking, ducking, raining showers of blows upon showers of blows and receiving showers of blows in return, and all the time the heart faithfully pumping the surging blood through the adequate veins. The veins, swollen at the time, had always shrunk down again, though not quite — each time, imperceptibly at first, remaining just a trifle larger than before. He stared at them and at his battered knuckles, and, for the moment, caught a vision of the youthful excellence of those hands before the first knuckle had been smashed on the head of Benny Jones, otherwise known as the Welsh Terror.

The impression of his hunger came back on him.

"Blimey, but couldn't I go a piece of steak!" he muttered aloud, clenching his huge fists and spitting out a smothered oath.

"I tried both Burke's an' Sawley's," his wife said half apologetically.

"An' they wouldn't?" he demanded.

"Not a ha'penny. Burke said — " She faltered.

"G'wan! Wot'd he say?"

"As how 'e was thinkin' Sandel 'ud do ye tonight, an' as how yer score was uncomfortable big as it was."

Tom King grunted but did not reply. He was busy thinking of the bull terrier he had kept in his younger days to which he had fed steaks without end. Burke would have given him credit for a thousand steaks — then. But times had changed. Tom King was getting old; and old men, fighting before second-rate clubs, couldn't expect to run bills of any size with the tradesmen.

He had got up in the morning with a longing for a piece of steak, and the longing had not abated. He had not had a fair training for this fight. It was a drought year in Australia, times were hard, and even the most irregular work was difficult to find. He had had no sparring partner, and his food had not been of the best nor always sufficient. He had done a few days' navvy work when he could get it, and he had run around the Domain in the early mornings to get his legs in shape. But it was hard, training without a partner and with a wife and two kiddies that must be fed. Credit with the tradesmen had undergone very slight expansion when he was matched with Sandel. The secretary of the Gayety Club had advanced him three pounds — the loser's end of the purse — and beyond that had refused to go. Now and again he had managed to borrow a few shillings from old pals, who would have lent more only that it was a drought year and they were hard put themselves. No — and there was no use disguising the fact — his training had not been satisfactory. He should have had better food and no worries. Besides, when a man is forty, it is harder to get into condition than when he is twenty.

"What time is it, Lizzie?" he asked.

His wife went across the hall to inquire, and came back.

"Quarter before eight."

"They'll be startin' the first bout in a few minutes," he said. "Only a try-out. Then there's a four-round spar 'tween Dealer Wells an' Gridley, an' a ten-round go 'tween Starlight an' some sailor bloke. I don't come on for over an hour." hour."

At the end of another silent ten minutes he rose to his feet.

"Truth is, Lizzie, I ain't had proper trainin'."

He reached for his hat and started for the door. He did not offer to kiss her — he never did on going out — but on this night she dared to kiss him, throwing her arms around him and compelling him to bend down to her face. She looked quite small against the massive bulk of the man.

"Good luck, Tom," she said. "You gotter do 'im."

"Ay, I gotter do 'im," he repeated. "That's all there is to it. I jus' gotter do 'im."

He laughed with an attempt at heartiness, while she pressed more closely against him. Across her shoulders he looked around the bare room. It was all he had in the world, with the rent overdue, and her and the kiddies. And he was leaving it to go out into the night to get meat for his mate and cubs — not like a modern working-man going to his machine grind, but in the old, primitive, royal, animal way, by fighting for it.

"I gotter do 'im," he repeated, this time a hint of desperation in his voice. "If it's a win, it's thirty quid — an' I can pay all that's owin', with a lump o' money left over. If it's a lose, I get naught — not even a penny for me to ride home on the tram. The secretary's give all that's comin' from a loser's end. Good-bye, old woman. I'll come straight home if it's a win."

"An' I'll be waitin' up," she called to him along the hall.

It was a full two miles to the Gayety, and as he walked along he remembered how in his palmy days — he had once been the heavyweight champion of New South Wales — he would have ridden in a cab to the fight, and how, most likely, some heavy backer would have paid for the cab and ridden with him. There were Tommy Burns and that Yankee, Jack Johnson — they rode about in motor-cars. And he walked! And, as any man knew, a hard two miles was not the best preliminary to a fight. He was an old 'un, and the world did not wag well with old 'uns. He was good for nothing now except navvy work, and his broken nose and swollen ear were against him even in that. He found himself wishing that he had learned a trade. It would have been better in the long run. But no one had told him, and he knew, deep down in his heart, that he would not have listened if they had. It had been so easy. Big money — sharp, glorious fights — periods of rest and loafing in between — a following of eager flatterers, the slaps on the back, the shakes of the hand, the toffs glad to buy him a drink for the privilege of five minutes' talk — and the glory of it, the yelling houses, the whirlwind finish, the referee's "King wins!" and his name in the sporting columns next day.

Those had been times! But he realized now, in his slow, ruminating way, that it was the old 'uns he had been putting away. He was Youth, rising; and they were Age, sinking. No wonder it had been easy — they with their swollen veins and battered knuckles and weary in the bones of them from the long battles they had already fought. He remembered the time he put out old Stowsher Bill, at Rush-Cutters Bay, in the eighteenth round, and how old Bill had cried afterwards in the dressing-room like a baby. Perhaps old Bill's rent had been overdue. Perhaps he'd had at home a missus an' a couple of kiddies. And perhaps Bill, that very day of the fight, had had a hungering for a piece of steak. Bill had fought game and taken incredible punishment. He could see now, after he had gone through the mill himself, that Stowsher Bill had fought for a bigger stake, that night twenty years ago, than had young Tom King, who had fought for glory and easy money. No wonder Stowsher Bill had cried afterwards in the dressing-room.

Well, a man had only so many fights in him, to begin with. It was the iron law of the game. One man might have a hundred hard fights in him, another man only twenty; each, according to the make of him and the quality of his fibre, had a definite number, and when he had fought them he was done. Yes, he had had more fights in him than most of them, and he had had far more than his share of the hard, gruelling fights — the kind that worked the heart and lungs to bursting, that took the elastic out of the arteries and made hard knots of muscle out of youth's sleek suppleness, that wore out nerve and stamina and made brain and bones weary from excess of effort and endurance overwrought. Yes, he had done better than all of them. There was none of his old fighting partners left. He was the last of the old guard. He had seen them all finished, and he had had a hand in finishing some of them.

They had tried him out against the old 'uns, and one after another he had put them away — laughing when, like old Stowsher Bill, they cried in the dressing-room. And now he was an old 'un, and they tried out the youngsters on him. There was that bloke Sandel. He had come over from New Zealand with a record behind him. But nobody in Australia knew anything about him, so they put him up against old Tom King. If Sandel made a showing, he would be given better men to fight, with bigger purses to win; so it was to be depended upon that he would put up a fierce battle. He had everything to win by it — money and glory and career; and Tom King was the grizzled old chopping block that guarded the highway to fame and fortune. And he had nothing to win except thirty quid, to pay to the landlord and the tradesmen. And as Tom King thus ruminated, there came to his stolid vision the form of youth, glorious youth, rising exultant and invincible, supple of muscle and silken of skin, with heart and lungs that had never been tired and torn and that laughed at limitation of effort. Yes, youth was the nemesis. It destroyed the old 'uns and recked not that, in so doing, it destroyed itself. It enlarged its arteries and smashed its knuckles, and was in turn destroyed by youth. For youth was ever youthful. It was only age that grew old.

At Castlereagh Street he turned to the left, and three blocks along came to the Gayety. A crowd of young larrikins hanging outside the door made respectful way for him, and he heard one say to another: "That's 'im! That's Tom King!"

Inside, on the way to his dressing-room, he encountered the secretary, a keen-eyed, shrewd-faced young man, who shook his hand.

"How are you feelin', Tom?" he asked.

"Fit as a fiddle," King answered, though he knew that he lied, and that if he had a quid he would give it right there for a good piece of steak.

When he emerged from the dressing-room, his seconds behind him, and came down the aisle to the squared ring in the centre of the hall, a burst of greeting and applause went up from the waiting crowd. He acknowledged salutations right and left, though few of the faces did he know. Most of them were the faces of kiddies unborn when he was winning his first laurels in the squared ring. He leaped lightly to the raised platform and ducked through the ropes to his corner, where he sat down on a folding stool. Jack Ball, the referee, came over and shook his hand. Ball was a broken-down pugilist who for over ten years had not entered the ring as a principal. King was glad that he had him for referee. They were both old 'uns. If he should rough it with Sandel a bit beyond the rules, he knew Ball could be depended upon to pass it by.

Aspiring young heavyweights, one after another, were climbing into the ring and being presented to the audience by the referee. Also he issued their challenges for them.

"Young Pronto," Bill announced, "from North Sydney, challenges the winner for fifty pounds side bet."

The audience applauded, and applauded again as Sandel himself sprang through the ropes and sat down in his corner. Tom King looked across the ring at him curiously, for in a few minutes they would be locked together in merciless combat, each trying with all the force of him to knock the other into unconsciousness. But little could he see, for Sandel, like himself, had trousers and sweater on over his ring costume. His face was strongly handsome, crowned with a curly mop of yellow hair, while his thick, muscular neck hinted at bodily magnificence.

Young Pronto went to one corner and then the other, shaking hands with the principals and dropping down out of the ring. The challenges went on. Ever youth climbed through the ropes — youth unknown but insatiable, crying out to mankind that with strength and skill it would match issues with the winner. A few years before, in his own heyday of invincibleness, Tom King would have been amused and bored by these preliminaries. But now he sat fascinated, unable to shake the vision of youth from his eyes. Always were these youngsters rising up in the boxing game, springing through the ropes and shouting their defiance; and always were the old 'uns going down before them. They climbed to success over the bodies of the old 'uns. And ever they came, more and more youngsters — youth unquenchable and irresistible — and ever they put the old 'uns away, themselves becoming old 'uns and travelling the same downward path, while behind them, ever pressing on them, was youth eternal — the new babies, grown lusty and dragging their elders down, with behind them more babies to the end of time — youth that must have its will and that will never die.

King glanced over to the press box, nodded to Morgan, of the *Sportsman,* and Corbett, of the *Referee.* Then he held out his hands, while Sid Sullivan and Charley Bates, his seconds, slipped on his gloves and laced them tight, closely watched by one of Sandel's seconds, who first examined critically the tapes on King's knuckles. A second of his own was in Sandel's corner, performing a like office. Sandel's trousers were pulled off, and as he stood up his sweater was skinned off over his head. And Tom King, looking, saw youth incarnate, deep-chested, heavy-thewed, with muscles that slipped and slid like live things under the white satin skin. The whole body was acrawl with life, and Tom King knew that it was a life that had never oozed its freshness out through the aching pores during the long fights wherein youth paid its toll and departed not quite so young as when it entered.

The two men advanced to meet each other, and as the gong sounded and the seconds clattered out of the ring with the folding stools, they shook hands and instantly took their fighting attitudes. And instantly, like a mechanism of steel and springs balanced on a hair trigger, Sandel was in and out and in again, landing a left to the eyes, a right to the ribs, ducking a counter, dancing lightly away and dancing menacingly back again. He was swift and clever. It was a dazzling exhibition. The house yelled its approbation. But King was not dazzled. He had fought too many fights and too many youngsters. He knew the blows for what they were — too quick and too deft to be dangerous. Evidently Sandel was going to rush things from the start. It was to be expected. It was the way of youth, expending its splendour and excellence in wild insurgence and furious onslaught, overwhelming opposition with its own unlimited glory of strength and desire.

Sandel was in and out, here, there, and everywhere, light-footed and eager-hearted, a living wonder of white flesh and stinging muscle that wove itself into a dazzling fabric of attack, slipping and leaping like a flying shuttle from action to action through a thousand actions, all of them centred upon the destruction of Tom King, who stood between him and fortune. And Tom King patiently endured. He knew his business, and he knew youth now that youth was no longer his. There was nothing to do till the other lost some of his steam, was his thought, and he grinned to himself as he deliberately ducked so as to receive a heavy blow on the top of his head. It was a wicked thing to do, yet eminently fair according to the rules of the boxing game. A man was supposed to take care of his own knuckles, and if he insisted on hitting an opponent on the top of the head he did so at his own peril. King could have ducked lower and let the blow whizz harmlessly past, but he remembered his own early fights and how he smashed his first knuckle on the head of the Welsh Terror. He was but playing the game. That duck had accounted for one of Sandel's knuckles. Not that Sandel would mind it now. He would go on, superbly regardless, hitting as hard as ever throughout the fight. But later on, when the long ring battles had begun to tell, he would regret that knuckle and look back and remember how he smashed it on Tom King's head.

The first round was all Sandel's, and he had the house yelling with the rapidity of his whirlwind rushes. He overwhelmed King with avalanches of punches, and King did nothing. He never struck once, contenting himself with covering up, blocking and ducking and clinching to avoid punishment. He occasionally feinted, shook his head when the weight of a punch landed, and moved stolidly about, never leaping or springing or wasting an ounce of strength. Sandel must foam the froth of youth away before discreet age could dare to retaliate. All King's movements were slow and methodical, and his heavy-lidded, slow-moving eyes gave him the appearance of being half asleep or dazed. Yet they were eyes that saw everything, that had been trained to see everything through all his twenty years and odd in the ring. They were eyes that did not blink or waver before an impending blow, but that coolly saw and measured distance.

Seated back in his corner for the minute's rest at the end of the round, he lay back with outstretched legs, his arms resting on the right-angle of the ropes, his chest and abdomen heaving frankly and deeply as he gulped down the air driven by the towels of his seconds. He listened with closed eyes to the voices of the house, "Why don't yeh fight, Tom?" many were crying. "Yeh ain't afraid of 'im, are yeh?"

"Muscle-bound," he heard a man on a front seat comment. "He can't move quicker. Two to one on Sandel, in quids."

The gong struck and the two men advanced from their corners. Sandel came forward fully three-quarters of the distance, eager to begin again; but King was content to advance the shorter distance. It was in line with his policy of economy. He had not been well trained, and he had not had enough to eat, and every step counted. Besides, he had already walked two miles to the ringside. It was a repetition of the first round, with Sandel attacking like a whirlwind and with the audience indignantly demanding why King did not fight. Beyond feinting and several slowly delivered and ineffectual blows he did nothing save block and stall and clinch. Sandel wanted to make the pace fast, while King, out of his wisdom, refused to accommodate him. He grinned with a certain wistful pathos in his ring-battered countenance, and went on cherishing his strength with the jealousy of which only age is capable. Sandel was youth, and he threw his strength away with the munificent abandon of youth. To King belonged the ring generalship, the wisdom bred of long, aching fights. He watched with cool eyes and head, moving slowly and waiting for Sandel's froth to foam away. To the majority of the onlookers it seemed as though King was hopelessly outclassed, and they voiced their opinion in offers of three to one on Sandel. But there were wise ones, a few, who knew King of old time, and who covered what they considered easy money.

The third round began as usual, one-sided, with Sandel doing all the leading and delivering all the punishment. A half minute had passed when Sandel, over-confident, left an opening. King's eyes and right arm flashed in the same instant. It was his first real blow — a hook, with the twisted arm of the arm to make it rigid, and with all the weight of the half-pivoted body behind it. It was like a sleepy-seeming lion suddenly thrusting out a lightning paw. Sandel, caught on the side of the jaw, was felled like a bullock. The audience gasped and murmured awe-stricken applause. The man was not muscle-bound, after all, and he could drive a blow like a trip hammer.

Sandel was shaken. He rolled over and attempted to rise, but the sharp yells from his seconds to take the count restrained him. He knelt on one knee, ready to rise, and waited, while the referee stood over him, counting the seconds loudly in his ear. At the ninth he rose in fighting attitude, and Tom King, facing him, knew regret that the blow had not been an inch nearer the point of the jaw. That would have been a knock-out, and he could have carried the thirty quid home to the missus and the kiddies.

The round continued to the end of its three minutes, Sandel for the first time respectful of his opponent and King slow of movement and sleepy-eyed as ever. As the round neared its close, King, warned of the fact by sight of the seconds crouching outside ready for the spring in through the ropes, worked the fight around to his own corner. And when the gong struck, he sat down immediately on the waiting stool, while Sandel had to walk all the way across the diagonal of the square to his own corner. It was a little thing, but it was the sum of little things that counted. Sandel was compelled to walk that many more steps, to give up that much energy, and to lose a part of the precious minute of rest. At the beginning of every round King loafed slowly out from his corner, forcing his opponent to advance the greater distance. The end of every round found the fight manœuvred by King into his own corner so that he could immediately sit down.

Two more rounds went by, in which King was parsimonious of effort and Sandel prodigal. The latter's attempt to force a fast pace made King uncomfortable, for a fair percentage of the multitudinous blows showered upon him went home. Yet King persisted in his dogged slowness, despite the crying of the young hotheads for him to go in and fight. Again, in the sixth round, Sandel was careless, again Tom King's fearful right flashed out to the jaw, and again Sandel took the nine seconds' count.

By the seventh round Sandel's pink of condition was gone, and he settled down to what he knew was to be the hardest fight in his experience. Tom King was an old 'un, but a better old 'un than he had ever encountered — an old 'un who never lost his head, who was remarkably able at defence, whose blows had the impact of a knotted club, and who had a knock-out in either hand. Nevertheless, Tom King dared not hit often. He never forgot his battered knuckles, and knew that every hit must count if the knuckles were to last out the fight. As he sat in his corner, glancing across at his opponent, the thought came to him that the sum of his wisdom and Sandel's youth would constitute a world's champion heavyweight. But that was the trouble. Sandel would never become a world champion. He lacked the wisdom, and the only way for him to get it was to buy it with youth; and when wisdom was his, youth would have been spent in buying it.

King took every advantage he knew. He never missed an opportunity to clinch, and in effecting most of the clinches his shoulder drove stiffly into the other's ribs. In the philosophy of the ring a shoulder was as good as a punch so far as damage was concerned, and a great deal better so far as concerned expenditure of effort. Also in the clinches King rested his weight on his opponent, and was loath to let go. This compelled the interference of the referee, who tore them apart, always assisted by Sandel, who had not yet learned to rest. He could not refrain from using those glorious flying arms and writhing muscles of his, and when the other rushed into a clinch, striking shoulder against ribs, and with head resting under Sandel's left arm, Sandel almost invariably swung his right behind his own back and into the projecting face. It was a clever stroke, much admired by the audience, but it was not dangerous, and was, therefore, just that much wasted strength. But Sandel was tireless and unaware of limitations, and King grinned and doggedly endured.

Sandel developed a fierce right to the body, which made it appear that King was taking an enormous amount of punishment, and it was only the old ringsters who appreciated the deft touch of King's left glove to the other's biceps just before the impact of the blow. It was true, the blow landed each time; but each time it was robbed of its power by that touch on the biceps. In the ninth round, three times inside a minute, King's right hooked its twisted arch to the jaw; and three times Sandel's body, heavy as it was, was levelled to the mat. Each time he took the nine seconds allowed him and rose to his feet, shaken and jarred, but still strong. He had lost much of his speed, and he wasted less effort. He was fighting grimly; but he continued to draw upon his chief asset, which was youth. King's chief asset was experience. As his vitality had dimmed and his vigour abated, he had replaced them with cunning, with wisdom born of the long fights and with a careful shepherding of strength. Not alone had he learned never to make a superfluous movement, but he had learned how to seduce an opponent into throwing his strength away. Again and again, by feint of foot and hand and body, he continued to inveigle Sandel into leaping back, ducking, or countering. King rested, but he never permitted Sandel to rest. It was the strategy of age.

Early in the tenth round King began stopping the other's rushes with straight lefts to the face, and Sandel, grown wary, responded by drawing the left, then by ducking it and delivering his right in a swinging hook to the side of the head. It was too high up to be vitally effective; but when it first landed King knew the old, familiar descent of the black veil of unconsciousness across his mind. For the instant, or for the slightest fraction of an instant, rather, he ceased. In the one moment he saw his opponent ducking out of his field of vision and the background of white, watching faces; in the next moment he again saw his opponent and the background of faces. It was as if he had slept for a time and just opened his eyes again, and yet the interval of unconsciousness was so microscopically short that there had been no time for him to fall. The audience saw him totter and his knees give, and then saw him recover and tuck his chin deeper into the shelter of his left shoulder.

Several times Sandel repeated the blow, keeping King partially dazed, and then the latter worked out his defence, which was also a counter. Feinting with his left, he took a half step backward, at the same time uppercutting with the whole strength of his right. So accurately was it timed that it landed squarely on Sandel's face in the full, downward sweep of the duck, and Sandel lifted in the air and curled backwards, striking the mat on his head and shoulders. Twice King achieved this, then turned loose and hammered his opponent to the ropes. He gave Sandel no chance to rest or to set himself, but smashed blow in upon blow till the house rose to its feet and the air was filled with an unbroken roar of applause. But Sandel's strength and endurance were superb, and he continued to stay on his feet. A knock-out seemed certain, and a captain of police, appalled at the dreadful punishment, arose by the ringside to stop the fight. The gong struck for the end of the round and Sandel staggered to his corner, protesting to the captain that he was sound and strong. To prove it, he threw two back air-springs, and the police captain gave in.

Tom King, leaning back in his corner and breathing hard, was disappointed. If the fight had been stopped, the referee, perforce, would have rendered him the decision and the purse would have been his. Unlike Sandel, he was not fighting for glory or career, but for thirty quid. And now Sandel would recuperate in the minute of rest.

Youth will be served — this saying flashed into King's mind, and he remembered the first time he had heard it, the night when he had put away Stowsher Bill. The toff who had bought him a drink after the fight and patted him on the shoulder had used those words. Youth will be served! The toff was right. And on that night in the long ago he had been youth. Tonight youth sat in the opposite corner. As for himself, he had been fighting for half an hour now, and he was an old man. Had he fought like Sandel, he would not have lasted fifteen minutes. But the point was that he did not recuperate. Those upstanding arteries and that sorely tried heart would not enable him to gather strength in the intervals between the rounds. And he had not had sufficient strength in him to begin with. His legs were heavy under him and beginning to cramp. He should not have walked those two miles to the fight. And there was the steak which he had got up longing for that morning. A great and terrible hatred rose up in him for the butchers who had refused him credit. It was hard for an old man to go into a fight without enough to eat. And a piece of steak was such a little thing, a few pennies at best; yet it meant thirty quid to him.

With the gong that opened the eleventh round Sandel rushed, making a show of freshness which he did not really possess. King knew it for what it was — a bluff as old as the game itself. He clinched to save himself, then, going free, allowed Sandel to get set. This was what King desired. He feinted with his left, drew the answering duck and swinging upward hook, then made the half step backward, delivered the uppercut full to the face and crumpled Sandel over to the mat. After that he never let him rest, receiving punishment himself, but inflicting far more, smashing Sandel to the ropes, hooking and driving all manner of blows into him, tearing away from his clinches or punching him out of attempted clinches, and ever when Sandel would have fallen, catching him with one uplifting hand and with the other immediately smashing him into the ropes where he could not fall.

The house by this time had gone mad, and it was his house, nearly every voice yelling: "Go it, Tom!" "Get 'im! Get' im!" "You've got 'im, Tom! You've got 'im!" It was to be a whirlwind finish, and that was what a ringside audience paid to see.

And Tom King, who for half an hour had conserved his strength, now expended it prodigally in the one great effort he knew he had in him. It was his one chance — now or not at all. His strength was waning fast, and his hope was that before the last of it ebbed out of him he would have beaten his opponent down for the count. And as he continued to strike and force, coolly estimating the weight of his blows and the quality of the damage wrought, he realized how hard a man Sandel was to knock out. Stamina and endurance were his to an extreme degree, and they were the virgin stamina and endurance of youth. Sandel was certainly a coming man. He had it in him. Only out of such rugged fibre were successful fighters fashioned.

Sandel was reeling and staggering, but Tom King's legs were cramping and his knuckles going back on him. Yet he steeled himself to strike the fierce blows, every one of which brought anguish to his tortured hands. Though now he was receiving practically no punishment, he was weakening as rapidly as the other. His blows went home, but there was no

longer the weight behind them, and each blow was the result
of a severe effort of will. His legs were like lead, and they
dragged visibly under him; while Sandel's backers, cheered
by this symptom, began calling encouragement to their
man.

King was spurred to a burst of effort. He delivered two
blows in succession — a left, a trifle too high, to the solar
plexus, and a right cross to the jaw. They were not heavy
blows, yet so weak and dazed was Sandel that he went down
and lay quivering. The referee stood over him, shouting the
count of the fatal seconds in his ear. If before the tenth second was called he did not rise, the fight was lost. The house
stood in hushed silence. King rested on trembling legs. A
mortal dizziness was upon him, and before his eyes the sea of
faces sagged and swayed, while to his ears, as from a remote
distance, came the count of the referee. Yet he looked upon
the fight as his. It was impossible that a man so punished
could rise.

Only youth could rise, and Sandel rose. At the fourth
second he rolled over on his face and groped blindly for the
ropes. By the seventh second he had dragged himself to his
knee, where he rested, his head rolling groggily on his shoulders. As the referee cried "Nine!" Sandel stood upright, in
proper stalling position, his left arm wrapped about his face,
his right wrapped about his stomach. Thus were his vital
points guarded, while he lurched towards King in the hope
of effecting a clinch and gaining more time.

At the instant Sandel arose, King was at him, but the two
blows he delivered were muffled on the stalled arms. The
next moment Sandel was in the clinch and holding on desperately while the referee strove to drag the two men apart.
King helped to force himself free. He knew the rapidity with
which youth recovered, and he knew that Sandel was his if

he could prevent that recovery. One stiff punch would do it. Sandel was his, indubitably his. He had outgeneralled him, outfought him, outpointed him. Sandel reeled out of the clinch, balanced on the hairline between defeat or survival. One good blow would topple him over and down and out. And Tom King, in a flash of bitterness, remembered the piece of steak and wished that he had it then behind that necessary punch he must deliver. He nerved himself for the blow, but it was not heavy enough nor swift enough. Sandel swayed but did not fall, staggering back to the ropes and holding on. King staggered after him, and, with a pang like that of dissolution, delivered another blow. But his body had deserted him. All that was left of him was a fighting intelligence that was dimmed and clouded from exhaustion. The blow that was aimed for the jaw struck no higher than the shoulder. He had willed the blow higher, but the tired muscles had not been able to obey. And, from the impact of the blow, Tom King himself reeled back and nearly fell. Once again he strove. This time his punch missed altogether, and from absolute weakness he fell against Sandel and clinched, holding on to him to save himself from sinking to the floor.

King did not attempt to free himself. He had shot his bolt. He was gone. And youth had been served. Even in the clinch he could feel Sandel growing stronger against him. When the referee thrust them apart, there, before his eyes, he saw youth recuperate. His punches, weak and futile at first, became stiff and accurate. Tom King's bleared eyes saw the gloved fist driving at his jaw, and he willed to guard it by interposing his arm. He saw the danger, willed the act; but the arm was too heavy. It seemed burdened with a hundredweight of lead. It would not lift itself, and he strove to lift it with his soul. Then the gloved fist landed home. He experienced a sharp snap that was like an electric spark, and simultaneously the veil of blackness enveloped him.

When he opened his eyes again he was in his corner, and he heard the yelling of the audience like the roar of the surf at Bondi Beach. A wet sponge was being pressed against the base of his brain, and Sid Sullivan was blowing cold water in a refreshing spray over his face and chest. His gloves had already been removed, and Sandel, being over him, was shaking his hand. He bore no ill will towards the man who had put him out, and he returned the grip with a heartiness that made his battered knuckles protest. Then Sandel stepped to the centre of the ring and the audience hushed its pandemonium to hear him accept young Pronto's challenge and offer to increase the side bet to one hundred pounds. King looked on apathetically while his seconds mopped the streaming water from him, dried his face, and prepared him to leave the ring. He felt hungry. It was not the ordinary, gnawing kind, but a great faintness, a palpitation at the pit of the stomach that communicated itself to all his body. He remembered back into the fight to the moment when he had Sandel swaying and tottering on the hairline balance of defeat. Ah, that piece of steak would have done it! He had lacked just that for the decisive blow, and he had lost. It was all because of the piece of steak.

His seconds were half supporting him as they helped him through the ropes. He tore free from them, ducked through the ropes unaided, and leaped heavily to the floor, following on their heels as they forced a passage for him down the crowded centre aisle. Leaving the dressing-room for the street, in the entrance to the hall, some young fellow spoke to him.

"W'y didn't yuh go in an' get 'im when yuh 'ad 'im?" the young fellow asked.

"Aw, go to hell!" said Tom King, and passed down the steps to the sidewalk.

The doors of the public house at the corner were swinging wide, and he saw the lights and the smiling barmaids, heard the many voices discussing the fight and the prosperous chink of money on the bar. Somebody called to him to have a drink. He hesitated perceptibly, then refused and went on his way.

He had not a copper in his pocket, and the two-mile walk home seemed very long. He was certainly getting old. Crossing the Domain he sat down suddenly on a bench, unnerved by the thought of the missus sitting up for him, waiting to learn the outcome of the fight. That was harder than any knock-out, and it seemed almost impossible to face.

He felt weak and sore, and the pain of his smashed knuckles warned him that, even if he could find a job at navvy work, it would be a week before he could grip a pick handle or a shovel. The hunger palpitation at the pit of the stomach was sickening. His wretchedness overwhelmed him, and into his eyes came an unwonted moisture. He covered his face with his hands, and, as he cried, he remembered Stowsher Bill and how he had served him that night in the long ago. Poor old Stowsher Bill! He could understand now why Bill had cried in the dressing-room.

**3** JACK LONDON FOLLOWED in the footsteps of Herman Melville and Robert Louis Stevenson when he sailed for Hawaii and the South Seas in 1907. With a crew of five which included his valet and wife, he sailed his small boat *Snark* from San Francisco across the Pacific as far as the Solomon Islands.

Ocean voyaging in those preradio days was of course highly dangerous, and life aboard the little ship was cramped and primitive. Nevertheless, London's confidence and ability kept morale high and turned the long and lonely voyage of the *Snark* into a romantic cruise whose progress was suspensefully followed by thousands of readers around the world. It was one of the great adventures of the day, rivaling endurance performances of auto and "aeroplane" daredevils in its imaginative appeal.

A self-taught but highly skillful navigator, London was an eager adventurer, tireless explorer, and keen student of native customs and mores. It was while visiting the legendary tropical island of Bora Bora that he was invited to participate in a communal fish hunt. The result, described in the following article, is one of the most exotic and amusing episodes of his South Seas odyssey.

*"The Stone-Fishing of Bora Bora" is reprinted
from* The Cruise of the Snark.
*Copyright 1911 by The Macmillan Company;
renewed 1939 by Charmian K. London.*

# The Stone-Fishing of Bora Bora

AT FIVE IN the morning the conches began to blow. From all along the beach the eerie sounds arose, like the ancient voice of War, calling to the fishermen to arise and prepare to go forth. We on the *Snark* likewise arose, for there could be no sleep in that mad din of conches. Also, we were going stone-fishing, though our preparations were few.

*Tautai-taora* is the name for stone-fishing, *tautai* meaning a "fishing instrument." And *taora* meaning "thrown." But *tautai-taora,* in combination, means "stone-fishing," for a stone is the instrument that is thrown. Stone-fishing is in reality a fish-drive, similar in principle to a rabbit-drive or a cattle-drive, though in the latter affairs drivers and driven operate in the same medium, while in the fish-drive the men must be in the air to breathe and the fish are driven through the water. It does not matter if the water is a hundred feet deep, the men, working on the surface, drive the fish just the same.

This is the way it is done. The canoes form in line, one hundred to two hundred feet apart. In the bow of each canoe a man wields a stone, several pounds in weight, which is attached to a short rope. He merely smites the water with the stone, pulls up the stone, and smites again. He goes on smiting. In the stern of each canoe, another man paddles, driving the canoe ahead and at the same time keeping it in the formation. The line of canoes advances to meet a second

line a mile or two away, the ends of the lines hurrying together to form a circle, the far edge of which is the shore.
The circle begins to contract upon the shore, where the
women, standing in a long row out into the sea, form a fence
of legs, which serves to break any rushes of the frantic fish.
At the right moment when the circle is sufficiently small, a
canoe dashes out from shore, dropping overboard a long
screen of cocoanut leaves and encircling the circle, thus
reenforcing the palisade of legs. Of course, the fishing is
always done inside the reef in the lagoon.

"*Tres jolie,*" the gendarme said, after explaining by signs
and gestures that thousands of fish would be caught of all
sizes from minnows to sharks, and that the captured fish
would boil up and upon the very sand of the beach.

It is a more successful method of fishing, while its nature
is more that of an outing festival, rather than of a prosaic,
food-getting task. Such fishing parties take place about once
a month at Bora Bora, and it is a custom that has descended
from old time. The man who originated it is not remembered. They always did this thing. But one cannot help wondering about that forgotten savage of the long ago, into
whose mind first flashed this scheme of easy fishing, of
catching huge quantities of fish without hook, or net, or
spear. One thing about him we can know: he was a radical.
And we can be sure that he was considered feather-brained
and anarchistic by his conservative tribesmen. His difficulty
was much greater than that of the modern inventor, who has
to convince in advance only one or two capitalists. That
early inventor had to convince his whole tribe in advance,
for without the cooperation of the whole tribe the device
could not be tested. One can well imagine the nightly pow-
wow-ings in that primitive island world, when he called his
comrades antiquated moss-backs, and they called him a

fool, a freak, and a crank, and charged him with having come from Kansas. Heaven alone knows at what cost of gray hairs and expletives he must finally have succeeded in winning over a sufficient number to give his idea a trial. At any rate, the experiment succeeded. It stood the test of truth — it worked! And thereafter, we can be confident, there was no man to be found who did not know all along that it was going to work.

Our good friends, Tehei and Bihaura, who were giving the fishing in our honor, had promised to come for us. We were down below when the call came from on deck that they were coming. We dashed up the companionway, to be overwhelmed by the sight of the Polynesian barge in which we were to ride. It was a long double canoe, the canoes lashed together by timbers with an interval of water between, and the whole decorated with flowers and golden grasses. A dozen flower-crowned Amazons were at the paddles, while at the stern of each canoe was a strapping steersman. All were garlanded with gold and crimson and orange flowers, while each wore about the hips a scarlet *pareu*. There were flowers everywhere, flowers, flowers, flowers, without end. The whole thing was an orgy of color. On the platform forward resting on the bows of the canoes, Tehei and Bihaura were dancing. All voices were raised in a wild song of greeting.

Three times they circled the *Snark* before coming alongside to take Charmian and me on board. Then it was away for the fishing-grounds, a five-mile paddle dead to windward. "Everybody is jolly in Bora Bora," is the saying throughout the Society Islands, and we certainly found everybody jolly. Canoe songs, shark songs, and fishing songs were sung to the dipping of the paddles, all joining in on the swinging choruses. Once in a while the cry *"Mao!"* was raised, whereupon all strained like mad at the paddles. *Mao* is shark, and when the deep-sea tigers appear, the natives paddle for dear life for the shore, knowing full well the danger they run of having their frail canoes overturned and of being devoured. Of course, in our case there were no sharks, but the cry of *mao* was used to incite them to paddle with as much energy as if a shark were really after them. *"Hoe! Hoe!"* was another cry that made us foam through the water.

On the platform Tehei and Bihaura danced, accompanied by songs and choruses or by rhythmic hand-clappings. At other times a musical knocking of the paddles against the sides of the canoes marked the accent. A young girl dropped her paddle, leaped to the platform, and danced a hula, in the midst of which, still dancing, she swayed and bent, and imprinted on our cheeks the kiss of welcome. Some of the songs, or *himines,* were religious, and they were especially beautiful, the deep bases of the men mingling with the altos and thin sopranos of the women and forming a combination of sound that irresistibly reminded one of an organ. In fact, "kanaka organ" is the scoffer's description of the *himine.* On the other hand, some of the chants or ballads were very barbaric, having come down from pre-Christian times.

And so, singing, dancing, paddling, these joyous Polynesians took us to the fishing. The gendarme, who is the French ruler of Bora Bora, accompanied us with his family in a double canoe of his own, paddled by his prisoners; for not only is he gendarme and ruler, but he is jailer as well, and in this jolly land when anybody goes fishing, all go fishing. A score of single canoes, with outriggers, paddled along with us. Around the point a big sailing-canoe appeared, running beautifully before the wind as it bore down to greet us. Balancing precariously on the outrigger, three young men saluted us with a wild rolling of drums.

The next point, half a mile farther on, brought us to the place of meeting. Here the launch, which had been brought along by Warren and Martin, attracted much attention.

The Bora Borans could not see what made it go. The canoes were drawn upon the sand, and all hands went ashore to drink cocoanuts and sing and dance. Here our numbers were added to by many who arrived on foot from near-by dwellings, and a pretty sight it was to see the flower-crowned maidens, hand in hand and two by two, arriving along the sands.

"They usually make a big catch," Allicot, a half-caste trader, told us. "At the finish the water is fairly alive with fish. It is lots of fun. Of course you know all the fish will be yours."

"All?" I groaned, for already the *Snark* was loaded down with lavish presents, by the canoe-load, of fruits, vegetables, pigs, and chickens.

"Yes, every last fish," Allicot answered. "You see, when the surround is completed, you, being the guest of honor, must take a harpoon and impale the first one. It is the custom. Then everybody goes in with their hands and throws the catch out on the sand. There will be a mountain of them. Then one of the chiefs will make a speech in which he presents you with the whole kit and boodle. But you don't have to take them all. You get up and make a speech, selecting what fish you want for yourself and presenting all the rest back again. Then everybody says you are very generous."

"But what would be the result if I kept the whole present?" I asked.

"It has never happened," was the answer. "It is the custom to give and give back again."

The native minister started with a prayer for success in the fishing, and all heads were bared. Next, the chief fishermen told off the canoes and allotted them their places. Then it was into the canoes and away. No women, however, came along, with the exception of Bihaura and Charmian. In the old days even they would have been tabooed. The women remained behind to wade out into the water and form the palisade of legs.

The big double canoe was left on the beach, and we went in the launch. Half the canoes paddled off to leeward, while we, with the other half, headed to windward a mile and a half, until the end of our line was in touch with the reef. The leader of the drive occupied a canoe midway in our line. He stood erect, a fine figure of an old man, holding a flag in his hand. He directed the taking of positions and the forming of the two lines by blowing on a conch. When all was ready, he waved his flag to the right. With a single splash the throwers in every canoe on that side struck the water with their stones. While they were hauling them back — a matter of a moment, for the stones scarcely sank beneath the surface — the flag waved to the left, and with admirable precision every stone on that side struck the water. So it went, back and forth, right and left; with every wave of the flag a long line of concussion smote the lagoon. At the same time the paddles drove the canoes forward; and what was being done in our line was being done in the opposing line of canoes a mile and more away.

On the bow of the launch, Tehei, with eyes fixed on the leader, worked his stone in unison with the others. Once, the stone slipped from the rope, and the same instant Tehei went overboard after it. I do not know whether or not that stone reached the bottom, but I do know that the next instant Tehei broke surface alongside with the stone in his hand. I noticed this same accident occur several times among the near-by canoes, but in each instance the thrower followed the stone and brought it back.

The reef ends of our lines accelerated, the shore ends lagged, all under the watchful supervision of the leader, until at the reef the two lines joined, forming the circle. Then the contraction of the circle began, the poor frightened fish harried shoreward by the streaks of concussion that smote the water. In the same fashion elephants are driven through the jungle by motes of men who crouch in the long grasses or behind trees and make strange noises. Already the palisade of legs had been built. We could see the heads of the women, in a long line, dotting the placid surface of the lagoon. The tallest women went farthest out, thus, with the exception of those close inshore, nearly all were up to their necks in water.

Still the circle narrowed, till canoes were almost touching. There was a pause. A long canoe shot out from shore, following the line of the circle. It went as fast as paddles could drive. In the stern a man threw overboard the long, continuous screen of cocoanut leaves. The canoes were no longer needed, and overboard went the men to reenforce the palisade with their legs. For the screen was only a screen, and not a net, and the fish could dash through it if they tried. Hence the need for legs that ever agitated the screen, and for hands that splashed and throats that yelled. Pandemonium reigned as the trap tightened.

But no fish broke surface or collided against the hidden legs. At last the chief fisherman entered the trap. He waded around everywhere, carefully. But there were no fish boiling up and out upon the sand. There was not a sardine, not a minnow, not a pollywog. Something must have been wrong with their prayer; or else, and more likely, as one grizzled fellow put it, the wind was not in its usual quarter and the fish were elsewhere in the lagoon. In fact, there had been no fish to drive.

"About once in five these drives are failures," Allicot consoled us.

Well, it was the stone-fishing that had brought us to Bora Bora, and it was our luck to draw the one chance in five. Had it been a raffle, it would have been the other way about. This is not pessimism. Nor is it an indictment of the plan of the universe. It is merely that feeling which is familiar to most fishermen at the empty end of a hard day.

4 THE METAPHOR OF man as gambler in the uncertain game of life became real enough to the young Jack London when, in the spring of 1897, he embarked along with thousands of other "sportsmen" on the glittering lottery of the Alaskan gold rush. Fortunes were made and lost overnight in the rough Klondike camps and boom towns which London visited, and he later saw similar scenes enacted in the pearl ports and isolated trading towns of the South Seas. It is not surprising, therefore, that one finds in his writing accounts of games and contests played for the highest imaginable stakes. For what were these games of chance if not symbols of the arbitrariness and precariousness of existence itself?

Set in Alaska or Polynesia, Jack London's gambling tales descend from a tradition in American literature which crossed the continent from Twain's colorful riverboat gamblers on the Mississippi to Crane's colorless dealer at Fort Romper's saloon to Harte's slick faro and pedro dealers of the Mother Lode. London's "A Goboto Night," "Shorty Dreams," and "The Race for Number Three" share in the tradition and extend it to farther frontiers and newer pioneers. They recall the spirit of those boom-or-bust "outposts of progress" where a man's wealth, reputation, or very life might depend on the turn of a card or spin of a wheel.

In "A Goboto Night," an intolerant young man's way of life is laid on the line in a game of cards. One of London's Klondike gamblers had placed his trust in a God who played loaded dice with the universe; here, his South Seas hero, David Grief, plays an unmarked deck for a no less important stake. The question is whether the game can mark a turning point in the career of one whose life urgently needs to be redealt. Fate is the dealer, a man's soul is the prize, and London's suspenseful tale is calculated to the last turn of the card.

# A Goboto Night

A T GOBOTO THE traders come off their schooners and the planters drift in from far, wild coasts, and one and all they assume shoes, white duck trousers, and various other appearances of civilization. At Goboto mail is received, bills are paid, and newspapers, rarely more than five weeks old, are accessible; the little island belted with coral reefs affords safe anchorage, is the steamer port of call, and serves as a distributing point for the whole wide-scattered island group.

Life at Goboto is heated, unhealthy and lurid, and for its size, asserts the distinction of more cases of acute alcoholism than any other spot in the world. Guvutu, over in the Solomons, claims that it drinks *between* drinks. Goboto does not deny this. It merely states in passing that in the Goboton chronology, no such interval as "between drinks" is known. It also points out its import statistics, which show a far greater per capita consumption of spirituous liquors. Guvutu explains this on the basis that Goboto does a larger business and has more visitors. Goboto retorts that its resident population is smaller and that its visitors are thirstier. And the discussion goes on interminably, principally because the disputants do not live long enough to settle it.

Goboto is not large. The island is only a quarter-mile in diameter, and on it are situated an Admiralty coal shed (where a few tons of coal have lain untouched for twenty years), the barracks for a handful of native laborers, a big store and warehouse with sheet-iron roofs, and a cottage

inhabited by the manager and his two clerks. They are the
white population. An average of one man out of the three is
always to be found down with fever. The job at Goboto is a
hard one. It is the policy of the company to treat its patrons
well, as invading companies have found out, and it is the
task of the manager and clerks to do the treating. Throughout the year traders and recruiters arrive from far, dry
cruises, and planters from equally distant and dry shores,
bringing with them magnificent thirsts. Goboto is the mecca
of sprees, and when they have spreed, they go back to their
schooners and plantations to recuperate.

Some of the less hardy require as much as six months between visits. But for the manager and his assistants there are
no such intervals. They are on the spot, and week by week,
blown in by monsoon or southeast trade, the schooners come
to anchor, cargo'd with copra, ivory nuts, pearl shell, hawks-
bill turtle, and thirst.

It is a very hard job at Goboto. That is why the pay is
twice that on other stations, and that is why the company
selects only courageous and intrepid men for this particular
station. They last no more than a year or so, when the wreck-
age of them is shipped back to Australia, or the remains of
them are buried in the sand across on the windward side of
the islet. Johnny Bassett, almost the legendary hero of
Goboto, broke all records. He was a remittance man with a
remarkable constitution, and he lasted seven years. His
dying request was duly observed by his clerks, who pickled
him in a cask of trade-rum (paid for out of their own sal-
aries) and shipped him back to his relatives in England.

Nevertheless, at Goboto, they tried to be gentlemen. For
that matter, though something was wrong with them, they
*were* gentlemen, and *had been* gentlemen. That was why
the great unwritten rule of Goboto was that visitors should

put on pants and shoes. Breech-clouts, lava-lavas, and bare legs were not tolerated. When Captain Jensen, wildest of the blackbirders though descended from old New York blue-blood stock, surged in, clad in loincloth, undershirt, two belted revolvers and a sheath knife, he was stopped at the beach. This was in the days of Johnny Bassett, ever a stickler in matters of etiquette. Captain Jensen stood up in the stern-sheets of his whaleboat and denied the existence of pants on his schooner. Also, he affirmed his intention of coming ashore. They of Goboto nursed him back to health from a bullet hole through his shoulder, and in addition handsome-ly begged his pardon, for no pants *had* they found on his schooner. And finally, on the first day he sat up, Johnny Basset kindly but firmly assisted his guest into a pair of pants of his own. This was the great precedent. In all the succeed-ing years it had never been violated. White men and pants were undivorceable. Only aborigines ran naked. Pants con-stituted caste.

On this night things were, with one exception, in nowise different from any other night. Seven of them, with glim-mering eyes and steady legs, had capped a day of Scotch with swizzle-sticked cocktails and sat down to dinner. Jack-eted, trousered, and shod, they were: Jerry McMurtrey, the manager; Eddy Little and Jack Andrews, clerks; Captain Stapler, of the recruiting ketch *Merry;* Darby Shryleton, planter from Tito-Ito; Peter Gee, a half-caste Chinese pearl buyer who ranged from Ceylon to the Tuamotus, and Alfred Deacon, a visitor who had stopped off from the last steamer. At first, wine was served by the native servants to those that drank it, though all quickly shifted back to Scotch and soda, pickling their food as they ate it, ere it entered their cal-cined, pickled stomachs.

Over their coffee, they heard the rumble of an anchor chain through a hawsehole, tokening the arrival of a vessel.

"It's David Grief," Peter Gee remarked.

"How do *you* know?" Deacon demanded truculently. "You fellows seem to think a stranger will fall for anything. I've done sailing myself, and naming a craft when its sail is only a blur, or naming a man by the sound of his anchor — it's — it's unadulterated poppycock."

Peter Gee, engaged in lighting a cigarette, did not answer.

"Some of the natives can do amazing things that way," McMurtrey interposed tactfully.

As with the others, this conduct of their young visitor jarred on the manager. From the moment of Peter Gee's arrival that afternoon Deacon had shown a tendency to pick on him. He had disputed his statements and been generally rude.

"Maybe it's because Peter's got Chinese blood in him," had been Andrews' hypothesis. "Deacon's South African, you know, and they're loony there about color."

"That's probably it," McMurtrey had agreed. "But we can't permit that sort of thing here, especially of a man like Peter Gee."

In this the manager had been in nowise wrong. Peter Gee was better educated than any man there, spoke better English as well as several other tongues, and knew and lived more of their own ideals of gentility than they did themselves. And, finally, he was a gentle soul. Violence he deprecated, though he had killed men in his time. Turbulence he abhorred — avoiding it like the plague.

Captain Stapler stepped in to assist McMurtrey:

"I remember, when I changed schooners and came into Altman, the natives knew it was me right off the bat. I wasn't expected, either, much less in another craft. They told the trader it was me. He used glasses, and still wouldn't believe them. But they knew. Told me afterward they could see it sticking out all over the schooner that I was running her."

Deacon ignored him, and returned to the attack on the pearl buyer.

"How do you know from the sound of his anchor that it is whatever-you-called-him?" he challenged.

"There are so many things that go to make up such a judgment," Peter Gee answered. "It's rather hard to explain. It would almost require a text book."

"I thought so," Deacon sneered. "Explanation that doesn't explain is easy."

"Who's for bridge?" Eddy Little, the second clerk, interrupted, looking up expectantly and starting to shuffle. "You'll play, won't you Peter?"

"If he does, he's a faker," Deacon cut back. "I'm tired of all this poppycock. Mr. Gee can surprise us all by telling how we knows who that man was that just dropped anchor. After that I'll play piquet."

"I'd prefer bridge," Peter answered. "It's something like this: By the sound it was a small craft — no square-rigger. No whistle, no siren, was blown — again a small craft. It anchored close in — still again a small craft, for steamers and big ships must drop hook outside the middle shoal. Now the entrance is tortuous. There is no recruiting nor trading captain around who dares run the passage after dark. Certainly no stranger would. There are two exceptions. The first was Margonville. But he was executed by the High Court at Fiji. Remains the other exception, David Grief. Night or day, in any weather, he runs the passage. This is well known to all. A possible factor, in case Grief were somewhere else, would be some young dare-devil of a skipper. In this connection, in the first place I don't know of any, nor does anybody else. In the second place, David Grief is in these waters, cruising on the *Gunga,* which is shortly scheduled to leave here for Karo-Karo. I spoke to Grief on the *Gunga* in Sandfly Passage, day before yesterday. He was putting a trader ashore on a new station. He said he was going to call in at Babo, and then come on to Goboto. He has had ample time to get here. I have heard an anchor drop. Who else than David Grief can it be? Captain Donovan is skipper of the *Gunga,* and I know him too well to believe that he'd run in to Goboto after dark unless his owner were in charge. In a few minutes David Grief will enter through that door and say, 'In Guvutu they merely drink *between* drinks.' I'll wager two hundred and fifty dollars he's the man that enters and that his words will be, 'In Guvutu they merely drink *between* drinks.' "

Deacon was for the moment crushed. The sullen blood rose darkly in his face.

"Well, he's answered you," McMurtrey laughed genially. "And I'll back his bet myself for a couple of bucks."

"Bridge! Who's going to take a hand?" Eddy Little cried impatiently. "Come on, Peter!"

"The rest of you play," Deacon said. "He and I are going to play piquet."

"I'd prefer bridge," Peter Gee said mildly.

"Don't you play piquet?"

The pearl buyer nodded.

"Then come on. Maybe I can show I know more about that than I do about anchors."

"Now look here—" McMurtrey began.

"You can play bridge," Deacon shut him off. "We prefer piquet."

Reluctantly, Peter Gee was bullied into a game that he knew would be unpleasant.

"Only a rubber," he said, as he cut for deal.

"For how much?" Deacon asked.

Peter Gee shrugged his shoulder. "As you please."

"Hundred up — twenty-five dollars a game?"

Peter Gee agreed.

"With default double, of course — fifty dollars?"

"All right," said Peter Gee.

At another table four of the others sat at bridge. Captain Stapler, no card-player, looked on and replenished the long glasses of Scotch that stood at each man's right hand. McMurtrey, with poorly concealed apprehension, followed as well as he could what went on at the piquet table. All were shocked by the behavior of the South African, and all were troubled by fear of some untoward act on his part. It was apparent that he was working up his animosity against the half-caste, and that the explosion might come any time.

"I hope Peter loses," McMurtrey said in an undertone.

"Not if he has any luck," Andrews answered. "He's a wizard at piquet. I know by experience."

That Peter Gee *was* lucky was obvious from the continual badgering by Deacon, who filled his glass frequently. He had lost the first game, and, from his remarks, was losing the second, when the door opened and David Grief entered.

"In Guvutu they merely drink *between* drinks," he remarked casually to the assembled company, and gripped the manager's hand. "Hello, Mac! My skipper's down in the whaleboat. He's got a silk shirt, a tie, and tennis shoes, all complete, but he wants you to send a pair of pants down. Mine are too small, but yours will fit him. Hello, Eddy! How's that *ngari-ngari?* You up, Jock? The miracle has happened. No one down with fever, and no one remarkably drunk." He sighed, "I suppose the night is young yet. Hello, Peter! You catch that big squall an hour after you left us? We had to let go the second anchor."

While he was being introduced to Deacon, McMurtrey dispatched a house boy with pants, and when Captain

Donovan came in it was as a gentlemen should — at least on Goboto.

Deacon lost the second game, and an outburst heralded the fact. Peter Gee devoted himself to lighting a cigarette and keeping quiet.

"What — quitting because you're ahead?" Deacon demanded.

Grief raised his eyebrows questioningly to McMurtrey, who frowned back his own disgust.

"I've won the rubber," Peter Gee explained.

"But I'm still entitled to win some money on a third hand. It's my deal. Come on!"

Peter Gee acquiesced, and the third game was on.

"Young punk — he needs a thrashing," McMurtrey muttered to Grief. "Come on, let's quit — I want to keep an eye on him. If he goes too far, I'll toss him out on the beach, Company instructions or no."

"Who is he?" Grief queried.

"A leftover from last steamer. Company's orders are to treat him nice; he's looking to invest in a plantation. Has a fifty thousand dollar letter of credit with him — and he's also got 'all-white South Africa' on the brain. Thinks because his skin is pure white and his father once was Attorney General in Pretoria, he can act like a louse. That's why he's picking on Peter, and you know Peter's the last man in the world to cause trouble. Damn the Company. I didn't engage to wet nurse infants with bank accounts. Come on, fill your glass, Grief. The man's contemptible."

"Maybe he's only young," Grief suggested.

"He can't hold his liquor — that's clear." The manager glared his disgust and wrath. "If he raises a hand to Peter, so help me, I'll give him a licking myself, the little overgrown punk!"

The pearl buyer pulled the pegs out of the cribbage board on which he was scoring and sat back. He had won the third game. He glanced across to Eddy Little, saying:

"I'm ready for bridge, now."

"I wouldn't be a quitter," Deacon snarled.

"Oh, really — I'm tired of the game," Peter Gee assured him with his habitual quietness.

"Come on," Deacon bullied. "One more. You can't take my money that way. I'm out seventy-five dollars. Double or nothing."

McMurtrey was about to interpose, but Grief restrained him with his eyes.

"If it positively is the last, all right," said Peter Gee, gathering up the cards. "It's my deal, I believe. As I understand it, this one is for seventy-five dollars. Either you owe me one hundred and fifty or we quit even?"

"That's it, friend. Either we break even or I pay you one hundred and fifty."

"Getting interesting, eh?" Grief remarked, drawing up a chair.

The other men stood or sat around the table, and Deacon played again in bad luck. That he was a good player was clear. The cards were merely running against him. That he could not take his ill luck with equanimity was equally clear. He was guilty of sharp, ugly curses which he snapped and growled at the imperturbable half-caste. In the end Peter Gee counted out, while Deacon had not even made his fifty points. He glowered speechlessly at his opponent.

"Looks like a default," said Grief.

"Which is double," said Peter Gee.

"No need telling me," Deacon snarled. "I've studied arithmetic. I owe you two hundred and twenty-five bucks. Take it!"

The way in which he flung the money on the table was an insult in itself. But Peter Gee was even quieter, and flew no signals of resentment.

"You've got fool's luck, but you can't play cards — I can tell you that much," Deacon went on. "I could teach you cards."

The half-caste smiled and nodded acquiescence as he folded up the money.

"There's a little game called cassino — I wonder if you ever heard of it — a child's game?"

"I've seen it played," the half-caste murmured gently.

"Maybe you think you can play it?" snapped Deacon.

"Oh, no, not at the moment. I'm afraid I'm not up to it."

"It's a jolly game, cassino," Grief broke in pleasantly. "*I* like it very much."

Deacon ignored him.

"I'll play you fifty bucks a game — thirty-one points out," was the challenge to Peter Gee. "And I'll show you how little you know about cards. Come on! Where's a full deck?"

"No, thanks," the half-caste answered. "They need a fourth here at bridge."

"Yes," Eddy Little begged eagerly. "Come on, Peter, let's get started."

"Afraid of a little game like cassino," Deacon sneered. "Maybe the stakes are too high. I'll play you for pennies — if you say so."

The man's conduct was an affront to all of them. McMurtrey could stand it no longer.

"Now hold on, Deacon. He says he doesn't want to play. Let him alone."

Deacon turned raging upon his host; but before he could blurt out his abuse, Grief had stepped into the breach.

"*I'd* like to play cassino with you," he said.

"What do *you* know about it?"

"Not much, but I'm willing to learn."

"Well, I'm not teaching for pennies tonight."

"Oh, that's all right," Grief answered. "I'll play for almost any sum—within reason, of course."

Deacon proceeded to dispose of this intruder with one stroke.

"I'll play you five hundred dollars a game, if that won't upset you."

Grief beamed his delight. "That will be fine. Let us begin. Do you count sweeps?"

Deacon was taken aback. He had not expected a Goboton trader to be anything but crushed by such a proposition.

"Do you count sweeps?" Grief repeated. Andrews had brought him a new deck, and he was throwing away the joker.

"Certainly not," Deacon answered. "That's a sissy game."

"I'm glad," Grief coincided. "I don't like sissy games either."

"You don't, eh? Well, then, I'll tell you what we'll do. We'll play for twenty-five hundred dollars a game."

Again Deacon was taken aback.

"I'm agreeable," Grief said, beginning to shuffle. " 'Cards' and 'spades' go out first, of course, and then 'big' and 'little cassino,' and the aces in the bridge order of value. Is that right?"

"You're a lot of comedians down here," Deacon laughed, but his laughter was strained. "How do I know you've got the money?"

"By the same token that I know you've got it. Mac, how's my credit with the Company?"

"All you want," the manager answered.

"You personally guarantee that?" Deacon demanded.

"I certainly do," McMurtrey said. "Depend upon it, the Company will honor his note up to and past your letter of credit."

"Low card deals," Grief said, placing the deck before Deacon on the table.

The latter hesitated in the midst of the cut and looked around with querulous misgiving at the faces of the others. The clerks and captains nodded.

"You're all strangers to me," Deacon complained. "How am I to know? Money on paper isn't always the real thing."

Then it was that Peter Gee, drawing a wallet from his pocket and borrowing a fountain pen from McMurtrey, went into action.

"I haven't started my buying yet," the half-caste explained, "so the account is intact. I'll just endorse it over to you, Grief. It's for seventy-five thousand."

Deacon intercepted the letter of credit as it was being passed across the table. He read it slowly, then glanced up at McMurtrey.

"Is this okay?"

"Yes. Just the same as your own, and just as good. The Company's paper is always good."

Deacon cut the cards, won the deal, and gave them a thorough shuffle. But luck was still against him, and he lost the game.

"Another game," he said. "We didn't say how many, and you can't quit with me a loser. I want action."

Grief shuffled and passed the cards for the cut.

"Let's play for five thousand," Deacon said, when he had lost the second game. And when the five thousand had gone the way of the two twenty-five hundred dollar bets, he proposed to play for ten thousand.

"That's progression,' " McMurtrey warned, and was rewarded by a glare from Deacon. But the manager was insistent. "You don't have to play progression, Grief, unless you're foolish."

"Who's playing this game?" Deacon flamed at his host; and then, to Grief: "I've lost ten thousand to you. Will you play for ten thousand?"

Grief nodded, the fourth game began, and Deacon won. The unfairness of such betting was obvious to all of them. Though he had lost three games out of four, Deacon had lost no money. By the child's device of doubling his wager with each loss, he was bound, with the first game he won, no matter how long delayed, to be even again.

He now evinced an unspoken desire to stop, but Grief passed the deck to be cut.

"What?" Deacon cried. "You want more?"

"Haven't had anything yet," Grief murmured whimsically, as he began to deal. "Back to the usual twenty-five hundred, I suppose?"

The same of what he had done must have even tingled in Deacon, for he answered, "No, we'll play for ten thousand. And say! Thirty-one points is too long. Why not twenty-one points out — if it isn't too rapid for you?"

"That will make it a nice, quick little game," Grief agreed.

The former method of play was repeated. Deacon lost two games, doubled the stake, and was again even. But Grief was patient, though the thing occurred several times in the next hour's play. Then happened what he was waiting for — a lengthening in the series of losing games for Deacon. The latter doubled to twenty thousand and lost, doubled to forty thousand and lost, and then proposed to double to eighty thousand.

Grief shook his head. "You can't do that, you know. You've only fifty thousand credit with the company."

"You mean you won't give me action?" Deacon asked hoarsely. "You mean that with forty thousand of my money you're going to quit?"

Grief smiled and shook his head.

"It's robbery, plain robbery," Deacon went on. "You take my money and won't give me action."

"No, you're wrong. I'm perfectly willing to give you whatever action you've got coming. You've got ten thousand dollars worth of action yet."

"Well, we'll play it," Deacon took him up. "You cut."

The game was played in silence, save for irritable remarks and curses from Deacon. Silently the onlookers filled and sipped their long Scotch glasses. Grief took no notice of his opponent's outbursts, but concentrated on the game. He was really playing cards, and there were fifty-two in the deck to keep track of, and of which he did keep track. Two-thirds of the way through the last deal he threw down his hand.

" 'Cards put me out," he said. "I have twenty-seven."

"If you've made a mistake," Deacon threatened, his face white and drawn.

"Then I shall have lost. Count them."

Grief passed over his stack of cards, and Deacon, with trembling fingers, verified the count. He half shoved his chair back from the table and emptied his glass. He looked about him at unsympathetic faces.

"I fancy I'll be catching the next steamer for Sydney," he said, for the first time his speech was quiet and without bluster.

As Grief told them afterward: "Had he whined or raised a roar I wouldn't have given him that last chance. As it was, he took his medicine like a man, and I had to do it.

Deacon glanced at his watch, simulated a weary yawn, and started to rise.

"Wait," Grief said. "Do you want further action?"

The other sank down in his chair, strove to speak, but could not, licked his dry lips, and nodded his head.

"Captain Donovan here sails at daylight in the *Gunga* for Karo-Karo," Grief began with seeming irrelevance. "Karo-Karo is a ring of sand in the sea, with a few thousand coconut trees. Pandanus grows there, but they can't grow sweet potatoes nor taro. There are about eight hundred natives, a king and two prime ministers. It's a Godforsaken little hole, and once a year I send a schooner up from Goboto. The drinking water is brackish, but old Tom Butler has survived on it for a dozen years. He's the only white man there. There are no missionaries. Two native Samoan teachers were clubbed to death on the beach when they landed several years ago.

"Naturally, you are wondering what this is all about. But have patience. As I have said, Captain Donovan sails on the annual trip to Karo-Karo at daylight tomorrow. Tom Butler is old, and getting quite helpless. I've tried to retire him to Australia, but he says he wants to remain and die on Karo-Karo, and he will in the next year or so. He's a queer old codger. Now the time is due for me to send someone else up to take the work off his hands. I wonder how you'd like the job. You'd have to stay two years.

"Hold on! I've not finished. You've talked frequently of action this evening. There's no action in betting away what you've never sweated for. The money you've lost to me was left you by your father or some other relative who did the sweating. But two years of work as trader on Karo-Karo would mean something.

"I'll bet the fifty thousand I've won from you against two years of your time. If you win, the money's yours. If you lose, you take the job at Karo-Karo and sail at daylight. Now that's what might be called real action. Will you play?"

Deacon could not speak. His throat lumped and he nodded his head as he reached for the cards.

"One thing more," Grief said. "I can do even better. If you lose, two years of your time are mine — naturally without wages. Nevertheless, I'll pay you wages. If your work is satisfactory, if you observe all instructions and rules, I'll pay you twenty-five thousand dollars a year for two years. The money will be deposited with the Company, to be paid to you, with interest, when the time expires. Is that all right?"

"Too much so," Deacon stammered. "You are unfair to yourself. A trader only gets fifty or seventy-five dollars a month."

"Put it down to action, then," Grief said, with an air of dismissal. "And before we begin, I'll jot down several of the rules. These you will repeat aloud every morning during the two years — if you lose. They are for the good of your soul. When you have repeated them aloud seven hundred and thirty Karo-Karo mornings I am confident they will be in your memory to stay. Lend me your pen, Mac. Now, let's see —"

He wrote steadily and rapidly for some minutes, then proceeded to read the matter aloud:

*I must always remember that one man is as good as another, even when he thinks he is better.*

*No matter how drunk I get I must not fail to be a gentleman. A gentleman is a man who is gentle.* NOTE: *It would be better not to get drunk.*

*When I play a man's game with men, I must play like a man.*

*A good curse, rightly used and rarely, is an efficient thing. Too many curses spoil the cursing.* NOTE: *A curse cannot change a card sequence nor cause the wind to blow.*

*There is no license for a man to be less than a man. Fifty thousand dollars cannot purchase such a license.*

At the beginning of the reading, Deacon's face had gone white with anger. Then had arisen, from neck to forehead, a slow and terrible flush that deepened to the end of the reading.

"There, that will be all," Grief said, as he folded the paper and tossed it to the center of the table. "Are you still ready to play the game?"

"I deserve it," Deacon muttered brokenly. "I've been a fool. Mr. Gee, before I know whether I win or lose, I want to apologize. Maybe it was the whiskey, I don't know, but I'm a damn fool."

He held out his hand, and the half-caste took it beamingly.

"Grief," Peter Gee blurted out, "the boy's all right. Call the whole thing off and let's forget it in a final nightcap."

Grief showed signs of debating, but Deacon cried:

"No; I won't permit it. I'm not a quitter. If it's Karo-Karo, it's Karo-Karo. That's all there is to it."

"Right," said Grief, as he began the shuffle. "If he's the right stuff to go to Karo-Karo, Karo-Karo won't do him any harm."

The game was close and hard. Three times they divided the deck between them and "cards" were not scored. At the beginning of the fifth and last deal, Deacon needed three points to go out, and Grief needed four. "Cards" alone would put Deacon out, and he played for "cards." He no longer muttered or cursed, and played his best game of the evening. Incidentally, he gathered in the two black aces and the ace of hearts.

"I suppose you can name the four cards I hold," he challenged, as the last of the deal was exhausted and he picked up his hand.

Grief nodded.

"Then name them."

"The jack of spades, the two of spades, the three of hearts, and the ace of diamonds," Grief answered.

Those behind Deacon and looking at his hand made no sign. Yet the naming had been correct.

"I fancy you play cassino better than I," Deacon acknowledged. "I can name only three of yours, a jack, an ace, and 'big cassino.' "

"Wrong. There aren't five aces in the deck. You've taken in three and you hold the fourth in your hand now."

"Say, you're right," Deacon admitted. "I did scoop in three. Anyway, I'll make 'cards' on you. That's all I need."

"I'll let you save 'little cassino' — " Grief paused to calculate. "Yes, and the ace as well, and I'll still make 'cards' and go out with 'big cassino.' Play."

"Nobody makes 'cards,' and I win!" Deacon exulted as the last of the hand was played. "I go out on 'little cassino' and the four aces. 'Big cassino' and 'spades' only bring you to twenty."

Grief shook his head. "Some mistake, I'm afraid."

"No," Deacon declared positively. "I counted every card I took in. That's the one thing I was correct on. *I've* twenty-six, and *you've* twenty-six."

"Count again," Grief said.

Carefully and slowly, with trembling fingers, Deacon counted the cards he had taken. There were twenty-five. He reached over to the corner of the table, took up the rules Grief had written, folded them, and put them in his pocket. Then he emptied his glass, and stood up. Captain Donovan looked at his watch, yawned, and also rose.

"Going aboard, Captain?" Deacon asked.

"Yes," was the answer. "What time shall I send the whaleboat for you?"

"I'll go with you now. We'll pick up my luggage from the *Billy* as we go by. I was sailing on her for Babo in the morning."

Deacon shook hands all around, after receiving final wishes of good luck on Karo-Karo.

"Does Tom Butler play cards?" he asked Grief.

"Solitaire," was the answer.

Deacon turned toward the door, where Captain Donovan waited.

"Then I'll teach him double solitaire," he said with a sigh.

5  WHEN THE DUKE of Edinburgh observed that "experience under sail is a highly desirable part of the training of men," he was unconsciously paraphrasing Jack London's view that "sailing a boat is the finest training in the world for boy and youth and man." And woman, too, as London proved by training and encouraging his wife Charmian to take the wheel of the small boats in which they explored the waters of the world.

Like the Duke, London spoke from personal experience. An enthusiastic sailor, he spent a considerable portion of his life on water. He knew the infinite variety of the sea from San Francisco to the Solomons, from Baltimore to the Bonins, from the tempestuous waves of Cape Horn to the icy currents of the Klondike.

Nowhere does London define his mariner's credo better than in the following report about small-boat sailing on San Francisco Bay and the inland waterways of California. Once he takes us into his confidence (and he does that almost immediately), the sailor-writer puts us on the deck with him, permitting us to share the difficulties as well as the delights of sail sport.

Time has been powerless to dim the candor, vigor, and robust charm of these nautical reminiscences, written seventy years ago by one whose name will forever be associated with the legends of the sea. But here, spreading sail and setting forth to adventure in his small boat, the myth talks like a man. Here, Jack London is a writer with a tale to tell and a sailor with a secret to confide.

*"Small-Boat Sailing" is reprinted
from* The Human Drift.
*Copyright 1917 by The Macmillan Company;
renewed 1945 by Charmian K. London.*

# Small Boat Sailing

A SAILOR IS BORN, not made. And by "sailor" is meant, not the average efficient and hopeless creature who is found to-day in the forecastle of deepwater ships, but the man who will take a fabric compounded of wood and iron and rope and canvas and compel it to obey his will on the surface of the sea. Barring captains and mates of big ships, the small-boat sailor is the real sailor. He knows — he must know — how to make the wind carry his craft from one given point to another given point. He must know about tides and rips and eddies, bar and channel markings, and day and night signals; he must be wise in weather-lore; and he must be sympathetically familiar with the peculiar qualities of his boat which differentiate it from every other boat that was ever built and rigged. He must know how to gentle her about, as one instance of a myriad, and to fill her on the other tack without deadening her way or allowing her to fall off too far.

The deepwater sailor of to-day needs know none of these things. And he doesn't. He pulls and hauls as he is ordered, swabs decks, washes paint, and chips iron-rust. He knows nothing, and cares less. Put him in a small boat and he is helpless. He will cut an even better figure on the hurricane deck of a horse.

I shall never forget my child-astonishment when I first encountered one of these strange beings. He was a runaway English sailor. I was a lad of twelve, with a decked-over, fourteen-foot, centre-board skiff which I had taught myself to sail. I sat at his feet as at the feet of a god, while he discoursed of strange lands and peoples, deeds of violence, and hair-raising gales at sea. Then, one day, I took him for a sail. With all the trepidation of the veriest little amateur, I hoisted sail and got under way. Here was a man, looking on critically, I was sure, who knew more in one second about boats and the water than I could ever know. After an interval, in which I exceeded myself, he took the tiller and the sheet. I sat on the little thwart amidships, open-mouthed, prepared to learn what real sailing was. My mouth remained open, for I learned what a real sailor was in a small boat. He couldn't trim the sheet to save himself, he nearly capsized several times in squalls, and, once again, by blunderingly jibing over; he didn't know what a centre-board was for, nor did he know that in running a boat before the wind one must sit in the middle instead of on the side; and finally, when we came back to the wharf, he ran the skiff in full tilt, shattering her nose and carrying away the mast-step. And yet he was a really truly sailor fresh from the vasty deep.

Which points my moral. A man can sail in the forecastles of big ships all his life and never know what real sailing is. From the time I was twelve, I listened to the lure of the sea. When I was fifteen I was captain and owner of an oyster-pirate sloop. By the time I was sixteen I was sailing in scow-schooners, fishing salmon with the Greeks up the Sacramento River, and serving as sailor on the Fish Patrol. And I was a good sailor, too, though all my cruising had been on San Francisco Bay and the rivers tributary to it. I had never been on the ocean in my life.

Then, the month I was seventeen, I signed before the mast as an able seaman on a three-topmast schooner bound on a seven-months' cruise across the Pacific and back again. As my shipmates promptly informed me, I had had my nerve with me to sign on as able seaman. Yet behold, I *was* an able seaman. I had graduated from the right school. It took no more than minutes to learn the names and uses of the few new ropes. It was simple. I did not do things blindly. As a small-boat sailor I had learned to reason out and know the *why* of everything. It is true, I had to learn how to steer by compass, which took maybe half a minute; but when it came to steering "full-and-by" and "close-and-by," I could beat the average of my shipmates, because that was the very way I had always sailed. Inside fifteen minutes I could box the compass around and back again. And there was little else to learn during that seven-months' cruise, except fancy rope-sailorising, such as the more complicated lanyard knots and the making of various kinds of sennit and rope-mats. The point of all of which is that it is by means of small-boat sailing that the real sailor is best schooled.

And if a man is a born sailor, and has gone to the school of the sea, never in all his life can he get away from the sea again. The salt of it is in his bones as well as his nostrils, and the sea will call to him until he dies. Of late years, I have found easier ways of earning a living. I have quit the forecastle for keeps, but always I come back to the sea. In my case it is usually San Francisco Bay, than which no lustier, tougher, sheet of water can be found for small-boat sailing.

It really blows on San Francisco Bay. During the winter, which is the best cruising season, we have southeasters, southwesters, and occasional howling northers. Throughout the summer we have what we call the "sea-breeze," an unfailing wind off the Pacific that on most afternoons in the week blows what the Atlantic Coast yachtsmen would name a gale. They are always surprised by the small spread of canvas our yachts carry. Some of them, with schooners they have sailed around the Horn, have looked proudly at their own lofty sticks and huge spreads, then patronisingly and even pityingly at ours. Then, perchance, they have joined in a club cruise from San Francisco to Mare Island. They found the morning run up the Bay delightful. In the afternoon, when the brave west wind ramped across San Pablo Bay and they faced it on the long beat home, things were somewhat different. One by one, like a flight of swallows, our more meagrely sparred and canvassed yachts went by, leaving them wallowing and dead and shortening down in what they called a gale but which we called a dandy sailing breeze. The next time they came out, we would notice their sticks cut down, their booms shortened, and their after-leeches nearer the luffs by whole cloths.

As for excitement, there is all the difference in the world between a ship in trouble at sea, and a small boat in trouble on land-locked water. Yet for genuine excitement and thrill, give me the small boat. Things happen so quickly, and there are always so few to do the work — and hard work, too, as the small-boat sailor knows. I have toiled all night, both watches on deck, in a typhoon off the coast of Japan, and been less exhausted than by two hours' work at reefing down a thirty-foot sloop and heaving up two anchors on a lee shore in a screaming southeaster.

Hard work and excitement? Let the wind baffle and drop in a heavy tide-way just as you are sailing your little sloop through a narrow drawbridge. Behold your sails, upon which you are depending, flap with sudden emptiness, and then see the impish wind, with a haul of eight points, fill your jib aback with a gusty puff. Around she goes, and sweeps, not through the open draw, but broadside on against the solid piles. Hear the roar of the tide, sucking through the trestle. And hear and see your pretty, fresh-painted boat crash against the piles. Feel her stout little hull give to the impact. See the rail actually pinch in. Hear your canvas tearing, and see the black, square-ended timbers thrusting holes through it. Smash! There goes your topmast stay, and the topmast reels over drunkenly above you. There is a ripping and crunching. If it continues, your starboard shrouds will be torn out. Grab a rope — any rope — and take a turn around a pile. But the free end of the rope is too short. You can't make it fast, and you hold on and wildly yell for your one companion to get a turn with another and longer rope. Hold on! You hold on till you are purple in the face, till it seems your arms are dragging out of their sockets, till the blood bursts from the ends of your fingers. But you hold, and your partner gets the longer rope and makes it fast. You straighten up and look at your hands. They are ruined. You can scarcely relax the crooks of the fingers. The pain is sickening. But there is no time. The skiff, which is always perverse, is pounding against the barnacles on the piles which threaten to scrape its gunwale off. It's drop the peak! Down jib! Then you run lines, and pull and haul and heave, and exchange unpleasant remarks with the bridge-tender who is always willing to meet you more than half way in such repartee. And finally, at the end of an hour, with aching back, sweat-soaked shirt, and slaughtered hands, you are through and swinging along on the placid, beneficent tide between narrow banks where the cattle stand knee-deep and gaze wonderingly at you. Excitement! Work! Can you beat it in a calm day on the deep sea?

I've tried it both ways. I remember labouring in a four-teen days' gale off the coast of New Zealand. We were a tramp collier, rusty and battered, with six thousand tons of coal in our hold. Life lines were stretched fore and aft; and on our weather side, attached to smokestack guys and rig-ging, were huge rope-nettings, hung there for the purpose of breaking the force of the seas and so saving our mess-room doors. But the doors were smashed and the mess-rooms washed out just the same. And yet, out of it all, arose but the one feeling, namely, of monotony.

In contrast with the foregoing, about the liveliest eight days of my life were spent in a small boat on the west coast of Korea. Never mind why I was thus voyaging up the Yellow Sea during the month of February in below-zero weather. The point is that I was in an open boat, a *sampan*, on a rocky coast where there were no light-houses and where the tides ran from thirty to sixty feet. My crew was Japanese fishermen. We did not speak each other's language. Yet there was nothing monotonous about that trip. Never shall I forget one particular cold bitter dawn, when, in the thick of driving snow, we took in sail and dropped our small anchor. The wind was howling out of the northwest, and we were on a lee shore. Ahead and astern, all escape was cut off by rocky headlands, against whose bases burst the unbroken seas. To windward a short distance, seen only between the snow-squalls, was a low rocky reef. It was this that inadequately protected us from the whole Yellow Sea that thundered in upon us.

The Japanese crawled under a communal rice mat and went to sleep. I joined them, and for several hours we dozed fitfully. Then a sea deluged us out with icy water, and we found several inches of snow on top the mat. The reef to windward was disappearing under the rising tide, and moment by moment the seas broke more strongly over the rocks. The fishermen studied the shore anxiously. So did I, and with a sailor's eye, though I could see little chance for a swimmer to gain that surf-hammered line of rocks. I made signs toward the headlands on either flank. The Japanese shook their heads. I indicated that dreadful lee shore. Still they shook their heads and did nothing. My conclusion was that they were paralysed by the hopelessness of the situation. Yet our extremity increased with every minute, for the rising tide was robbing us of the reef that served as buffer. It soon became a case of swamping at our anchor. Seas were splashing on board in growing volume, and we baled constantly. And still my fishermen crew eyed the surf-battered shore and did nothing.

At last, after many narrow escapes from complete swamping, the fishermen got into action. All hands tailed on to the anchor and hove it up. For'ard, as the boat's head paid off, we set a patch of sail about the size of a flour-sack. And we headed straight for shore. I unlaced my shoes, unbuttoned my great-coat and coat, and was ready to make a quick partial strip a minute or so before we struck. But we didn't strike, and, as we rushed in, I saw the beauty of the situation. Before us opened a narrow channel, frilled at its mouth with breaking seas. Yet, long before, when I had scanned the shore closely, there had been no such channel. *I had forgotten the thirty-foot tide.* And it was for this tide that the Japanese had so precariously waited. We ran the frill of breakers, curved into a tiny sheltered bay where the water was scarcely flawed by the gale, and landed on a beach where the salt sea of the last tide lay frozen in long curving lines. And this was one gale of three in the course of those eight days in the *sampan.* Would it have been beaten on a ship? I fear me the ship would have gone aground on the outlying reef and that its people would have been incontinently and monotonously drowned.

There are enough surprises and mishaps in a three-days' cruise in a small boat to supply a great ship on the ocean for a full year. I remember, once, taking out on her trial trip a little thirty-footer I had just bought. In six days we had two stiff blows, and, in addition, one proper southwester and one ripsnorting southeaster. The slight intervals between these blows were dead calms. Also, in the six days, we were aground three times. Then, too, we tied up to the bank in the Sacramento River, and, grounding by an accident on the steep slope on a falling tide, nearly turned a side somersault down the bank. In a stark calm and a heavy tide in the Carquinez Straits, where anchors skate on the channel-scoured bottom, we were sucked against a big dock and smashed and bumped down a quarter of a mile of its length before we could get clear. Two hours afterward, on San Pablo Bay, the wind was piping up and we were reefing down. It is no fun to pick up a skiff adrift in a heavy sea and gale. That was our next task, for our skiff, swamping, parted both towing painters we had bent on. Before we recovered it we had nearly killed ourselves with exhaustion, and we certainly had strained the sloop in every part from keelson to truck. And to cap it all, coming into our home port, beating up the narrowest part of the San Antonio Estuary, we had a shave of inches from collision with a big ship in tow of a tug. I have sailed the ocean in far larger craft a year at a time, in which period occurred no such chapter of moving incident.

After all, the mishaps are almost the best part of small-boat sailing. Looking back, they prove to be punctuations of joy. At the time they try your mettle and your vocabulary, and may make you so pessimistic as to believe that God has a grudge against you — but afterward, ah, afterward, with what pleasure you remember them and with what gusto do you relate them to your brother skippers in the fellowhood of small-boat sailing.

A narrow, winding slough; a half tide, exposing mud surfaced with gangrenous slime; the water itself filthy and discoloured by the waste from the vats of a near-by tannery;

the marsh grass on either side mottled with all the shades of a decaying orchid; a crazy, ramshackled, ancient wharf; and at the end of the wharf a small, white-painted sloop. Nothing romantic about it. No hint of adventure. A splendid pictorial argument against the alleged joys of small-boat sailing. Possibly that is what Cloudesley and I thought, that sombre, leaden morning as we turned out to cook breakfast and wash decks. The latter was my stunt, but one look at the dirty water overside and another at my fresh-painted deck, deterred me. After breakfast, we started a game of chess. The tide continued to fall, and we felt the sloop begin to list. We played on until the chess men began to fall over. The list increased, and we went on deck. Bow-line and stern-line were drawn taut. As we looked the boat listed still farther with an abrupt jerk. The lines were now very taut.

"As soon as her belly touches the bottom she will stop," I said.

Cloudesley sounded with a boat hook along the outside.

"Seven feet of water," he announced. "The bank is almost up and down. The first thing that touches will be her mast when she turns bottom up."

An omnious, minute snapping noise came from the stern-line. Even as we looked, we saw a strand fray and part. Then we jumped. Scarcely had we bent another line between the stern and the wharf, when the original line parted. As we bent another line for'ard, the original one there crackled and parted. After that, it was an inferno of work and excitement. We ran more and more lines, and more and more lines continued to part, and more and more the pretty boat went over on her side. We bent all our spare lines; we unrove sheets and halyards; we used our two-inch hawser; we fastened lines part way up the mast, half way up, and everywhere else. We toiled and sweated and enounced our mutual and sincere conviction that God's grudge still held against us. Country yokels came down on the wharf and sniggered at us. When Cloudesley let a coil of rope slip down the inclined deck into the vile slime and fished it out with seasick countenance, the yokels sniggered louder and it was all I could do to prevent him from climbing up on the wharf and committing murder.

By the time the sloop's deck was perpendicular, we had unbent the boom-lift from below, made it fast to the wharf, and, with the other end fast nearly to the mast head, heaved it taut with block and tackle. The lift was of steel wire. We were confident that it could stand the strain, but we doubted the holding-power of the stays that held the mast.

The tide had two more hours to ebb (and it was the big run-out), which meant that five hours must elapse ere the returning tide would give us a chance to learn whether or not the sloop would rise to it and right herself. The bank was almost up and down, and at the bottom, directly beneath us, the fast-ebbing tide left a pit of the vilest, illest-smelling muck to be seen in many a day's ride. Said Cloudesley to me gazing down into it:

"I love you as a brother. I'd fight for you. I'd face roaring lions, and sudden death by field and flood. But just the same, don't you fall into that." He shuddered nauseously. "For if you do, I haven't the grit to pull you out. I simply couldn't. You'd be awful. The best I could do would be to take a boat-hook and shove you down out of sight."

We sat on the upper side-wall of the cabin, dangled our legs down the top of the cabin, leaned our backs against the deck, and played chess until the rising tide and the block and tackle on the boom-lift enabled us to get her on a respectable keel again. Years afterward, down in the South Seas, on the island of Ysabel, I was caught in a similar predicament. In order to clean her copper, I had careened the *Snark* broadside on to the beach and outward. When the tide rose, she refused to rise. The water crept in through the scuppers, mounted over the rail, and the level of the ocean slowly crawled up the slant of the deck. We battened down the engine room hatch, and the sea rose to it and over it and climbed perilously near to the cabin companionway and sky-light. We were all sick with fever, but we turned out in the blazing tropic sun and toiled madly for several hours. We carried our heaviest lines ashore from our mast-heads and heaved with our heaviest purchase until everything crackled including ourselves. We would spell off and lie down like dead men, then get up and heave and crackle again. And in the end, our lower rail five feet under water and the wavelets lapping the companionway combing, the sturdy little craft shivered and shook herself and pointed her masts once more to the zenith.

There is never lack of exercise in small-boat sailing, and the hard work is not only part of the fun of it, but it beats the doctors. San Francisco Bay is no mill pond. It is a large and draughty and variegated piece of water. I remember, one winter evening, trying to enter the mouth of the Sacramento. There was a freshet on the river, the flood tide from the bay had been beaten back into a strong ebb, and the lusty west wind died down with the sun. It was just sunset, and with a fair to middling breeze, dead aft, we stood still in the rapid current. We were squarely in the mouth of the river; but there was no anchorage and we drifted backward, faster and faster, and dropped anchor outside as the last breath of wind left us. The night came on, beautiful and warm and starry. My one companion cooked supper, while on deck I put everything in shape Bristol fashion. When we turned in at nine o'clock the weather-promise was excellent.

(If I had carried a barometer I'd have known better.) By two in the morning our shrouds were thumming in a piping breeze, and I got up and gave her more scope on her hawser. Inside another hour there was no doubt that we were in for a southeaster.

It is not nice to leave a warm bed and get out of a bad anchorage in a black blowy night, but we arose to the occasion, put in two reefs, and started to heave up. The winch was old, and the strain of the jumping head sea was too much for it. With the winch out of commission, it was impossible to heave up by hand. We knew, because we tried it and slaughtered our hands. Now a sailor hates to lose an anchor. It is a matter of pride. Of course, we could have buoyed ours and slipped it. Instead, however, I gave her still more hawser, veered her, and dropped the second anchor.

There was little sleep after that, for first one and then the other of us would be rolled out of our bunks. The increasing size of the seas told us we were dragging, and when we struck the scoured channel we could tell by the feel of it that our two anchors were fairly skating across. It was a deep channel, the farther edge of it rising steeply like the wall of a canyon, and when our anchors started up that wall they hit it and held. Yet, when we fetched up, through the darkness we could hear the seas breaking on the solid shore astern, and so near was it that we shortened the skiff's painter.

Daylight showed us that between the stern of the skiff and destruction was no more than a score of feet. And how it did blow! There were times, in the gusts, when the wind must have approached a velocity of seventy or eighty miles an hour. But the anchors held, and so nobly that our final anxiety was that the for'ard bitts would be jerked clean out of the boat. All day the sloop alternately ducked her nose under and sat down on her stern; and it was not till late afternoon that the storm broke in one last and worst mad gust. For a full five minutes an absolute dead calm prevailed, and then, with the suddenness of a thunderclap, the wind snorted out of the southwest — a shift of eight points and a boisterous gale. Another night of it was too much for us, and we hove up by hand in a cross head-sea. It was not stiff work. It was heartbreaking. And I know we were both near to crying from the hurt and the exhaustion. And when we did get the first anchor up-and-down we couldn't break it out. Between seas we snubbed her nose down to it, took plenty of turns, and stood clear as she jumped. Almost everything smashed and parted except the anchor-hold. The chocks were jerked out, the rail torn off, and the very covering-board splintered, and still the anchor held. At last, hoisting the reefed mainsail and slacking off a few of the hard-won feet of the chain, we sailed the anchor out. It was nip and tuck, though, and there were times when the boat was knocked down flat. We repeated the manœuvre with the remaining anchor, and in the gathering darkness fled into the shelter of the river's mouth.

I was born so long ago that I grew up before the era of gasoline. As a result, I am old-fashioned. I prefer a sail-boat to a motor-boat, and it is my belief that boat-sailing is a finer, more difficult, and sturdier art than running a motor. Gasoline engines are becoming fool proof, and while it is unfair to say that any fool can run an engine, it is fair to say that almost any one can. Not so, when it comes to sailing a boat. More skill, more intelligence, and a vast deal more training are necessary. It is the finest training in the world for boy and youth and man. If the boy is very small, equip him with a small, comfortable skiff. He will do the rest. He won't need to be taught. Shortly he will be setting a tiny leg-of-mutton and steering with an oar. Then he will begin to talk keels and centreboards and want to take his blankets out and stop aboard all night.

But don't be afraid for him. He is bound to run risks and encounter accidents. Remember, there are accidents in the nursery as well as out on the water. More boys have died from hothouse culture than have died on boats large and small; and more boys have been made into strong and reliant men by boat-sailing than by lawn-croquet and dancing school.

And once a sailor, always a sailor. The savour of the salt never stales. The sailor never grows so old that he does not care to go back for one more wrestling bout with wind and wave. I know it of myself. I have turned rancher, and live beyond sight of the sea. Yet I can stay away from it only so long. After several months have passed, I begin to grow restless. I find myself day-dreaming over incidents of the last cruise, or wondering if the striped bass are running on Wingo Slough, or eagerly reading the newspapers for reports of the first northern flights of ducks. And then, suddenly, there is a hurried packing of suit-cases and overhauling of gear, and we are off for Vallejo where the little *Roamer* lies, waiting, always waiting, for the skiff to come alongside, for the lighting of the fire in the galley-stove, for the pulling off of gaskets, the swinging up of the mainsail, and the rat-tat-tat of the reef-points, for the heaving short and the breaking out, and for the twirling of the wheel as she fills away and heads up Bay or down.

On Board *Roamer*,
Sonoma Creek,
April 15, 1911.

6 UNLIKE HEMINGWAY, AN earnest and eloquent aficionado of the sport, Jack London had little love for bullfighting. He was not one of the many Americans who enjoy the ritualized and purgative danger of the corrida, but a critic who saw its stylized ceremony as mere window dressing for an unequal combat whose purpose was to enrage, frustrate, and slaughter a dumb beast.

The effect of such blood sport on animals was plain enough, London observed, but what about its less visible effect on human beings? His strong curiosity and indignation fueled this story of a seemingly normal American visitor who, like the bull, is slowly exasperated and provoked into violence.

The question with which London leaves us in this disturbing tale is whether the madness he describes belongs only to those few nonconformists who (like John Harned) jeer blood sport, or to the multitude of fans who cheer it. It is a pertinent question for our own age of mass spectator sports, and one which might well be asked about audiences at the increasingly violent spectacles of professional sport in contemporary America.

Described in language whose idiom, precision, and tension unmistakably foreshadow the Hemingway style, here is an early experiment in crowd psychology which describes what happens when the dangerous emotions of one spectator are not purged by the events of the arena. The strange conduct of the gringo who avenges a bull and a horse is described by a narrator who is unable to understand it; one man's madness is another's favorite sport. London wisely leaves such interpretation to the only true judge of events — the reader.

# The Madness of John Harned

I TELL THIS FOR a fact. It happened in the bull-ring at Quito. I sat in the box with John Harned, and with Maria Valenzuela, and with Luis Cervallos. I saw it happen. I saw it all from first to last. I was on the steamer *Ecuadore* from Panama to Guayaquil. Maria Valenzuela is my cousin. I have known her always. She is very beautiful. I am a Spaniard — an Ecuadoriano, true, but I am descended from Pedro Patino, who was one of Pizarro's captains. They were brave men. They were heroes. Did not Pizarro lead three hundred and fifty Spanish cavaliers and four thousand Indians into the far Cordilleras in search of treasure? And did not all the four thousand Indians and three hundred of the brave cavaliers die on that vain quest? But Pedro Patino did not die. He it was that lived to found the family of the Patino. I am Ecuadoriano, true, but I am Spanish. I am Manuel de Jesus Patino. I own many haciendas, and ten thousand Indians are my slaves, though the law says they are free men who work by freedom of contract. The law is a funny thing. We Ecuadorianos laugh at it. It is our law. We make it for ourselves. I am Manuel de Jesus Patino. Remember that name. It will be written some day in history. There are revolutions in Ecuador. We call them elections. It is a good joke is it not — what you call a pun?

John Harned was an American. I met him first at the Tivoli Hotel in Panama. He had much money — this I have heard. He was going to Lima, but he met Maria Valenzuela in the Tivoli Hotel. Maria Valenzuela is my cousin, and she is beautiful. It is true, she is the most beautiful woman in Ecuador. But also is she most beautiful in every country — in Paris, in Madrid, in New York, in Vienna. Always do all men look at her, and John Harned looked long at her at Panama. He loved her, that I know for a fact. She was Ecuadoriano, true — but she was of all countries; she was of all the world. She spoke many languages. She sang — ah! like an artiste. Her smile — wonderful, divine. Her eyes — ah! have I not seen men look in her eyes? They were what you English call amazing. They were promises of paradise. Men drowned themselves in her eyes.

Maria Valenzuela was rich — richer than I, who am accounted very rich in Ecuador. But John Harned did not care for her money. He had a heart — a funny heart. He was a fool. He did not go to Lima. He left the steamer at Guayaquil and followed her to Quito. She was coming home from Europe and other places. I do not see what she found in him, but she liked him. This I know for a fact, else he would not have followed her to Quito. She asked him to come. Well do I remember the occasion. She said —

"Come to Quito and I will show you the bullfight — brave, clever, magnificent!"

But he said: "I go to Lima, not Quito. Such is my passage engaged on the steamer."

"You travel for pleasure — no?" said Maria Valenzuela; and she looked at him as only Maria Valenzuela could look, her eyes warm with the promise.

And he came. No; he did not come for the bull-fight. He came because of what he had seen in her eyes. Women like Maria Valenzuela are born once in a hundred years. They are of no country and no time. They are what you call universal. They are goddesses. Men fall down at their feet. They play with men and run them through their pretty fingers like sand. Cleopatra was such a woman they say: and so was Circe. She turned men into swine. Ha! ha! It is true — no?

It all came about because Maria Valenzuela said —

"You English people are — what shall I say? — savage — no? You prize-fight. Two men each hit the other with their fists till their eyes are blinded and their noses are broken. Hideous! And the other men who look on cry out loudly and are made glad. It is barbarous — no?"

"But they are men," said John Harned; "and they prize-fight out of desire. No one makes them prize-fight. They do it because they desire it more than anything else in the world."

Maria Valenzuela — there was scorn in her smile as she said —

"They kill each other often — is it not so? I have read it in the papers."

"But the bull," said John Harned. "The bull is killed many times in the bull-fight, and the bull does not come into the ring out of desire. It is not fair to the bull. He is compelled to fight. But the man in the prize-fight — no; he is not compelled."

"He is the more brute therefore," said Maria Valenzuela. "He is savage. He is primitive. He is animal. He strikes with his paws like a bear from a cave, and he is ferocious. But the bull-fight — ah! You have not seen the bull-fight — no? The toreador is clever. He must have skill. He is modern. He is romantic. He is only a man, soft and tender, and he faces the wild bull in conflict. And he kills with a sword, a slender sword, with one thrust, so, to the heart of the great beast. It is delicious. It makes the heart beat to behold — the small man, the great beast, the wide level sand, the thousands that look on without breath; the great beast rushes to the attack, the small man stands like a statue; he does not move, he is unafraid, and in his hand is the slender sword flashing like silver in the sun; nearer and nearer rushes the great beast with its sharp horns, the man does not move, and then — so — the sword flashes, the thrust is made, to the heart, to the hilt, the bull falls to the sand and is dead, and the man is unhurt. It is brave. It is magnificent! Ah! — I could love the toreador. But the man of the prize-fight — he is the brute, the human beast, the savage primitive, the maniac, that receives many blows in his stupid face and rejoices. Come to Quito and I will show you the brave sport, the sport of men, the toreador and the bull."

But John Harned did not go to Quito for the bull-fight. He went because of Maria Valenzuela. He was a large man, more broad of shoulder than we Ecuadorianos, more tall, more heavy of limb and bone. True, he was larger even than most men of his own race. His eyes were blue, though I have seen them grey, and, sometimes, like cold steel. His features were large, too — not delicate like ours, and his jaw was very strong to look at. Also, his face was smooth-shaven like a priest's. Why should a man feel shame for the hair on his face? Did not God put it there? Yes, I believe in God. I am not a pagan like many of you English. God is good. He made me an Ecuadoriano with ten thousand slaves. And when I die I shall go to God. Yes, the priests are right.

But John Harned. He was a quiet man. He talked always in a low voice, and he never moved his hands when he talked. One would have thought his heart was a piece of ice; yet he did have a streak of warm in his blood, for he followed Maria Valenzuela to Quito. Also, and for all that he talked low without-moving his hands, he was an animal, as you shall see — the beast primitive, the stupid, ferocious savage of the long ago that dressed in wild skins and lived in the caves along with the bears and wolves.

Luis Cervallos is my friend, the best of Ecuadorianos. He owns three cacao plantations at Naranjito and Chobo. At

Milagro is his big sugar plantation. He has large haciendas at Ambato and Latacunga, and down the coast is he interested in oil-wells. Also he has spent much money in planting rubber along the Guayas. He is modern, like the Yankee; and, like the Yankee, full of business. He has much money, but it is in many ventures, and ever he needs more money for new ventures and for the old ones. He has been everywhere and seen everything. When he was a very young man he was in the Yankee military academy what you call West Point. There was trouble. He was made to resign. He does not like Americans. But he did like Maria Valenzuela, who was of his own country. Also, he needed her money for his ventures and for his gold mine in eastern Ecuador where the painted Indians live. I was his friend. It was my desire that he should marry Maria Valenzuela. Further, much of my money had I invested in his ventures, more so in his gold mine which was very rich but which first required the expense of much money before it would yield forth its riches. If Luis Cervallos married Maria Valenzuela I should have more money very immediately.

But John Harned followed Maria Valenzuela to Quito, and it was quickly clear to us — to Luis Cervallos and me — that she looked upon John Harned with great kindness. It is said that a woman will have her will, but this is a case not in point, for Maria Valenzuela did not have her will — at least not with John Harned. Perhaps it would all have happened as it did, even if Luis Cervallos and I had not sat in the box that day at the bull-ring in Quito. But this I know: we *did* sit in the box that day. And I shall tell you what happened.

The four of us were in the one box, guests of Luis Cervallos. It was next to the Presidente's box. On the other side was the box of General José Eliceo Salazar. With him were Joaquin Endara and Urcisino Castillo, both generals, and Colonel Jacinto Fierro and Captain Baltazar de Echeverria.

Only Luis Cervallos had the position and influence to get that box next to the Presidente. I know for a fact that the Presidente himself expressed the desire to the management that Luis Cervallos should have that box.

The band finished playing the national hymn of Ecuador. The procession of the toreadors was over. The Presidente nodded to begin. The bugles blew, and the bull dashed in — you know the way, excited, bewildered, the darts in its shoulder burning like fire, itself seeking madly whatever enemy to destroy. The toreadors hid behind their shelters and waited. Suddenly they appeared forth, the capadors, five of them, from every side, their coloured capes flinging wide. The bull paused at sight of such a generosity of enemies, unable in his own mind to know which to attack. Then advanced one of the capadors alone to meet the bull. The bull was very angry. With its forelegs it pawed the sand of the arena till the dust rose all about it. Then it charged, with lowered head, straight for the lone capador.

It is always of interest, the first charge of the first bull. After a time it is natural that one should grow tired, a trifle, that the keenness should lose its edge. But that first charge of the first bull! John Harned was seeing it for the first time, and he could not escape the excitement — the sight of the man, armed only with a piece of cloth, and of the bull rushing upon him across the sand with sharp horns, wide-spreading.

"See!" cried Maria Valenzuela. "Is it not superb?"

John Harned nodded, but did not look at her. His eyes were sparkling, and they were only for the bull-ring. The capador stepped to the side, with a twirl of the cape eluding the bull and spreading the cape on his own shoulders.

"What do you think?" asked Maria Valenzuela. "Is it not a — what-you-call — sporting proposition — no?"

"It is certainly," said John Harned. "It is very clever."

She clapped her hands with delight. They were little hands. The audience applauded. The bull turned and came back. Again the capador eluded him, throwing the cape on his shoulders, and again the audience applauded. Three times did this happen. The capador was very excellent. Then he retired, and the other capadors played with the bull. After that they placed the banderillos in the bull, in the shoulders, on each side of the backbone, two at a time. Then stepped forward Ordonez, the chief matador, with the long sword and the scarlet cape. The bugles blew for the death. He is not so good as Matestini. Still he is good, and with one thrust he drove the sword to the heart, and the bull doubled his legs under him and lay down and died. It was a pretty thrust, clean and sure; and there was much applause, and many of the common people threw their hats into the ring. Maria Valenzuela clapped her hands with the rest, and John Harned, whose cold heart was not touched by the event, looked at her with curiosity.

"You like it?" he asked.

"Always," she said, still clapping her hands.

"From a little girl," said Luis Cervallos. "I remember her first fight. She was four years old. She sat with her mother, and just now she clapped her hands. She is a proper Spanish woman."

"You have seen it," said Maria Valenzuela to John Harned, as they fastened the mules to the dead bull and dragged it out. "You have seen the bull-fight and you like it — no? What do you think?"

"I think the bull had no chance," he said. "The bull was doomed from the first. The issue was not in doubt. Every one knew, before the bull entered the ring, that it was to die. To be a sporting proposition, the issue must be in doubt. It was one stupid bull who had never fought a man against five wise men who had fought many bulls. It would be possibly a little bit fair if it were one man against one bull."

"Or one man against five bulls," said Maria Valenzuela; and we all laughed, and Luis Cervallos laughed loudest.

"Yes," said John Harned, "against five bulls, and the man, like the bulls, never in the bull-ring before — a man like yourself, Senor Cervallos."

"Yet we Spanish like the bull-fight," said Luis Cervallos; and I swear the devil was whispering then in his ear, telling him to do that which I shall relate.

"Then it must be a cultivated taste," John Harned made answer. "We kill bulls by the thousand every day in Chicago, yet no one cares to pay admittance to see."

"That is butchery," said I; "but this — ah, this is an art. It is delicate. It is fine. It is rare."

"Not always," said Luis Cervallos. "I have seen clumsy matadors, and I tell you it is not nice."

He shuddered, and his face betrayed such what-you-call disgust, that I knew, then, that the devil was whispering and that he was beginning to play a part.

"Senor Harned may be right," said Luis Cervallos. "It may not be fair to the bull. For is it not known to all of us that for twenty-four hours the bull is given no water, and that immediately before the fight he is permitted to drink his fill?"

"And he comes into the ring heavy with water?" said John Harned quickly; and I saw that his eyes were very grey and very sharp and very cold.

"It is necessary for the sport," said Luis Cervallos. "Would you have the bull so strong that he would kill the toreadors?"

"I would that he had a fighting chance," said John Harned, facing the ring to see the second bull come in.

It was not a good bull. It was frightened. It ran around

the ring in search of a way to get out. The capadors stepped forth and flared their capes, but he refused to charge upon them.

"It is a stupid bull," said Maria Valenzuela.

"I beg pardon," said John Harned; "but it would seem to me a wise bull. He knows he must not fight man. See! He smells death there in the ring."

True. The bull, pausing where the last one had died, was smelling the wet sand and snorting. Again he ran around the ring, with raised head, looking at the faces of the thousands that hissed him, that threw orange-peel at him and called him names. But the smell of blood decided him, and he charged a capador, so without warning that the man just escaped. He dropped his cape and dodged into the shelter. The bull struck the wall of the ring with a crash. And John Harned said, in a quiet voice, as though he talked to himself—

"I will give one thousand sucres to the lazar-house of Quito if a bull kills a man this day."

"You like bulls?" said Maria Valenzuela with a smile.

"I like such men less," said John Harned. "A toreador is not a brave man. He surely cannot be a brave man. See, the bull's tongue is already out. He is tired and he has not yet begun."

"It is the water," said Luis Cervallos.

"Yes, it is the water," said John Harned. "Would it not be safer to hamstring the bull before he comes on?"

Maria Valenzuela was made angry by this sneer in John Harned's words. But Luis Cervallos smiled so that only I could see him, and then it broke upon my mind surely the game he was playing. He and I were to be banderilleros. The big American bull was there in the box with us. We were to stick the darts in him till he became angry, and then there might be no marriage with Maria Valenzuela. It was a good sport. And the spirit of bull-fighters was in our blood.

The bull was now angry and excited. The capadors had great game with him. He was very quick, and sometimes he turned with such sharpness that his hind legs lost their footing and he ploughed the sand with his quarter. But he charged always the flung capes and committed no harm.

"He has no chance," said John Harned. "He is fighting wind."

"He thinks the cape is his enemy," explained Maria Valenzuela. "See how cleverly the capador deceives him."

"It is his nature to be deceived," said John Harned. "Wherefore he is doomed to fight wind. The toreadors know it, the audience knows it, you know it, I know it — we all know from the first that he will fight wind. He only does not know it. It is his stupid beast-nature. He has no chance."

"It is very simple," said Luis Cervallos. "The bull shuts his eyes when he charges. Therefore —"

"The man steps out of the way and the bull rushes by," John Harned interrupted.

"Yes," said Luis Cervallos; "that is it. The bull shuts his eyes, and the man knows it."

"But cows do not shut their eyes," said John Harned. "I know a cow at home that is a Jersey and gives milk, that would whip the whole gang of them."

"But the toreadors do not fight cows," said I.

"They are afraid to fight cows," said John Harned.

"Yes," said Luis Cervallos; "they are afraid to fight cows. There would be no sport in killing toreadors."

"There would be some sport," said John Harned, "if a toreador were killed once in a while. When I become an old man, and mayhap a cripple, and should I need to make a living and be unable to do hard work, then would I become a bull-fighter. It is a light vocation for elderly gentlemen and pensioners!"

"But see!" said Maria Valenzuela, as the bull charged bravely and the capador eluded it with a fling of his cape. "It requires skill so to avoid the beast."

"True," said John Harned. "But believe me, it requires a thousand times more skill to avoid the many and quick punches of a prize-fighter who keeps his eyes open and strikes with intelligence. Furthermore, this bull does not want to fight. Behold, he runs away."

It was not a good bull, for again it ran around the ring, seeking to find a way out.

"Yet these bulls are sometimes the most dangerous," said Luis Cervallos. "It can never be known what they will do next. They are wise. They are half cow. The bull-fighters never like them. See! He has turned!"

Once again, baffled and made angry by the walls of the ring that would not let him out, the bull was attacking his enemies valiantly.

"His tongue is hanging out," said John Harned. "First, they fill him with water. Then they tire him out, one man and then another, persuading him to exhaust himself by fighting wind. While some tire him, others rest. But the bull they never let rest. Afterwards, when he is quite tired and no longer quick, the matador sticks the sword into him."

The time had now come for the banderillos. Three times one of the fighters endeavoured to place the darts, and three times did he fail. He but stung the bull and maddened it. The banderillos must go in, you know, two at a time, into the shoulders, on each side of the backbone and close to it. If but one be placed, it is a failure. The crowd hissed and called for Ordonez. And then Ordonez did a great thing. Four times he stood forth, and four times, at the first attempt, he stuck in the banderillos, so that eight of them, well placed, stood out in the back of the bull at one time. The crowd went mad, and a rain of hats and money fell upon the sand of the ring.

And just then the bull charged unexpectedly one of the capadors. The man slipped and lost his head. The bull caught him — fortunately, between his wide horns. And while the audience watched, breathless and silent, John Harned stood up and yelled with gladness. And he yelled for the bull. As you see yourself, John Harned wanted the man killed. His was a brutal heart. This bad conduct made those angry that sat in the box of General Salazar, and they cried out against John Harned. And Urcisino Castillo told him to his face that he was a dog of a Gringo and other things. Only it was in Spanish, and John Harned did not understand. He stood and yelled, perhaps for the time of ten seconds, when the bull was enticed into charging the other capadors and the man arose unhurt.

"The bull has no chance," John Harned said with sadness as he sat down. "The man was uninjured. They fooled the bull away from him." Then he turned to Maria Valenzuela and said: "I beg your pardon. I was excited."

She smiled and in reproof tapped his arm with her fan.

"It is your first bull-fight," she cried. "After you have seen more you will not cry for the death of the man. You Americans, you see, are more brutal than we. It is because of your prize-fighting. We come only to see the bull killed."

"But I would the bull had some chance," he answered. "Doubtless, in time, I shall cease to be annoyed by the men who take advantage of the bull."

The bugles blew for the death. Ordonez stood forth with the sword and the scarlet cloth. But the bull had changed again, and did not want to fight. Ordonez stamped his foot in the sand, and cried out, and waved the scarlet cloth. Then the bull charged, but without heart. There was no weight to the charge. It was a poor thrust. The sword struck a bone and bent. Ordonez took a fresh sword. The bull, again stung to fight, charged once more. Five times Ordonez essayed the thrust, and each time the sword went but part way in or struck bone. The sixth time, the sword went in to the hilt. But it was a bad thrust. The sword missed the heart and stuck out half a yard through the ribs on the opposite side. The audience hissed the matador. I glanced at John Harned. He sat silent, without movement; but I could see his teeth were set, and his hands were clenched tight on the railing of the box.

All fight was now out of the bull, and, though it was no vital thrust, he trotted lamely because of the sword that stuck through him, in one side and out the other. He ran away from the matador and the capadors, and circled the edge of the ring, looking up at the many faces.

"He is saying: 'For God's sake let me out of this; I don't want to fight,' " said John Harned.

That was all. He said no more, but sat and watched, though sometimes he looked sideways at Maria Valenzuela to see how she took it. She was angry with the matador. He was awkward, and she had desired a clever exhibition.

The bull was now very tired, and weak from loss of blood, though far from dying. He walked slowly around the wall of the ring, seeking a way out. He would not charge. He had had enough. But he must be killed. There is a place, in the neck of a bull behind the horns, where the cord of the spine is unprotected and where a short stab will immediately kill. Ordonez stepped in front of the bull and lowered his scarlet cloth to the ground. The bull would not charge. He stood still and smelled the cloth, lowering his head to do so. Ordonez stabbed between the horns at the spot in the neck. The bull jerked his head up. The stab had missed. Then the bull watched the sword. When Ordonez moved the cloth on the ground, the bull forgot the sword and lowered his head to smell the cloth. Again Ordonez stabbed, and again he failed. He tried many times. It was stupid. And John Harned said nothing. At last a stab went home, and the bull fell to the sand, dead immediately, and the mules were made fast and he was dragged out.

"The Gringos say it is a cruel sport — no?" said Luis Cervallos. "That it is not humane. That it is bad for the bull. No?"

"No," said John Harned. "The bull does not count for much. It is bad for those that look on. It is degrading to those that look on. It teaches them to delight in animal suffering. It is cowardly for five men to fight one stupid bull. Therefore those that look on learn to be cowards. The bull dies, but those that look on live and the lesson is learned. The bravery of men is not nourished by scenes of cowardice."

Maria Valenzuela said nothing. Neither did she look at him. But she heard every word and her cheeks were white with anger. She looked out across the ring and fanned herself, but I saw that her hand trembled. Nor did John Harned look at her. He went on as though she were not there. He, too, was angry, coldly angry.

"It is the cowardly sport of a cowardly people," he said.

"Ah," said Luis Cervallos softly, "you think you understand us."

"I understand now the Spanish Inquisition," said John Harned. "It must have been more delightful than bullfighting."

Luis Cervallos smiled but said nothing. He glanced at Maria Valenzuela, and knew that the bull-fight in the box was won. Never would she have further to do with the Gringo who spoke such words. But neither Luis Cervallos nor I was prepared for the outcome of the day. I fear we do not understand the Gringos. How were we to know that John Harned, who was so coldly angry, should go suddenly mad? But mad he did go, as you shall see. The bull did not count for much — he said so himself. Then why should the horse count for so much? That I cannot understand. The mind of John Harned lacked logic. That is the only explanation.

"It is not usual to have horses in the bull-ring at Quito," said Luis Cervallos, looking up from the programme. "In Spain they always have them. But to-day, by special permission we shall have them. When the next bull comes on there will be horses and picadors — you know, the men who carry lances and ride the horses."

"The bull is doomed from the first," said John Harned. "Are the horses then likewise doomed?"

"They are blindfolded so that they may not see the bull," said Luis Cervallos. "I have seen many horses killed. It is a brave sight."

"I have seen the bull slaughtered," said John Harned. "I will now see the horse slaughtered, so that I may understand more fully the fine points of this noble sport."

"They are old horses," said Luis Cervallos, "that are not good for anything else."

"I see," said John Harned.

The third bull came on, and soon against it were both capadors and picadors. One picador took his stand directly below us. I agree, it was a thin and aged horse he rode, a bag of bones covered with mangy hide.

"It is a marvel that the poor brute can hold up the weight of the rider," said John Harned. "And now that the horse fights the bull, what weapons has it?"

"The horse does not fight the bull," said Luis Cervallos.

"Oh," said John Harned, "then is the horse there to be gored? That must be why it is blindfolded, so that it shall not see the bull coming to gore it."

"Not quite so," said I. "The lance of the picador is to keep the bull from goring the horse."

"Then are horses rarely gored?" asked John Harned.

"No," said Luis Cervallos. "I have seen, at Seville, eighteen horses killed in one day, and the people clamoured for more horses."

"Were they blindfolded like this horse?" asked John Harned.

"Yes," said Luis Cervallos.

After that we talked no more, but watched the fight. And John Harned was going mad all the time, and we did not know. The bull refused to charge the horse. And the horse stood still, and because it could not see it did not know that the capadors were trying to make the bull charge upon it. The capadors teased the bull with their capes, and when it charged them they ran towards the horse and into their shelters. At last the bull was well angry, and it saw the horse before it.

"The horse does not know, the horse does not know," John Harned whispered like to himself, unaware that he voiced his thought aloud.

The bull charged, and of course the horse knew nothing till the picador failed and the horse found himself impaled on the bull's horns from beneath. The bull was magnificently strong. The sight of its strength was splendid to see. It lifted the horse clear into the air; and as the horse fell to its side on the ground the picador landed on his feet and escaped, while the capadors lured the bull away. The horse was emptied of its essential organs. Yet did it rise to its feet screaming. It was the scream of the horse that did it, that made John Harned completely mad; for he, too, started to rise to his feet. I heard him curse low and deep. He never took his eyes from the horse, which, still screaming, strove to run, but fell down instead and rolled on its back so that all its four legs were kicking in the air. Then the bull charged it and gored it again and again until it was dead.

John Harned was now on his feet. His eyes were no longer cold like steel. They were blue flames. He looked at Maria Valenzuela, and she looked at him, and in his face was a great loathing. The moment of his madness was upon him. Everybody was looking, now that the horse was dead; and John Harned was a large man and easy to be seen.

"Sit down," said Luis Cervallos, "or you will make a fool of yourself."

John Harned replied nothing. He struck out his fist. He smote Luis Cervallos in the face so that he fell like a dead man across the chairs and did not rise again. He saw nothing of what followed. But I saw much. Urcisino Castillo, leaning forward from the next box, with his cane struck John Harned full across the face. And John Harned smote him with his fist so that in falling he overthrew General Salazar. John Harned was now in what-you-call Berserker rage — no? The beast primitive in him was loose and roaring — the beast primitive of the holes and caves of the long ago.

"You came for a bull-fight," I heard him say, "and by God I'll show you a man-fight!"

It was a fight. The soldiers guarding the Presidente's box leapèd across, but from one of them he took a rifle and beat them on their heads with it. From the other box Colonel Jacinto Fierro was shooting at him with a revolver. The first shot killed a soldier. This I know for a fact. I saw it. But the second shot struck John Harned in the side. Whereupon he swore, and with a lunge drove the bayonet of his rifle into Colonel Jacinto Fierro's body. It was horrible to behold. The Americans and the English are a brutal race. They sneer at our bull-fighting, yet do they delight in the shedding of blood. More men were killed that day because of John Harned than were ever killed in all the history of the bull-ring of Quito, yes, and of Guayaquil and all Ecuador.

It was the scream of the horse that did it. Yet why did not John Harned go mad when the bull was killed? A beast is a beast, be it bull or horse. John Harned was mad. There is no other explanation. He was blood-mad, a beast himself. I leave it to your judgment. Which is worse — the goring of the horse by the bull, or the goring of Colonel Jacinto Fierro by the bayonet in the hands of John Harned? And John Harned gored others with that bayonet. He was full of devils. He fought with many bullets in him, and he was hard to kill. And Marie Valenzuela was a brave woman. Unlike the other women, she did not cry out or faint. She sat still in her box, gazing out across the bull-ring. Her face was white and she fanned herself, but she never looked around.

From all sides came the soldiers and officers and the common people bravely to subdue the mad Gringo. It is true — the cry went up from the crowd to kill all the Gringos. It is an old cry in Latin-American countries, what of the dislike for the Gringos and their uncouth ways. It is true, the cry went up. But the brave Ecuadorianos killed only John Harned, and first he killed seven of them. Besides, there were many hurt. I have seen many bull-fights, but never have I seen anything so abominable as the scene in the boxes when the fight was over. It was like a field of battle. The dead lay around everywhere, while the wounded sobbed and groaned and some of them died. One man, whom John Harned had thrust through the belly with the bayonet, clutched at himself with both his hands and screamed. I tell you for a fact it was more terrible than the screaming of a thousand horses.

No, Maria Valenzuela did not marry Luis Cervallos. I am sorry for that. He was my friend, and much of my money was invested in his ventures. It was five weeks before the surgeons took the bandages from his face. And there is a scar there to this day, on the cheek, under the eye. Yet John Harned struck him but once and struck him only with his naked fist. Maria Valenzuela is in Austria now. It is said she is to marry an Archduke or some high nobleman. I do not know. I think she liked John Harned before he followed her to Quito to see the bull-fight. But why the horse? That is what I desire to know. Why should he watch the bull and say that it did not count, and then go immediately and most horribly mad because a horse screamed? There is no understanding the Gringos. They are barbarians.

7 ONLY A WRITER like Jack London could fashion an adventure out of the unpromising prospect of a volcanic mountain whose isolation and desolation had discouraged climbers and writers alike. Haleakala was no ordinary mountain, even for Hawaii, but then London was no ordinary writer. His progress up and down the forbidding mountain on horse and foot is as much the record of a romanticist embarked on an epic tour as it is the chronicle of a sportsman's journey of exploration and discovery.

London's account of his passage through "The House of the Sun" recalls Hemingway's description of the lonely and hazardous sport of a writer's artistic renewal. In competition with others, if not himself, the writer puts his resources to the ultimate test, "driven far out past where he can go, out to where no one can help him." By doing so, he reaches a place without precedence in his experience and becomes an interpreter of it.

The test of man against mountain in "The House of the Sun" parallels the struggle of the writer to acquire his materials, refine his perceptions, and master the imperfect medium of his craft. Photography cannot do justice to Haleakala, London tells us, but as a writer he is also painfully aware that "words are a vain thing and drive [the writer] to despair."

Despite his misgivings, London's word picture of the mountain is a confident and precise one. In it is all the living immediacy and shared intimacy of experience that we could come to expect in his best writing.

And there is more. For, to the extent that we accompany and encourage the writer-explorer upon his mythic journey, we are also, to paraphrase Hemingway, going where we have not gone before. And when we return from that place, there is always the possibility that, like the writer, we can also be interpreters.

# The House of the Sun

THERE ARE HOSTS of people who journey like restless spirits round and about this earth in search of seascapes and landscapes and the wonders and beauties of nature. They overrun Europe in armies; they can be met in droves and herds in Florida and the West Indies, at the pyramids, and on the slopes and summits of the Canadian and American Rockies; but in the House of the Sun they are as rare as live and wriggling dinosaurs. Haleakala is the Hawaiian name for "the house of the sun." It is a noble dwelling, situated on the island of Maui; but so few tourists have ever peeped into it, much less entered it, that their number may be practically reckoned as zero. Yet I venture to state that for natural beauty and wonder the nature-lover may see dissimilar things as great as Haleakala, but no greater, while he will never see elsewhere anything more beautiful or wonderful. Honolulu is six days' steaming from San Francisco; Maui is a night's run on the steamer from Honolulu; and six hours more if he is in a hurry, can bring the traveller to Kolikoli, which is ten thousand and thirty-two feet above the sea and which stands hard by the entrance portal to the House of the Sun. Yet the tourist comes not, and Haleakala sleeps on in lonely and unseen grandeur.

Not being tourists, we of the *Snark* went to Haleakala. On the slopes of that monster mountain there is a cattle ranch of some fifty thousand acres, where we spent the night at an altitude of two thousand feet. The next morning it was boots and saddles, and with cow-boys and packhorses we climbed to Ukulele, a mountain ranch-house, the altitude of which, fifty-five hundred feet, gives a severely temperate climate, compelling blankets at night and a roaring fireplace in the living-room. Ukulele, by the way, is the Hawaiian for "jumping flea" as it is also the Hawaiian for a certain musical instrument that may be likened to a young guitar. It is my opinion that the mountain ranch-house was named after the young guitar. We were not in a hurry, and we spent the day at Ukulele, learnedly discussing altitudes and barometers and shaking our particular barometer whenever any one's argument stood in need of demonstration. Our barometer was the most graciously acquiescent instrument I have ever seen. Also, we gathered mountain raspberries, large as hen's eggs and larger, gazed up the pasture-covered lava slopes to the summit of Haleakala, forty-five hundred feet above us, and looked down upon a mighty battle of the clouds that was being fought beneath us, ourselves in the bright sunshine.

Every day and every day this unending battle goes on. Ukiukiu is the name of the trade-wind that comes raging down out of the northeast and hurls itself upon Haleakala. Now Haleakala is so bulky and tall that it turns the northeast trade-wind aside on either hand, so that in the lee of Haleakala no trade-wind blows at all. On the contrary, the wind blows in the counter direction, in the teeth of the northeast trade. This wind is called Naula. And day and night and always Ukiukiu and Naulu strive with each other, advancing, retreating, flanking, curving, curling, and turning and twisting, the conflict made visible by the cloud-masses plucked from the heavens and hurled back and forth in squadrons, battalions, armies, and great mountain ranges. Once in a while, Ukiukiu, in mighty gusts, flings immense cloud-masses clear over the summit of Haleakala; whereupon Naulu craftily captures them, lines them up in new battle-formation, and with them smites back at his ancient and eternal antagonist. Then Ukiukiu sends a great cloud-army around the eastern side of the mountain. It is a flanking movement, well executed. But Naulu, from his lair on the leeward side, gathers the flanking army in, pulling and twisting and dragging it, hammering it into shape, and sends it charging back against Ukiukiu around the western side of the mountain. And all the while, above and below the main battle-field, high up the slopes toward the sea, Ukiukiu and Naulu are continually sending out little wisps of cloud, in ragged skirmish line, that creep and crawl over the ground, among the trees and through the canyons, and that spring upon and capture one another in sudden ambuscades and sorties. And sometimes Ukiukiu or Naulu, abruptly sending out a heavy charging column, captures the ragged little skirmishers or drives them skyward, turning over and over, in vertical whirls, thousands of feet in the air.

But it is on the western slopes of Haleakala that the main battle goes on. Here Naulu masses his heaviest formations and wins his greatest victories. Ukiukiu grows weak toward late afternoon, which is the way of all trade-winds, and is driven backward by Naulu. Naulu's generalship is excellent. All day he has been gathering and packing away immense reserves. As the afternoon draws on, he welds them into a solid column, sharp-pointed, miles in length, a mile in width, and hundreds of feet thick. This column he slowly thrusts forward into the broad battle-front of Ukiukiu, and slowly and surely Ukiukiu, weakening fast, is split asunder. But it is not all bloodless. At times Ukiukiu struggles wildly, and with fresh accessions of strength from the limitless northeast, smashes away half a mile at a time of Naulu's column and sweeps it off and away toward West Maui. Sometimes, when the two charging armies meet end-on, a tremendous perpendicular whirl results, the cloud-masses, locked together, mounting thousands of feet into the air and turning over and over. A favorite device of Ukiukiu is to send a low, squat formation, densely packed, forward along the ground and under Naulu. When Ukiukiu is under, he proceeds to buck. Naulu's mighty middle gives to the blow and bends upward, but usually he turns the attacking column back upon itself and sets it milling. And all the while the ragged little skirmishers, stray and detached, sneak through the trees and canyons, crawl along and through the grass, and surprise one another with unexpected leaps and rushes; while above, far above, serene and lonely in the rays of the setting sun, Haleakala looks down upon the conflict. And so, the night. But in the morning, after the fashion of trade-winds, Ukiukiu gathers strength and sends the hosts of Naulu rolling back in confusion and rout. And one day is like another day in the battle of the clouds, where Ukiukiu and Naulu strive eternally on the slopes of Haleakala.

Again in the morning, it was boots and saddles, cow-boys and packhorses, and the climb to the top began. One pack-horse carried twenty gallons of water, slung in five-gallon bags on either side; for water is precious and rare in the crater itself, in spite of the fact that several miles to the north and east of the crater-rim more rain comes down than in any other place in the world. The way led upward across countless lava flows, without regard for trails, and never have I seen horses with such perfect footing as that of the thirteen that composed our outfit. They climbed or dropped down perpendicular places with the sureness and coolness of mountain goats, and never a horse fell or balked.

There is a familiar and strange illusion experienced by all who climb isolated mountains. The higher one climbs, the more of the earth's surface becomes visible, and the effect of this is that the horizon seems up-hill from the observer. This illusion is especially notable on Haleakala, for the old volcano rises directly from the sea, without buttresses or connecting ranges. In consequence, as fast as we climbed up the grim slope of Haleakala, still faster did Haleakala, ourselves, and all about us, sink down into the centre of what appeared a profound abyss. Everywhere, far above us, towered the horizon. The ocean sloped down from the horizon to us. The higher we climbed, the deeper did we seem to sink down, the farther above us shone the horizon, and the steeper pitched the grade up to that horizontal line where the sky and ocean met. It was weird and unreal, and vagrant thoughts of Simm's Hole and of the volcano through which Jules Verne journeyed to the centre of the earth flitted through one's mind.

And then, when at last we reached the summit of that monster mountain, which summit was like the bottom of an inverted cone situated in the centre of an awful cosmic pit, we found that we were at neither top nor bottom. Far above us was the heaven-towering horizon, and far beneath us, where the top of the mountain should have been, was a deeper deep, the great crater, the House of the Sun. Twenty-three miles around stretched the dizzy walls of the crater. We stood on the edge of the nearly vertical western wall, and the floor of the crater lay nearly half a mile beneath. This floor, broken by lava-flows and cinder-cones, was as red and fresh and uneroded as if it were but yesterday that the fires went out. The cinder-cones, the smallest over four hundred feet in height and the largest over nine hundred, seemed no more than puny little sand-hills, so mighty was the magnitude of the setting. Two gaps, thousands of feet deep, broke the rim of the crater, and through these Ukiukiu vainly strove to drive his fleecy herds of trade-wind clouds. As fast as they advanced through the gaps, the heat of the crater dissipated them into thin air, and though they advanced always, they got nowhere.

It was a scene of vast bleakness and desolation, stern, forbidding, fascinating. We gazed down upon a place of fire and earthquake. The tie-ribs of earth lay bare before us. It was a workshop of nature still cluttered with the raw beginnings of world-making. Here and there great dikes of primordial rock had thrust themselves up from the bowels of earth, straight through the molten surface-ferment that had evidently cooled only the other day. It was all unreal and unbelievable. Looking upward, far above us (in reality beneath us) floated the cloud-battle of Ukiukiu and Naulu. And higher up the slope of the seeming abyss, above the cloud-battle, in the air and sky, hung the islands of Lanai and Molokai. Across the crater, to the southeast, still apparently looking upward, we saw ascending, first, the turquoise sea, then the white surf-line of the shore of Hawaii; above that the belt of trade-clouds, and next, eighty miles away, rearing their stupendous bulks out of the azure sky, tipped with snow, wreathed with cloud, trembling like a mirage, the peaks of Mauna Kea and Mauna Loa hung posed on the wall of heaven.

It is told that long ago, one Maui, the son of Hina, lived on what is now known as West Maui. His mother, Hina, employed her time in the making of *kapas*. She must have made them at night, for her days were occupied in trying to dry the *kapas*. Each morning, and all morning, she toiled at spreading them out in the sun. But no sooner were they out, then she began taking them in, in order to have them all under shelter for the night. For know that the days were shorter then than now. Maui watched his mother's futile toil and felt sorry for her. He decided to do something — oh, no, not to help her hang out and take in the *kapas*. He was too clever for that. His idea was to make the sun go slower. Perhaps he was the first Hawaiian astronomer. At any rate, he took a series of observations of the sun from various parts of the island. His conclusion was that the sun's path was directly across Haleakala. Unlike Joshua, he stood in no need of divine assistance. He gathered a hugh quantity of cocoanuts, from the fiber of which he braided a stout cord, and in one end of which he made a noose, even as the cowboys of Haleakala do to this day. Next he climbed into the House of the Sun and laid in wait. When the sun came tearing along the path, bent on completing its journey in the shortest time possible, the valiant youth threw his lariat around one of the sun's largest and strongest beams. He made the sun slow down some; also, he broke the beam short off. And he kept on roping and breaking off beams till the sun said it was willing to listen to reason. Maui set forth his terms of peace, which the sun accepted, agreeing to go more slowly thereafter. Wherefore Hina had ample time in which to dry her *kapas,* and the days are longer than they used to be, which last is quite in accord with the teachings of modern astronomy.

We had a lunch of jerked beef and hard *poi* in a stone corral, used of old time for the night-impounding of cattle being driven across the island. Then we skirted the rim for half a mile and began the descent into the crater. Twenty-five hundred feet beneath lay the floor, and down a steep slope of loose volcanic cinders we dropped, the sure-footed horses slipping and sliding, but always keeping their feet. The black surface of the cinders, when broken by the horses' hoofs, turned to a yellow ochre dust, virulent in appearance and acid of taste, that arose in clouds. There was a gallop across a level stretch to the mouth of a convenient blowhole, and then the descent continued in clouds of volcanic dust, winding in and out among cinder-cones, brick-red, old rose, and purplish black of color. Above us, higher and higher, towered the crater-walls, while we journeyed on across innumerable lava-flows, turning and twisting a devious way among the adamantine billows of a petrified sea. Saw-toothed waves of lava vexed the surface of this weird ocean, while on either hand arose jagged crests and spiracles of fantastic shape. Our way led on past a bottomless pit and along and over the main stream of the latest lava-flow for seven miles.

At the lower end of the crater was our camping spot, in a small grove of *olapa* and *kolea* trees, tucked away in a corner of the crater at the base of walls that rose perpendicularly fifteen hundred feet. Here was pasturage for the horses, but no water, and first we turned aside and picked our way across a mile of lava to a known water-hole in a crevice in the crater-wall. The water-hole was empty. But on climbing fifty feet up the crevice, a pool was found containing half a dozen barrels of water. A pail was carried up, and soon a steady stream of the precious liquid was running down the rock and filling the lower pool, while the cow-boys below were busy fighting the horses back, for there was room for one only to drink at a time. Then it was on to camp at the foot of the wall, up which herds of wild goats scrambled and blatted, while the tent arose to the sound of rifle-firing. Jerked beef, hard *poi,* and broiled kid was the menu. Over the crest of the crater, just above our heads, rolled a sea of clouds, driven on by Ukiukiu. Though this sea rolled over the crest unceasingly, it never blotted out nor dimmed the moon, for the heat of the crater dissolved the clouds as fast as they rolled in. Through the moonlight, attracted by the camp-fire, came the crater cattle to peer and challenge.

They were rolling fat, though they rarely drank water, the morning dew on the grass taking its place. It was because of this dew that the tent made a welcome bedchamber, and we fell asleep to the chanting of *hulas* by the unwearied Hawaiian cow-boys, in whose veins, no doubt, ran the blood of Maui, their valiant forebear.

The camera cannot do justice to the House of the Sun. The sublimated chemistry of photography may not lie, but it certainly does not tell all the truth. The Koolau Gap is faithfully reproduced, just as it impinged on the retina of the camera, yet in the resulting picture the gigantic scale of things is missing. Those walls that seem several hundred feet in height are almost as many thousand; that entering wedge of cloud is a mile and a half wide in the gap itself, while beyond the gap it is a veritable ocean; and that foreground of cinder-cone and volcanic ash, mushy and colorless in appearance, is in truth gorgeous-hued in brick-red, terracotta, rose, yellow ochre, and purplish black. Also, words are a vain thing and drive to despair. To say that a crater-wall is two thousand feet high is to say just precisely that it is two thousand feet high; but there is a vast deal more to that crater-wall than a mere statistic. The sun is ninety-three millions of miles distant, but to mortal conception the adjoining county is farther away. This frailty of the human brain is hard on the sun. It is likewise hard on the House of the Sun. Haleakala has a message of beauty and wonder for the human soul that cannot be delivered by proxy. Kolikoli is six hours from Kahului; Kahului is a night's run from Honolulu; Honolulu is six days from San Francisco; and there you are.

We climbed the crater-walls, put the horses over impossible places, rolled stones, and shot wild goats. I did not get any goats. I was too busy rolling stones. One spot in particular I remember, where we started a stone the size of a horse. It began the descent easy enough, rolling over, wobbling, and threatening to stop; but in a few minutes it was soaring through the air two hundred feet at a jump. It grew rapidly smaller until it struck a slight slope of volcanic sand, over which it darted like a startled jackrabbit, kicking up behind it a tiny trail of yellow dust. Stone and dust diminished in size, until some of the party said the stone had stopped. That was because they could not see it any longer. It had vanished into the distance beyond their ken. Others saw it rolling farther on — I know I did; and it is my firm conviction that that stone is still rolling.

Our last day in the crater, Ukiukiu gave us a taste of his strength. He smashed Naulu back all along the line, filled the House of the Sun to overflowing with clouds, and drowned us out. Our rain-gauge was a pint cup under a tiny hole in the tent. That last night of storm and rain filled the cup, and there was no way of measuring the water that spilled over into the blankets. With the rain-gauge out of business there was no longer any reason for remaining; so we broke camp in the wet-gray of dawn, and plunged eastward across the lava to the Kaupo Gap. East Maui is nothing more or less than the vast lava stream that flowed long ago through the Kaupo Gap; and down this stream we picked our way from an altitude of six thousand five hundred feet to the sea. This was a day's work in itself for the horses; but never were there such horses. Safe in the bad places, never rushing, never losing their heads, as soon as they found a trail wide and smooth enough to run on, they ran. There was no stopping them until the trail became bad again, and then they stopped of themselves. Continuously, for days, they had performed the hardest kind of work, and fed most of the time on grass foraged by themselves at night while we slept, and yet that day they covered twenty-eight leg-breaking miles and galloped into Hana like a bunch of colts. Also, there were several of them, reared in the dry region on the leeward side of Haleakala, that had never worn shoes in all their lives. Day after day, and all day long, unshod, they had travelled over the sharp lava, with the extra weight of a man on their backs, and their hoofs were in better condition than those of the shod horses.

The scenery between Vieiras's (where the Kaupo Gap empties into the sea) and Hana, which we covered in half a day, is well worth a week or a month; but, wildly beautiful as it is, it becomes pale and small in comparison with the wonderland that lies beyond the rubber plantations between Hana and the Honomanu Gulch. Two days were required to cover this marvellous stretch, which lies on the windward side of Haleakala. The people who dwell there call it the "ditch country," an unprepossessing name, but it has no other. Nobody else ever comes there. Nobody else knows anything about it. With the exception of a handful of men, whom business has brought there, nobody has heard of the ditch country of Maui. Now a ditch is a ditch, assumably muddy, and usually tranversing uninteresting and monotonous landscapes. But the Nahiku Ditch is not an ordinary ditch. The windward side of Haleakala is serried by a thousand precipitous gorges, down which rush as many torrents, each torrent of which achieves a score of cascades and waterfalls before it reaches the sea. More rain comes down here than in any other region in the world. In 1904 the year's downpour was four hundred and twenty inches. Water means sugar, and sugar is the backbone of the territory of Hawaii, wherefore the Nahiku Ditch, which is not a ditch, but a chain of tunnels. The water travels underground, appearing only at intervals to leap a gorge, travelling high in the air on a giddy flume and plunging into and through the opposing mountain. This magnificent waterway is called a "ditch," and with equal appropriateness can Cleopatra's barge be called a box-car.

There are no carriage roads through the ditch country, and before the ditch was built, or bored, rather, there was no horse-trail. Hundreds of inches of rain annually, on fertile soil, under a tropic sun, means a steaming jungle of vegetation. A man, on foot, cutting his way through, might advance a mile a day, but at the end of a week he would be a wreck, and he would have to crawl hastily back if he wanted to get out before the vegetation overran the passage way he had cut. O'Shaughnessy was the daring engineer who conquered the jungle and the gorges, ran the ditch, and made the horse-trail. He built enduringly, in concrete and masonry, and made one of the most remarkable water-farms in the world. Every little runlet and dribble is harvested and conveyed by subterranean channels to the main ditch. But so heavily does it rain at times, that countless spillways let the surplus escape to the sea.

The horse-trail is not very wide. Like the engineer who built it, it dares anything. Where the ditch plunges through the mountain, it climbs over; and where the ditch leaps a gorge on a flume, the horse-trail takes advantage of the ditch and crosses on top of the flume. That careless trail thinks nothing of travelling up or down the faces of precipices. It gouges its narrow way out of the wall, dodging around waterfalls or passing under them where they thunder down in white fury; while straight overhead the wall rises hundreds of feet, and straight beneath it sinks a thousand. And those marvellous mountain horses are as unconcerned as the trail. They fox-trot along it as a matter of course, though the footing is slippery with rain, and they will gallop

with their hind feet slipping over the edge if you let them. I
advise only those with steady nerves and cool heads to tackle
the Nahiku Ditch trail. One of our cow-boys was noted as
the strongest and bravest on the big ranch. He had ridden
mountain horses all his life on the rugged western slope of
Haleakala. He was first in the horse-breaking; and when the
others hung back, as a matter of course, he would go in to
meet a wild bull in the cattle-pen. He had a reputation. But
he had never ridden over the Nahiku Ditch. It was there he
lost his reputation. When he faced the first flume, spanning
a hair-raising gorge, narrow, without railings, with a bellowing waterfall above, another below, and directly beneath a
wild cascade, the air filled with driving spray and rocking to
the clamor and rush of sound and motion — well, that cow-
boy dismounted from his horse, explained briefly that he
had a wife and two children, and crossed over on foot,
leading the horse behind him.

The only relief from the flumes was the precipices; and
the only relief from the precipices was the flumes, except
where the ditch was far under ground, in which case we
crossed one horse and rider at a time, on primitive log-
bridges that swayed and teetered and threatened to carry
away. I confess that at first I rode such places with my feet
loose in the stirrups, and that on the sheer walls I saw to it,
by a definite, conscious act of will, that the foot in the outside stirrup, overhanging the thousand feet of fall, was
exceedingly loose. I say "at first"; for, as in the crater itself
we quickly lost our conception of magnitude, so, on the
Nahiku Ditch, we quickly lost our apprehension of depth.
The ceaseless iteration of height and depth produced a state
of consciousness in which height and depth were accepted as
the ordinary conditions of existence; and from the horse's
back to look sheer down four hundred or five hundred feet

became quite commonplace and non-productive of thrills. And as carelessly as the trail and the horses, we swung along the dizzy heights and ducked around or through the waterfalls.

And such a ride! Falling water was everywhere. We rode above the clouds, under the clouds, and through the clouds! And every now and then a shaft of sunshine penetrated like a search-light to the depths yawning beneath us, or flashed upon some pinnacle of the crater-rim thousands of feet above. At every turn of the trail a waterfall or a dozen waterfalls, leaping hundreds of feet through the air, burst upon our vision. At our first night's camp, in the Keanæ Gulch, we counted thirty-two waterfalls from a single viewpoint. The vegetation ran riot over that wild land. There were forests of koa and kolea trees, and candlenut trees; and then there were the trees called ohia-ai, which bore red mountain apples, mellow and juicy and most excellent to eat. Wild bananas grew everywhere, clinging to the sides of the gorges, and, overborne by their great bunches of ripe fruit, falling across the trail and blocking the way. And over the forest surged a sea of green life, the climbers of a thousand varieties, some that floated airily, in lacelike filaments, from the tallest branches; others that coiled and wound about the trees like huge serpents; and one, the ei-ei, that was for all the world like a climbing palm, swinging on a thick stem from branch to branch and tree to tree and throttling the supports whereby it climbed. Through the sea of green, lofty tree-ferns thrust their great delicate fronds, and the lehua flaunted its scarlet blossoms. Underneath the climbers, in no less profusion, grew the warm-colored, strangely-marked plants that in the United States one is accustomed to seeing preciously conserved in hot-houses. In fact, the ditch country of Maui is nothing more nor less than a huge conservatory. Every familiar variety of fern flourishes, and more varieties that are unfamiliar, from the tiniest maidenhair to the gross and voracious staghorn, the latter the terror of the woodsmen, interlacing with itself in tangled masses five or six feet deep and covering acres.

Never was there such a ride. For two days it lasted, when we emerged into rolling country, and, along an actual wagon-road, came home to the ranch at a gallop. I know it was cruel to gallop the horses after such a long, hard journey; but we blistered our hands in vain effort to hold them in. That's the sort of horses they grow on Haleakala. At the ranch there was great festival of cattle-driving, branding, and horse-breaking. Overhead Ukiukiu and Naulu battled valiantly, and far above, in the sunshine, towered the mighty summit of Haleakala.

London's yacht *Roamer*, on which he explored the inland waterways of San Francisco Bay.

Across the Pacific: the view from the bow of the *Snark*.

JAMES MONTGOMERY FLAGG

JACK LONDON

The master of San
Francisco Bay (note the
awe-struck seagull!).

"For those in peril on the sea": A mid-Pacific conference
aboard the *Snark*.

Jack London's writing desk. Note the manuscripts in the "in" and "out" wire baskets at left. Behind them are the alphabetically-arranged card file cabinets in which ideas and story notes were preserved.

Original illustration for "A Goboto Night" (*Saturday Evening Post*, September 30, 1911).

Jack London's boxing gloves and fencing rapiers recall two of the writer's favorite sports.

Original illustration for "Shorty Dreams" (*Cosmopolitan*, September 1911).

Duck for dinner? Jack takes careful aim with his favorite Winchester.

Somewhere in the South Pacific, "the amateur navigator" attempts to fix his ship's position.

Jack teaching Charmian the manly (and womanly) art of self-defense.

Original illustration for *The Game*, *(Metropolitan Magazine*, May 1905)

Always a "good sport," Jack was never too busy to smile for the many fans who lined up with their cameras for a souvenir.

The Londons' "little grass shack" on the beach at Waikiki.

The author of *The Call of the Wild* returns to the snow country.

Learning the proper way to parry from fencing master Spiro Orfans.

Waikiki Beach, 1915

**8** ATHLETES FOR WHOM victory in a contest is also victory for a cause have become legend in both life and literature. In "The Mexican," London's hero, Felipe Rivera, must wage the fight of his life for the guns and ammunition that will topple a dictator. Rivera is so badly outmatched that democracy looks like a bad bet.

The fate of a nation hangs in the balance as the two fighters climb into the ring. One is desperate to be champion. One is determined to get the guns to liberate his people.

And only one man can win.

# The Mexican

NOBODY KNEW HIS history — they of the Junta least of all. He was their "little mystery," their "big patriot," and in his way he worked as hard for the coming Mexican Revolution as did they. They were tardy in recognizing this, for not one of the Junta liked him. The day he first drifted into their crowded, busy rooms they all suspected him of being a spy — one of the bought tools of the Diaz secret service. Too many of the comrades were in civil and military prisons scattered over the United States, and others of them, in irons, were even then being taken across the border to be lined up against adobe walls and shot.

At the first sight the boy did not impress them favourably. Boy he was, not more than eighteen and not over-large for his years. He announced that he was Felipe Rivera, and that it was his wish to work for the revolution. That was all — not a wasted word, no further explanation. He stood waiting. There was no smile on his lips, no geniality in his eyes. Big, dashing Paulino Vera felt an inward shudder. Here was something forbidding, terrible, inscrutable. There was something venomous and snakelike in the boy's black eyes. They burned like cold fire, as with a vast, concentrated bitterness. He flashed them from the faces of the conspirators to the typewriter which little Mrs. Sethby was industriously operating. His eyes rested on hers but an instant — she had chanced to look up — and she, too, sensed the nameless something that made her pause. She was compelled to read back in order to regain the swing of the letter she was writing.

123

Paulino Vera looked questioningly at Arrellano and Ramos, and questioningly they looked back and to each other. The indecision of doubt brooded in their eyes. This slender boy was the Unknown. He was unrecognizable, something quite beyond the ken of honest, ordinary revolutionists whose fiercest hatred for Diaz and his tyranny after all was only that of honest and ordinary patriots. Here was something else, they knew not what. But Vera, always the most impulsive, the quickest to act, stepped into the breach.

"Very well," he said coldly. "You say you want to work for the revolution. Take off your coat. Hang it over there. I will show you — come — where are the buckets and cloths. The floor is dirty. You will begin by scrubbing it, and by scrubbing the floors of the other rooms. The spittoons need to be cleaned. Then there are the windows."

"Is it for the revolution?" the boy asked.

"It is for the revolution," Vera answered.

Riviera looked cold suspicion at all of them, then proceeded to take off his coat.

"It is well," he said.

And nothing more. Day after day he came to his work — sweeping, scrubbing, cleaning. He emptied the ashes from the stoves, brought up the coal and kindling, and lighted the fires before the most energetic one of them was at his desk.

"Can I sleep here?" he asked once.

Aha! So that was it — the hand of Diaz showing through! To sleep in the rooms of the Junta meant access to their secrets, to the lists of names, to the addresses of comrades down on Mexican soil. The request was denied, and Rivera never spoke of it again. He slept they knew not where, and ate they knew not where or how. Once Arrellano offered him a couple of dollars. Rivera declined the money with a shake of the head. When Vera joined in and tried to press it upon him, he said:

"I am working for the revolution."

It takes money to raise a modern revolution, and always the Junta was pressed. The members starved and toiled, and the longest day was none too long, and yet there were times when it appeared as if the revolution stood or fell on no more than the matter of a few dollars. Once, the first time, when the rest of the house was two months behind and the landlord was threatening dispossession, it was Felipe Rivera, the scrub boy in the poor, cheap clothes, worn and thread-bare, who laid sixty dollars in gold on May Sethby's desk. There were other times. Three hundred letters, clicked out on the busy typewriters (appeals for assistance, for sanctions from the organized labour groups, requests for square news deals to the editors of newspapers, protests against the high-handed treatment of revolutionists by the United States courts), lay unmailed, awaiting postage. Vera's watch had disappeared — the old-fashioned gold repeater that had been his father's. Likewise had gone the plain gold band from May Sethby's third finger. Things were desperate. Ramos and Arrellano pulled their long moustaches in despair. The letters must go off, and the post office allowed no credit to purchasers of stamps. Then it was that Rivera put on his hat and went out. When he came back he laid a thousand two-cent stamps on May Sethby's desk.

"I wonder if it is the cursed gold of Diaz?" said Vera to the comrades.

They elevated their brows and could not decide. And Felipe Rivera, the scrubber for the revolution, continued, as occasion arose, to lay down gold and silver for the Junta's use.

And still they could not bring themselves to like him. They did not know him. His ways were not theirs. He gave no confidences. He repelled all probing. Youth that he was, they could never nerve themselves to dare to question him.

"A great and lonely spirit, perhaps. I do not know, I do not know," Arrellano said helplessly.

"He is not human," said Ramos.

"His soul has been seared," said May Sethby. "Light and laughter have been burned out of him. He is like one dead, and yet he is fearfully alive."

"He has been through hell," said Vera. "No man could look like that who has not been through hell — and he is only a boy."

Yet they could not like him. He never talked, never inquired, never suggested. He would stand listening, expressionless, a thing dead, save for his eyes, coldly burning, while their talk of the revolution ran high and warm. From face to face and speaker to speaker his eyes would turn, boring like gimlets of incandescent ice, disconcerting and perturbing.

"He is no spy," Vera confided to May Sethby. "He is a patriot — mark me, the greatest patriot of all. I know it, I feel it, here in my heart and head I feel it. But him I know not at all."

"He has a bad temper," said May Sethby.

"I know," said Vera with a shudder. "He has looked at me with those eyes of his. They do not love; they threaten; they are savage as a wild tiger's. I know, if I should prove unfaithful to the cause, that he would kill me. He has no heart. He is pitiless as steel, keen and cold as frost. He is like moonshine in a winter night when a man freezes to death on some lonely mountain top. I am not afraid of Diaz and all his killers; but this boy, of him am I afraid. I tell you true. I am afraid. He is the breath of death."

Yet Vera it was who persuaded the others to give the first trust to Rivera. The line of communication between Los Angeles and Lower California had broken down. Three of the comrades had dug their own graves and been shot into them. Two more were United States prisoners in Los Angeles. Juan Alvarado, the federal commander, was a monster. All their plans did he checkmate. They could no longer gain access to the active revolutionists, and the incipient ones, in Lower California.

Young Rivera was given his instructions and dispatched south. When he returned, the line of communication was re-established, and Juan Alvarado was dead. He had been found in bed, a knife hilt-deep in his breast. This had exceeded Rivera's instructions, but they of the Junta knew the times of his movements. They did not ask him. He said nothing. But they looked at one another and conjectured.

"I have told you," said Vera. "Diaz has more to fear from this youth than from any man. He is implacable. He is the hand of God."

The bad temper, mentioned by May Sethby, and sensed by them all, was evidenced by physical proofs. Now he appeared with a cut lip, a blackened cheek, or a swollen ear. It was patent that he brawled, somewhere in that outside world where he ate and slept, gained money, and moved in ways unknown to them. As the time passed he had come to set type for the little revolutionary sheet they published weekly. There were occasions when he was unable to set type, when his knuckles were bruised and battered, when his thumbs were injured and helpless, when one arm or the other hung wearily at his side while his face was drawn with unspoken pain.

"A wastrel," said Arrellano.

"A frequenter of low places," said Ramos.

"But where does he get the money?" Vera demanded. "Only today, just now, have I learned that he paid the bill for white paper — one hundred and forty dollars."

"There are his absences," said May Sethby. "He never explains them."

"We should set a spy upon him," Ramos propounded.

"I should not care to be that spy," said Vera. "I fear you would never see me again, save to bury me. He has a terrible passion. Not even God would he permit to stand between him and the way of his passion."

"I feel like a child before him," Ramos confessed.

"To me he is power — he is the primitive, the wild wolf, the striking rattlesnake, the stinging centipede," said Arrellano.

"He is the revolution incarnate," said Vera. "He is the flame and the spirit of it, the insatiable cry for vengeance that makes no cry but that slays noiselessly. He is a destroying angel moving through the still watches of the night."

"I could weep over him," said May Sethby. "He knows nobody. He hates all people. Us he tolerates, for we are the way of his desire. He is alone . . . lonely." Her voice broke in a half sob and there was dimness in her eyes.

Rivera's ways and times were truly mysterious. There were periods when they did not see him for a week at a time. Once he was away a month. These occasions were always capped by his return, when, without advertisement or speech, he laid gold coins on May Sethby's desk. Again, for days and weeks, he spent all his time with the Junta. And yet again, for irregular periods, he would disappear through the heart of each day, from early morning until late afternoon. At such times he came early and remained late. Arrellano had found him at midnight, setting type with fresh-swollen knuckles, or mayhap it was his lip, new-split, that still bled.

## II

The time of the crisis approached. Whether or not the revolution would be depended upon the Junta, and the Junta was hard-pressed. The need for money was greater than ever before, while money was harder to get. Patriots had given their last cent and now could give no more. Section-gang labourers — fugitive peons from Mexico — were contributing half their scanty wages. But more than that was needed. The heartbreaking, conspiring, undermining toil of years approached fruition. The time was ripe. The revolution hung on the balance. One shove more, one last heroic effort, and it would tremble across the scales to victory. They knew their Mexico. Once started, the revolution would take care of itself. The whole Diaz machine would go down like a house of cards. The border was ready to rise. One Yankee, with a hundred I.W.W. men, waited the word to cross over the border and begin the conquest of Lower California. But he needed guns. And clear across to the Atlantic, the Junta in touch with them all and all of them needing guns, mere adventurers, soldiers of fortune, bandits, disgruntled American union men, socialists, anarchists, roughnecks, Mexican exiles, peons escaped from bondage, whipped miners from the bullpens of Cœur d'Alene and Colorado who desired only the more vindictively to fight — all the flotsam and jetsam of wild spirits from the madly complicated modern world. And it was guns and ammunition, ammunition and guns — the unceasing and eternal cry.

Fling this heterogeneous, bankrupt, vindictive mass across the border, and the revolution was on. The custom-house, the northern ports of entry, would be captured. Diaz could not resist. He dared not throw the weight of his armies against them, for he must hold the south. And through the south the flame would spread despite. The people would rise. The defences of city after city would crumple up. State after state would totter down. And at last, from every side, the victorious armies of the revolution would close in on the city of Mexico itself, Diaz's last stronghold.

But the money. They had the men, impatient and urgent, who would use the guns. They knew the traders who would sell and deliver the guns. But to culture the revolution thus far had exhausted the Junta. The last dollar had been spent, the last resource and the last starving patriot milked dry, and the great adventure still trembled on the scales. Guns and ammunition! The ragged battalions must be armed. But how? Ramos lamented his confiscated estates. Arrellano wailed the spendthriftness of his youth. May Sethby wondered if it would have been different had they of the Junta been more economical in the past.

"To think that the freedom of Mexico should stand or fall on a few paltry thousands of dollars," said Paulino Vera.

Despair was in all their faces. Jose Amarillo, their last hope, a recent convert who had promised money, had been apprehended at his hacienda in Chihuahua and shot against his own stable wall. The news had just come through.

Rivera, on his knees, scrubbing, looked up, with suspended brush, his bare arms flecked with soapy, dirty water.

"Will five thousand do it?" he asked.

They looked their amazement. Vera nodded and swallowed. He could not speak, but he was on the instant invested with a vast faith.

"Order the guns," Rivera said, and thereupon was guilty of the longest flow of words they had ever heard him utter. "The time is short. In three weeks I shall bring you the five thousand. It is well. The weather will be warmer for those who fight. Also, it is the best I can do."

Vera fought his faith. It was incredible. Too many fond hopes had been shattered since he had begun to play the revolution game. He believed this threadbare scrubber of the revolution, and yet he dared not believe.

"You are crazy," he said.

"In three weeks," said Rivera. "Order the guns."

He got up, rolled down his sleeves, and put on his coat.

"Order the guns," he said. "I am going now."

### III

After hurrying and scurrying, much telephoning and bad language, a night session was held in Kelly's office. Kelly was rushed with business; also, he was unlucky. He had brought Danny Ward out from New York, arranged the fight for him with Billy Carthey, the date was three weeks away, and for two days now, carefully concealed from the sporting writers, Carthey had been lying up, badly injured. There was no one to take his place. Kelly had been burning the wires east to every eligible lightweight, but they were tied up with dates and contracts. And now hope had revived, though faintly.

"You've got a hell of a nerve," Kelly addressed Rivera, after one look, as soon as they got together.

Hate that was malignant was in Rivera's eyes, but his face remained impassive.

"I can lick Ward," was all he said.

"How do you know? Ever see him fight?"

Rivera shook his head.

"Haven't you anything to say?" the fight promoter snarled.

"I can lick him."

"Who'd you ever fight, anyway?" Michael Kelly demanded. Michael was the promoter's brother, and ran the

Yellowstone Poolrooms, where he made goodly sums on the fight game.

Rivera favoured him with a bitter, unanswering stare.

The promoter's secretary, a distinctively sporty young man, sneered audibly.

"Well, you know Roberts," Kelly broke the hostile silence. "He ought to be here. I've sent for him. Sit down and wait, though from the looks of you, you haven't got a chance. I can't throw the public down with a bum fight. Ringside seats are selling at fifteen dollars, you know that."

When Roberts arrived it was patent that he was mildly drunk. He was a tall, lean, slack-jointed individual, and his walk, like his talk, was a smooth and languid drawl.

Kelly went straight to the point.

"Look here, Roberts, you've been braggin' you discovered this little Mexican. You know Carthey's broken his arm. Well, this little yellow streak has the gall to blow in today and say he'll take Carthey's place. What about it?"

"It's all right, Kelly," came the slow response. "He can put up a fight."

"I suppose you'll be sayin' next that he can lick Ward," Kelly snapped.

Roberts considered judicially.

"No, I won't say that. Ward's a topnotcher and a ring general. But he can't hash-house Rivera in short order. I know Rivera. Nobody can get his goat. He ain't got a goat that I could ever discover. And he's a two-handed fighter. He can throw in the sleep-makers from any position."

"Never mind that. What kind of a show can he put up? You've been conditioning and training fighters all your life. I take off my hat to your judgment. Can he give the public a run for its money?"

"He sure can, and he'll worry Ward a mighty heap on top of it. You don't know that boy. I do. I discovered him. He ain't got a goat. He's a devil. He's a wizzy-wooz if anybody should ask you. He'll make Ward sit up with a show of local talent that'll make the rest of you sit up. I won't say he'll lick Ward, but he'll put up such a show that you'll all know he's a comer."

"All right." Kelly turned to his secretary. "Ring up Ward. I warned him to show up if I thought it worth while. He's right across at the Yellowstone, throwin' chests and doing the popular." Kelly turned back to the conditioner. "Have a drink?"

Roberts sipped his highball and unburdened himself.

"Never told you how I discovered the little cuss. It was a couple of years ago he showed up out at the quarters. I was getting Prayne ready for his fight with Delaney. Prayne's wicked. He ain't got a tickle of mercy in his make-up. He'd chop up his pardners something cruel, and I couldn't find a willing boy that'd work with him. I'd noticed this little starved Mexican kid hanging around, and I was desperate. So I grabbed him, slammed on the gloves, and put him in. He was tougher'n rawhide, but weak. And he didn't know the first letter in the alphabet of boxing. Prayne chopped him to ribbons. But he hung on for two sickening rounds, when he fainted. Starvation, that was all. Battered? You couldn't have recognized him. I gave him half a dollar and a square meal. You oughta seen him wolf it down. He hadn't had a bite for a couple of days. That's the end of him, thinks I. But next day he showed up, stiff an' sore, ready for another half and a square meal. And he done better as time went by. Just a born fighter, and tough beyond belief. He hasn't a heart. He's a piece of ice. And he never talked eleven words in a string since I know him. He saws wood and does his work."

"I've seen 'm," the secretary said. "He's worked a lot for you."

"All the big little fellows has tried out on him," Roberts answered. "And he's learned from 'em. I've seen some of them he could lick. But his heart wasn't in it. I reckoned he never liked the game. He seemed to act that way."

"He's been fighting some before the little clubs the last few months," Kelly said.

"Sure. But I don't know what struck 'm. All of a sudden his heart got into it. He just went out like a streak and cleaned up all the little local fellows. Seemed to want the money, and he's won a bit, though his clothes don't look it. He's peculiar. Nobody knows his business. Nobody knows how he spends his time. Even when he's on the job, he plumb up and disappears most of each day soon as his work is done. Sometimes he just blows away for weeks at a time. But he don't take advice. There's a fortune in it for the fellow that gets the job of managin' him, only he won't consider it. And you watch him hold out for the cash money when you get down to terms."

It was at this stage that Danny Ward arrived. Quite a party he was. His manager and trainer were with him, and he breezed in like a gust draught of geniality, good nature, and all-conqueringness. Greetings flew about, a joke here, a retort there, a smile or a laugh for everybody. Yet it was his way, and only partly sincere. He was a good actor, and he had found geniality a most valuable asset in the game of getting on in the world. But down underneath he was the deliberate, cold-blooded fighter and businessman. The rest was a mask. Those who knew him or trafficked with him said that when it came to brass tacks he was Danny on the Spot. He was invariably present at all business discussions, and it was urged by some that his manager was a blind whose only function was to serve as Danny's mouthpiece.

Rivera's way was different. Indian blood, as well as Spanish, was in his veins, and he sat back in a corner, silent, immobile, only his black eyes passing from face to face and noting everything.

"So that's the guy," Danny said, running an appraising eye over his proposed antagonist. "How de do, old chap?"

Rivera's eyes burned venomously, but he made no sign of acknowledgment. He disliked all gringos, but this gringo he hated with an immediacy that was unusual in him.

"Gawd!" Danny protested facetiously to the promoter. "You ain't expectin' me to fight a deef mute." When the laughter subsided he made another hit. "Los Angeles must be on the dink when this is the best you can scare up. What kindergarten did you get 'm from?"

"He's a good little boy, Danny, take it from me," Roberts defended. "Not as easy as he looks."

"And half the house is sold already," Kelly pleaded. "You'll have to take 'm on, Danny. It's the best we can do."

Danny ran another careless and unflattering glance over Rivera and sighed.

"I gotta be easy with 'm, I guess. If only he don't blow up."

Roberts snorted.

"You gotta be careful," Danny's manager warned. "No taking chances with a dub that's likely to sneak a lucky one across."

"Oh, I'll be careful all right, all right," Danny smiled. "I'll get 'm at the start and' nurse 'm along for the dear public's sake. What d'ye say to fifteen rounds, Kelly — an' then the hay for him?"

"That'll do," was the answer. "As long as you make it realistic."

"Then let's get down to biz." Danny paused and calculated. "Of course, sixty-five per cent of gate receipts, same as with Carthey. But the split'll be different. Eighty will just about suit me." And to his manager, "That right?"

The manager nodded.

"Here, you, did you get that?" Kelly asked Rivera.

Rivera shook his head.

"Well, it's this way," Kelly exposited. "The purse'll be sixty-five per cent of the gate receipts. You're a dub, and an unknown. You and Danny split, twenty per cent goin' to you, an' eighty to Danny. That's fair, isn't is, Roberts?"

"Very fair," Roberts agreed. "You see, you ain't got a reputation yet."

— "What will sixty-five per cent of the gate receipts be?" Rivera demanded.

"Oh, maybe five thousand, maybe as high as eight thousand," Danny broke in to explain. "Something like that. Your share'll come to something like a thousand or sixteen hundred. Pretty good for takin' a licking from a guy with my reputation. What d'ye say?"

Then Rivera took their breaths away.

"Winner takes all," he said with finality.

A dead silence prevailed.

"It's like candy from a baby," Danny's manager proclaimed.

Danny shook his head.

"I've been in the game too long," he explained. "I'm not casting reflections on the referee or the present company.

I'm not sayin' nothing about bookmakers an' frame-ups that sometimes happen. But what I do say is that it's poor business for a fighter like me. I play safe. There's no tellin'. Mebbe I break my arm, eh? Or some guy slips me a bunch of dope." He shook his head solemnly. "Win or lose, eighty is my split. What d'ye say, Mexican?"

Rivera shook his head.

Danny exploded. He was getting down to brass tacks now.

"Why, you dirty little greaser! I've a mind to knock your block off right now."

Roberts drawled his body to interposition between hostilities.

"Winner takes all," Rivera repeated sullenly.

"Why do you stand out that way?" Danny asked.

"I can lick you," was the straight answer.

Danny half started to take off his coat. But, as his manager knew, it was grandstand play. The coat did not come off, and Danny allowed himself to be placated by the group. Everybody sympathized with him. Rivera stood alone.

"Look here, you little fool," Kelly took up the argument. "You're nobody. We know what you've been doing the last few months — putting away little local fighters. But Danny is class. His next fight after this will be for the championship. And you're unknown. Nobody ever heard of you out of Los Angeles."

"They will," Rivera answered with a shrug, "after this fight."

"You think for a second you can lick me?" Danny blurted in.

Rivera nodded.

"Oh, come; listen to reason," Kelly pleaded. "Think of the advertising."

"I want the money," was Rivera's answer.

"You couldn't win from me in a thousand years," Danny assured him.

"Then what are you holding out for?" Rivera countered. "If the money's that easy, why don't you go after it?"

"I will, so help me!" Danny cried with abrupt conviction. "I'll beat you to death in the ring, my boy — you monkeyin' with me this way. Make out the articles, Kelly. Winner take all. Play it up in the sportin' columns. Tell 'em it's a grudge fight. I'll show this fresh kid a few."

Kelly's secretary had begun to write, when Danny interrupted.

"Hold on!" He turned to Rivera. "Weights?"

"Ringside," came the answer.

"Not on your life, fresh kid. If winner takes all, we weigh in at 10 A.M."

"And winner takes all?" Rivera queried.

Danny nodded. That settled it. He would enter the ring in his full ripeness of strength.

"Weigh in at ten," Rivera said.

The secretary's pen went on scratching.

"It means five pounds," Roberts complained to Rivera. "You've given too much away. You've thrown the fight right there. Danny'll be as strong as a bull. You're a fool. He'll lick you sure. You ain't got the chance of a dewdrop in hell."

Rivera's answer was a calculated look of hatred. Even this gringo he despised, and him had he found the whitest gringo of them all.

IV

Barely noticed was Rivera as he entered the ring. Only a very slight and very scattering ripple of half-hearted hand-clapping greeted him. The house did not believe in him. He was the lamb led to slaughter at the hands of the great Danny. Besides, the house was disappointed. It had expected a rushing battle between Danny Ward and Billy Carthey, and here it must put up with this poor little tyro. Still further, it had manifested its disapproval of the change by betting two, and even three, to one on Danny. And where a betting audience's money is, there is its heart.

The Mexican boy sat down in his corner and waited. The slow minutes lagged by. Danny was making him wait. It was an old trick, but ever it worked on the young, new fighters. They grew frightened, sitting thus and facing their own apprehensions and a callous, tobacco-smoking audience. But for once the trick failed. Roberts was right. Rivera had no goat. He, who was more delicately co-ordinated, more finely nerved and strung than any of them, had no nerves of this sort. The atmosphere of foredoomed defeat in his own corner had no effect on him. His handlers were gringos and strangers. Also they were scrubs — the dirty driftage of the fight game, without honour, without efficiency. And they were chilled, as well, with certitude that theirs was the losing corner.

"Now you gotta be careful," Spider Hagerty warned him. Spider was his chief second. "Make it last as long as you can — them's my instructions from Kelly. If you don't, the papers'll call it another bum fight and give the game a bigger black eye in Los Angeles."

All of which was not encouraging. But Rivera took no notice. He despised prize fighting. It was the hated game of the hated gringo. He had taken up with it, as a chopping block for others in the training quarters, solely because he was starving. The fact that he was marvellously made for it had meant nothing. He hated it. Not until he had come in to the Junta had he fought for money, and he had found the money easy. Not first among the sons of men had he been to find himself successful at a despised vocation.

He did not analyse. He merely knew that he must win this fight. There could be no other outcome. For behind him, nerving him to this belief, were profounder forces than any the crowded house dreamed. Danny Ward fought for money and for the easy ways of life that money would bring. But the things Rivera fought for burned in his brain — blazing and terrible visions, that, with eyes wide open, sitting lonely in the corner of the ring and waiting for his tricky antagonist, he saw as clearly as he had lived them.

He saw the white-walled, water-power factories of Rio Blanco. He saw the six thousand workers, starved and wan, and the little children, seven and eight years of age, who toiled long shifts for ten cents a day. He saw the perambulating corpses, the ghastly death's heads of men who laboured in the dye rooms. He remembered that he had heard his father call the dye rooms the "suicide holes," where a year was death. He saw the little patio, and his mother cooking and moiling at crude housekeeping and finding time to caress and love him. And his father he saw, large, big-moustached, and deep-chested, kindly above all men, who loved all men and whose heart was so large that there was love to overflowing still left for the mother and the little *muchacho* playing in the corner of the patio. In those days his name had not been Felipe Rivera. It had been Fernandez, his father's and mother's name. Him had they called Juan. Later he had changed it himself, for he had found the name of Fernandez hated by prefects of police, *jefes politicos,* and *rurales.*

Big, hearty Joaquin Fernandez! A large place he occupied in Rivera's visions. He had not understood at the time, but, looking back, he could understand. He could see him setting type in the little printery, or scribbling endless hasty, nervous lines on the much-cluttered desk. And he could see the strange evenings, when workmen, coming secretly in the dark like men who did ill deeds, met with his father and talked long hours where he, the muchacho, lay not always asleep in the corner.

As from a remote distance he could hear Spider Hagerty saying to him: "No layin' down at the start. Them's instructions. Take a beatin' and earn your dough."

Ten minutes had passed, and he still sat in his corner. There were no signs of Danny, who was evidently playing the trick to the limit.

But more visions burned before the eye of Rivera's memory. The strike, or, rather, the lock-out, because the workers of Rio Blanco had helped their striking brothers of Puebla. The hunger, the expeditions in the hills for berries, the roots and herbs that all ate and that twisted and pained the stomachs of all of them. And then the nightmare; the waste of ground before the company's store; the thousands of starving workers; General Rosalio Martinez and the soldiers of Porfirio Diaz; and the death-spitting rifles that seemed never to cease spitting, while the workers' wrongs were washed and washed again in their own blood. And that night! He saw the flat cars, piled high with the bodies of the slain, consigned to Vera Cruz, food for the sharks of the bay. Again he crawled over the grisly heaps, seeking and finding, stripped and mangled, his father and mother. His mother he especially remembered — only her face projecting, her body burdened by the weight of dozens of bodies. Again the rifles of the soldiers of Porfirio Diaz cracked, and again he dropped to the ground and slunk away like some hunted coyote of the hills.

To his ears came a great roar, as of the sea, and he saw Danny Ward, leading his retinue of trainers and seconds,

coming down the centre aisle. The house was in wild uproar
for the popular hero who was bound to win. Everybody proclaimed him. Everybody was for him. Even Rivera's own
seconds warmed to something akin to cheerfulness when
Danny ducked jauntily through the ropes and entered the
ring. His face continually spread to an unending succession
of smiles, and when Danny smiled he smiled in every feature,
even to the laughter wrinkles of the corners of the eyes and
into the depths of the eyes themselves. Never was there so
genial a fighter. His face was a running advertisement of
good feeling, of good-fellowship. He knew everybody. He
joked, and laughed, and greeted his friends through the
ropes. Those farther away, unable to suppress their admiration, cried loudly: "Oh, you Danny!" It was a joyous ovation
of affection that lasted a full five minutes.

Rivera was disregarded. For all that the audience noticed,
he did not exist. Spider Hagerty's bloated face bent down
close to his.

"No gettin' scared," the Spider warned. "An' remember
instructions. You gotta last. No layin' down. If you lay
down, we got instructions to beat you up in the dressing-
rooms. Savvy? You just gotta fight."

The house began to applaud. Danny was crossing the ring
to him. Danny bent over him, caught Rivera's right hand in
both his own and shook it with impulsive heartiness. Danny's
smile-wreathed face was close to his. The audience yelled its
appreciation of Danny's display of sporting spirit. He was
greeting his opponent with the fondness of a brother. Danny's lips moved, and the audience, interpreting the unheard
words to be those of a kindly-natured sport, yelled again.
Only Rivera heard the low words.

"You little Mexican rat," hissed from between Danny's
gaily smiling lips, "I'll fetch the yellow outa you."

Rivera made no move. He did not rise. He merely hated
with his eyes.

"Get up, you dog!" some man yelled through the ropes
from behind.

The crowd began to hiss and boo him for his unsportsmanlike conduct, but he sat unmoved. Another great outburst of applause was Danny's as he walked back across the
ring.

When Danny stripped, there were ohs! and ahs! of delight. His body was perfect, alive with easy suppleness and
health and strength. The skin was white as a woman's, and
as smooth. All grace, and resilience, and power resided
therein. He had proved it in scores of battles. His photographs were in all the physical-culture magazines.

A groan went up as Spider Hagerty peeled Rivera's
sweater over his head. His body seemed leaner because of
the swarthiness of the skin. He had muscles, but they made
no display like his opponent's. What the audience neglected
to see was the deep chest. Nor could it guess the toughness of
the fibre of the flesh, the instantaneousness of the cell explo-
sions of the muscles, the fineness of the nerves that wired
every part of him into a splendid fighting mechanism. All
the audience saw was a brown-skinned boy of eighteen with
what seemed the body of a boy. With Danny it was different.
Danny was a man of twenty-four, and his body was a man's
body. The contrast was still more striking as they stood
together in the centre of the ring receiving the referee's last
instructions.

Rivera noticed Roberts sitting directly behind the newspapermen. He was drunker than usual, and his speech was
correspondingly slower.

"Take it easy, Rivera," Roberts drawled. "He can't kill
you, remember that. He'll rush you at the go-off, but don't

get rattled. You just cover up, and stall, and clinch. He can't hurt you much. Just make believe to yourself that he's choppin' out on you at the trainin' quarters."

Rivera made no sign that he had heard.

"Sullen little devil," Roberts muttered to the man next to him. "He always was that way."

But Rivera forgot to look his usual hatred. A vision of countless rifles blinded his eyes. Every face in the audience, as far as he could see, to the high dollar seats, was transformed into a rifle. And he saw the long Mexican border arid and sun-washed and aching, and along it he saw the ragged bands that delayed only for the guns.

Back in his corner he waited, standing up. His seconds had crawled out through the ropes, taking the canvas stool with them. Diagonally across the squared ring, Danny faced him. The gong struck, and the battle was on. The audience howled its delight. Never had it seen a battle open more convincingly. The papers were right. It was a grudge fight. Three-quarters of the distance Danny covered in the rush to get together, his intention to eat up the Mexican lad plainly advertised. He assailed with not one blow, nor two, nor a dozen. He was a gyroscope of blows, a whirlwind of destruction. Rivera was nowhere. He was overwhelmed, buried beneath avalanches of punches delivered from every angle and position by a past master in the art. He was overborne, swept back against the ropes, separated by the referee, and swept back against the ropes again.

It was not a fight. It was a slaughter, a massacre. Any audience, save a prize-fighting one, would have exhausted its emotions in that first minute. Danny was certainly showing what he could do — a splendid exhibition. Such was the certainty of the audience, as well as its excitement and favouritism, that it failed to notice that the Mexican still stayed on his feet. It forgot Rivera. It rarely saw him, so closely was he enveloped in Danny's man-eating attack. A minute of this went by, and two minutes. Then, in a separation, it caught a clear glimpse of the Mexican. His lip was cut, his nose was bleeding. As he turned and staggered into a clinch the welts of oozing blood, from his contacts with the ropes, showed in red bars across his back. But what the audience did not notice was that his chest was not heaving and that his eyes were coldly burning as ever. Too many aspiring champions, in the cruel welter of the training camps, had practised this man-eating attack on him. He had learned to live through for a compensation of from half a dollar a go up to fifteen dollars a week — a hard school, and he was schooled hard.

Then happened the amazing thing. The whirling, blur-ring mix-up ceased suddenly. Rivera stood alone. Danny, the redoubtable Danny, lay on his back. His body quivered as consciousness strove to return to it. He had not staggered and sunk down, nor had he gone over in a long slumping fall. The right hook of Rivera had dropped him in mid-air with the abruptness of death. The referee shoved Rivera back with one hand and stood over the fallen gladiator counting the seconds. It is the custom of prize-fighting audiences to cheer a clean knock-down blow. But this audi-ence did not cheer. The thing had been too unexpected. It watched the toll of the seconds in tense silence, and through this silence the voice of Roberts rose exultantly:

"I told you he was a two-handed fighter!"

By the fifth second Danny was rolling on his face, and when seven was counted he rested on one knee, ready to rise after the count of nine and before the count of ten. If his knee still touched the floor at "ten" he was considered "down" and also "out." The instant his knee left the floor he was considered "up," and in that instant it was Rivera's right to try and put him down again. Rivera took no chances. The moment that knee left the floor he would strike again. He circled around, but the referee circled in between, and Rivera knew that the seconds he counted were very slow. All gringos were against him, even the referee.

At "nine" the referee gave Rivera a sharp thrust back. It was unfair, but it enabled Danny to rise, the smile back on his lips. Doubled partly over, with arms wrapped about face and abdomen, he cleverly stumbled into a clinch. By all the rules of the game the referee should have broken it, but he did not, and Danny clung on like a surf-battered barnacle and moment by moment recuperated. The last minute of the round was going fast. If he could live to the end he would have a full minute in his corner to revive. And live to the end he did, smiling through all desperateness and extremity.

"The smile that won't come off!" somebody yelled, and the audience laughed loudly in its relief.

"The kick that greaser's got is something God-awful," Danny gasped in his corner to his adviser while his handlers worked frantically over him.

The second and third rounds were tame. Danny, a tricky and consummate ring general, stalled and blocked and held on, devoting himself to recovering from the dazing first-round blow. In the fourth round he was himself again. Jarred and shaken, nevertheless his good condition had enabled him to regain his vigour. But he tried no man-eating tactics. The Mexican had proved a tartar. Instead he brought to bear his best fighting powers. In tricks and skill and experience he was the master, and though he could land nothing vital, he proceeded scientifically to chop and wear down his opponent. He landed three blows to Rivera's one, but they were punishing blows only, and not deadly. It was the sum of many of them that constituted deadliness. He was respectful of this two-handed dub with the amazing short-arm kicks in both his fists.

In defence Rivera developed a disconcerting straight left. Again and again, attack after attack he straight-lefted away from him with accumulated damage to Danny's mouth and nose. But Danny was protean. That was why he was the coming champion. He could change from style to style of fighting at will. He now devoted himself to in-fighting. In this he was particularly wicked, and it enabled him to avoid the other's straight left. Here he set the house wild repeatedly, capping it with a marvellous lock-break and life of an inside uppercut that raised the Mexican in the air and dropped him to the mat. Rivera rested on one knee, making the most of the count, and in the soul of him knew the referee was counting short seconds on him.

Again, in the seventh, Danny achieved the diabolical inside uppercut. He succeeded only in staggering Rivera, but in the ensuing moment of defenceless helplessness he smashed him with another blow through the ropes. Rivera's body bounced on the heads of the newspapermen below, and they boosted him back to the edge of the platform outside the ropes. Here he rested on one knee, while the referee raced off the seconds. Inside the ropes, through which he must duck to enter the ring, Danny waited for him. Nor did the referee intervene or thrust Danny back.

The house was beside itself with delight.

"Kill 'm, Danny, kill 'm!" was the cry.

Scores of voices took it up until it was like a war chant of wolves.

Danny did his best, but Rivera, at the count of eight, instead of nine, came unexpectedly through the ropes and safely into a clinch. Now the referee worked, tearing him away so that he could be hit, giving Danny every advantage that an unfair referee can give.

But Rivera lived, and the daze cleared from his brain. It was all of a piece. They were the hated gringos and they were unfair. And in the worst of it visions continued to flash and sparkle in his brain — long lines of railroad track that simmered across the desert; *rurales* and American constables; prisons and calabooses; tramps at water tanks — all the squalid and painful panorama of his odyssey after Rio Blanco and the strike. And, resplendent and glorious, he saw the great red revolution sweeping across his land. The guns were there before him. Every hated face was a gun. It was for the guns he fought. He was the guns. He was the revolution. He fought for all Mexico.

The audience began to grow incensed with Rivera. Why didn't he take the licking that was appointed him? Of course he was going to be licked, but why should he be so obstinate about it? Very few were interested in him, and they were the certain, definite percentage of a gambling crowd that plays long shots. Believing Danny to be the winner, nevertheless they had put their money on the Mexican at four to ten and one to three. More than a trifle was up on the point of how many rounds Rivera could last. Wild money had appeared at the ringside proclaiming that he could not last seven rounds, or even six. The winners of this, now that their cash risk was happily settled, had joined in cheering on the favourite.

Rivera refused to be licked. Through the eighth round his opponent strove vainly to repeat the uppercut. In the ninth Rivera stunned the house again. In the midst of a clinch he broke the lock with a quick, lithe movement, and in the narrow space between their bodies his right lifted from the waist. Danny went to the floor and took the safety of the count. The crowd was appalled. He was being bested at his own game. His famous right uppercut had been worked back on him. Rivera made no attempt to catch him as he arose at "nine." The referee was openly blocking that play, though he stood clear when the situation was reversed and it was Rivera who required to rise.

Twice in the tenth Rivera put through the right uppercut, lifted from waist to opponent's chin. Danny grew desperate. The smile never left his face, but he went back to his man-eating rushes. Whirlwind as he would, he could not damage Rivera, while Rivera, through the blur and whirl, dropped him to the mat three times in succession. Danny did not recuperate so quickly now, and by the eleventh round he was in a serious way. But from then till the fourteenth he put up the gamest exhibition of his career. He stalled and block-ed, fought parsimoniously, and strove to gather strength. Also he fought as foully as a successful fighter knows how. Every trick and device he employed, butting in the clinches with the seeming of accident, pinioning Rivera's glove be-tween arm and body, heeling his glove on Rivera's mouth to clog his breathing. Often, in the clinches, through his cut and smiling lips he snarled insults unspeakable and vile in Rivera's ear. Everybody, from the referee to the house, was with Danny and was helping Danny. And they knew what he had in mind. Bested by this surprise box of an unknown, he was pinning all on a single punch. He offered himself for punishment, fished, and feinted, and drew, for that one opening that would enable him to whip a blow through with all his strength and turn the tide. As another and greater fighter had done before him, he might do — a right and left, to solar plexus and across the jaw. He could do it, for he was noted for the strength of punch that remained in his arms as long as he could keep his feet.

Rivera's seconds were not half caring for him in the inter-vals between rounds. Their towels made a showing but drove little air into his panting lungs. Spider Hagerty talked advice to him, but Rivera knew it was wrong advice. Everybody was against him. He was surrounded by treachery. In the fourteenth round he put Danny down again, and himself stood resting, hand dropped at side, while the referee counted. In the other corner Rivera had been noting suspicious whisperings. He saw Michael Kelly make his way to Roberts and bend and whisper. Rivera's ears were a cat's, desert-trained, and he caught snatches of what was said. He wanted to hear more, and when his opponent arose he manœuvred the fight into a clinch over against the ropes.

"Got to," he could hear Michael, while Roberts nodded. "Danny's got to win — I stand to lose a mint. I've got a ton of money covered — my own. If he lasts the fifteenth I'm bust. The boy'll mind you. Put something across."

And thereafter Rivera saw no more visions. They were trying to job him. Once again he dropped Danny and stood resting, his hands at his side. Roberts stood up.

"That settled him," he said. "Go to your corner."

He spoke with authority, as he had often spoken to Rivera at the training quarters. But Rivera looked hatred at him and waited for Danny to rise. Back in his corner in the minute interval, Kelly, the promoter, came and talked to Rivera.

"Throw it, damn you," he rasped in a harsh low voice. "You gotta lay down, Rivera. Stick with me and I'll make your future. I'll let you lick Danny next time. But here's where you lay down."

Rivera showed with his eyes that he heard, but he made neither sign of assent nor dissent.

"Why don't you speak?" Kelly demanded angrily.

"You lose anyway," Spider Hagerty supplemented. "The referee'll take it away from you. Listen to Kelly and lay down."

"Lay down, kid," Kelly pleaded, "and I'll help you to the championship."

Rivera did not answer.

"I will, so help me, kid."

At the strike of the gong Rivera sensed something impending. The house did not. Whatever it was, it was there inside the ring with him and very close. Danny's early surety seemed returned to him. The confidence of his advance frightened Rivera. Some trick was about to be worked. Danny rushed, but Rivera refused the encounter. He sidestepped away into safety. What the other wanted was a clinch. It was in some way necessary to the trick. Rivera backed and circled away, yet he knew, sooner or later, the clinch and the trick would come. Desperately he resolved to draw it. He made as if to effect the clinch with Danny's next rush. Instead, at the last instant, just as their bodies should have come together, Rivera darted nimbly back. And in the same instant Danny's corner raised a cry of foul. Rivera had fooled them. The referee paused irresolutely. The decision that trembled on his lips was never uttered, for a shrill, boy's voice from the gallery piped, "Raw work!"

Danny cursed Rivera openly, and forced him, while Rivera danced away. Also Rivera made up his mind to strike no more blows at the body. In this he threw away half his chance of winning, but he knew if he was to win at all it was with the outfighting that remained to him. Given the least opportunity, they would lie a foul on him. Danny threw all caution to the winds. For two rounds he tore after and into the boy who dared not meet him at close quarters. Rivera was struck again and again; he took blows by the dozens to avoid the perilous clinch. During this supreme final rally of Danny's the audience rose to its feet and went mad. It did not understand. All it could see was that its favourite was winning after all.

"Why don't you fight?" it demanded wrathfully of Rivera. "You're yellow! You're yellow!" "Open up, you cur! Open up!" "Kill 'm, Danny! Kill 'm!" "You sure got 'm! Kill 'm!"

In all the house, bar none, Rivera was the only cold man. By temperament and blood he was the hottest-passioned there; but he had gone through such vastly greater heats that this collective passion of ten thousand throats, rising surge on surge, was to his brain no more than the velvet cool of a summer twilight.

Into the seventeenth round Danny carried his rally. Rivera, under a heavy blow, drooped and sagged. His hands dropped helplessly as he reeled backwards. Danny thought it was his chance. The boy was at his mercy. Thus Rivera, feigning, caught him off his guard, lashing out a clean drive to the mouth. Danny went down. When he arose Rivera felled him with a down-chop of the right on neck and jaw. Three times he repeated this. It was impossible for any referee to call these blows foul.

"Oh, Bill! Bill!" Kelly pleaded to the referee.

"I can't," that official lamented back. "He won't give me a chance."

Danny, battered and heroic, still kept coming up. Kelly and others near to the ring began to cry out to the police to stop it, though Danny's corner refused to throw in the towel. Rivera saw the fat police captain starting awkwardly to climb through the ropes, and was not sure what it meant. There were so many ways of cheating in this game of the gringos. Danny, on his feet, tottered groggily and helplessly before him. The referee and the captain were both reaching for Rivera when he struck the last blow. There was no need to stop the fight, for Danny did not rise.

"Count!" Rivera cried hoarsely to the referee.

And when the count was finished Danny's seconds gathered him up and carried him to his corner.

"Who wins?" Rivera demanded.

Reluctantly the referee caught his gloved hand and held it aloft.

There was no congratulations for Rivera. He walked to his corner unattended, where his seconds had not yet placed his stool. He leaned backwards on the ropes and looked his hatred at them, swept it on and about him till the whole ten thousand gringos were included. His knees trembled under him, and he was sobbing from exhaustion. Before his eyes the hated faces swayed back and forth in the giddiness of nausea. Then he remembered they were the guns. The guns were his. The revolution could go on.

9   "NAVIGATION *IS* EASY," Jack London wrote, "I shall always contend that; but when a man is taking three gasolene engines and a wife around the world and is writing hard every day to keep the engines supplied with gasolene and the wife with pearls and volcanoes, he hasn't much time left in which to study navigation."

How London found the time to study, let alone write about, the complex science of navigation is one of the major marvels of his ocean odyssey aboard the *Snark*. The mysteries of deep sea reckoning have seldom been more entertainingly revealed than in the following account. It is the story of an intrepid sportsman who, by default of three incompetent captains, was compelled to become a self-instructed and self-tormented "amateur navigator." Will his feverish calculations lead his party correctly to the pearl ports and volcanic isles they seek, or to the less happy prospect of being lost at sea?

The ease and charm of London's writing almost blind us to the fact that in plotting his course, he is also plotting his story, transposing his navigational difficulties to the substance of his art. In this, he proves himself less the baffled amateur he seems (or wishes to appear), than an accomplished professional. The enigma of compass, sextant, and chronometer offer another bond, another intimacy, another adventure to be shared with his reader.

London gives his inanimate sailing instruments a life of their own. He imparts form and color to the dreary (and fallible) mathematics of reckoning a course. He evokes his navigational "nightmares" for our pleasure. It is the game of a master mariner. It is the business of a master writer.

# The Amateur Navigator

THERE ARE CAPTAINS and captains, and some
mighty fine captains, I know; but the run of the
captains on the *Snark* has been remarkably otherwise. My
experience with them has been that it is harder to take care
of one captain on a small boat than of two small babies. Of
course, this is no more than is to be expected. The good men
have positions, and are not likely to forsake their one-
thousand-to-fifteen-thousand-ton billets for the *Snark* with
her ten tons net. The *Snark* has had to cull her navigators
from the beach, and the navigator on the beach is usually a
congenital inefficient — the sort of man who beats about for
a fortnight trying vainly to find an ocean isle and who
returns with his schooner to report the island sunk with all
on board, the sort of man whose temper or thirst for strong
waters works him out of billets faster than he can work into
them.

The *Snark* has had three captains, and by the grace of
God she shall have no more. The first captain was so senile
as to be unable to give a measurement for a boom-jaw to a
carpenter. So utterly agedly helpless was he, that he was
unable to order a sailor to throw a few buckets of salt water
on the *Snark's* deck. For twelve days, at anchor, under an
overhead tropic sun, the deck lay dry. It was a new deck. It
cost me one hundred and thirty-five dollars to recalk it. The
second captain was angry. He was born angry. "Papa is
always angry," was the description given him by his half-
breed son. The third captain was so crooked that he couldn't

hide behind a corkscrew. The truth was not in him, common honesty was not in him, and he was as far away from fair play and square-dealing as he was from his proper course when he nearly wrecked the *Snark* on the Ringgold Isles.

It was at Suva, in the Fijis, that I discharged my third and last captain and took up again the role of amateur navigator. I had assayed it once before, under my first captain, who, out of San Francisco, jumped the *Snark* so amazingly over the chart that I really had to find out what was doing. It was fairly easy to find out, for we had a run of twenty-one hundred miles before us. I knew nothing of navigation; but, after several hours of reading up and half an hour's practice with the sextant, I was able to find the *Snark's* latitude by meridian observation and her longitude by the simple method known as "equal altitudes." This is not a correct method. It is not even a safe method, but my captain was attempting to navigate by it, and he was the only one on board who should have been able to tell me that it was a method to be eschewed. I brought the *Snark* to Hawaii, but the conditions favored me. The sun was in northern declination and nearly overhead. The legitimate "chronometer-sight" method of ascertaining the longitude I had not heard of — yes, I had heard of it. My first captain mentioned it vaguely, but after one or two attempts at practice of it he mentioned it no more.

I had time in the Fijis to compare my chronometer with two other chronometers. Two weeks previous, at Pago Pago, in Samoa, I had asked my captain to compare our chronometers on the American cruiser, the *Annapolis*. This he told me he had done — of course he had done nothing of the sort; and he told me that the difference he had ascertained was only a small fraction of a second. He told it to me with finely simulated joy and with words of praise for my splendid

time-keeper. I repeat it now, with words of praise for his
splendid and unblushing unveracity. For behold, fourteen
days later, in Suva, I compared the chronometer with the
one on the *Atua,* an Australian steamer, and found that
mine was thirty-one seconds fast. Now thirty-one seconds of
time, converted into arc, equals seven and one-quarter
miles. That is to say, if I were sailing west, in the night-time,
and my position, according to my dead reckoning from my
afternoon chronometer sight, was shown to be seven miles
off the land, why, at that very moment I would be crashing
on the reef. Next I compared my chronometer with Captain
Wooley's. Captain Wooley, the harbormaster, gives the time
to Suva, firing a gun signal at twelve, noon, three times a
week. According to his chronometer mine was fifty-nine
seconds fast, which is to say, that, sailing west, I should be
crashing on the reef when I thought I was fifteen miles off
from it.

I compromised by subtracting thirty-one seconds from
the total of my chronometer's losing error, and sailed away
for Tanna, in the New Hebrides, resolved, when nosing
around the land on dark nights, to bear in mind the other
seven miles I might be out according to Captain Wooley's instrument. Tanna lay some six hundred miles west-southwest
from the Fijis, and it was my belief that while covering that
distance I could quite easily knock into my head sufficient
navigation to get me there. Well, I got there, but listen first
to my troubles. Navigation *is* easy, I shall always contend
that; but when a man is taking three gasolene engines and a
wife around the world and is writing hard every day to keep
the engines supplied with gasolene and the wife with pearls
and volcanoes, he hasn't much time left in which to study
navigation. Also, it is bound to be easier to study said science
ashore, where latitude and longitude are unchanging, in a

house whose position never alters, than it is to study navigation on a boat that is rushing along day and night toward land that one is trying to find and which he is liable to find disastrously at a moment when he least expects it.

To begin with, there are the compasses and the setting of the courses. We sailed from Suva on Saturday afternoon, June 6, 1908, and it took us till after dark to run the narrow, reef-ridden passage between the islands of Viti Levu and Mbengha. The open ocean lay before me. There was nothing in the way with the exception of Vatu Leile, a miserable little island that persisted in poking up through the sea some twenty miles to the west-southwest — just where I wanted to go. Of course, it seemed quite simple to avoid it by steering a course that would pass it eight or ten miles to the north. It was a black night, and we were running before the wind. The man at the wheel must be told what direction to steer in order to miss Vatu Leile. But what direction? I turned me to the navigation books. "True Course" I lighted upon. The very thing! What I wanted was the true course. I read eagerly on:

*The True Course is the angle made with the meridian by a straight line on the chart drawn to connect the ship's position with the place bound to.*

Just what I wanted. The *Snark's* position was at the western entrance of the passage between Viti Levu and Mbengha. The immediate place she was bound to was a place on the chart ten miles north of Vatu Leile. I pricked that place off on the chart with my dividers, and with my parallel rulers found that west-by-south was the true course. I had but to give it to the man at the wheel and the *Snark* would win her way to the safety of the open sea.

But alas and alack and lucky for me, I read on. I discovered that the compass, that trusty, everlasting friend of the mariner, was not given to pointing north. It varied. Sometimes it pointed east of north, sometimes west of north, and on occasion it even turned tail on north and pointed south. The variation at the particular spot on the globe occupied by the *Snark* was 9° 40′ easterly. Well, that had to be taken into account before I gave the steering course to the man at the wheel. I read:

> *The Correct Magnetic Course is derived from the True Course by applying it to the variation.*

Therefore, I reasoned, if the compass points 9° 40′ *eastward of north, and I wanted to sail due north, I should have to steer 9° 40′* westward of the north indicated by the compass and which was not north at all. So I added 9° 40′ to the left of my west-by-south course, thus getting my correct Magnetic Course, and was ready once more to run to open sea.

Again alas and alack! The Correct Magnetic Course was not the Compass Course. There was another sly little devil lying in wait to trip me up and land me smashing on the reefs of Vatu Leile. This little devil went by the name of Deviation. I read:

> *The Compass Course is the course to steer, and is derived from the Correct Magnetic Course by applying to it the Deviation.*

Now Deviation is the variation in the needle caused by the distribution of iron on board ship. This purely local variation I derived from the deviation card of my standard compass and then applied to the Correct Magnetic Course. The result was the Compass Course. And yet, not yet. My standard compass was amidships on the companionway. My steering compass was aft, in the cockpit, near the wheel. When the steering compass pointed west–by–south–three-quarters–south (the steering course), the standard compass pointed west–one-half–north, which was certainly not the steering course. I kept the *Snark* up till she was heading west–by–south–three-quarters–south on the standard compass, which gave, on the steering compass, southwest-by-west.

The foregoing operations constitute the simple little matter of setting a course. And the worst of it is that one must perform every step correctly or else he will hear "Breakers ahead!" some pleasant night, receive a nice sea-bath, and be given the delightful diversion of fighting his way to the shore through a horde of man-eating sharks.

Just as the compass is tricky and strives to fool the mariner by pointing in all directions except north, so does that guide-post of the sky, the sun, persist in not being where it ought to be at a given time. This carelessness of the sun is the cause of more trouble — at least it caused trouble for me. To find out where one is on the earth's surface, he must know, at precisely the same time, where the sun is in the heavens. That is to say, the sun, which is the timekeeper for men, doesn't run on time. When I discovered this, I fell into deep gloom and all the Cosmos was filled with doubt. Immutable laws, such as gravitation and the conservation of energy, became wobbly, and I was prepared to witness their violation at any moment and to remain unastonished. For see, if the compass lied and the sun did not keep its engagements, why should not objects lose their mutual attraction and why should not a few bushel baskets of force be annihilated? Even perpetual motion became possible, and I was in a frame of mind prone to purchase Keeley-Motor stock from

the first enterprising agent that landed on the *Snark's* deck.
And when I discovered that the earth really rotated on its
axis 366 times a year, while there were only 365 sunrises and
sunsets, I was ready to doubt my own identity.

This is the way of the sun. It is so irregular that it is impossible for man to devise a clock that will keep the sun's
time. The sun accelerates and retards as no clock could be
made to accelerate and retard. The sun is sometimes ahead
of its schedule; at other times it is lagging behind; and at
still other times it is breaking the speed limit in order to
overtake itself, or, rather, to catch up with where it ought to
be in the sky. In this last case it does not slow down quick
enough, and, as a result, goes dashing ahead of where it
ought to be. In fact, only four days in a year do the sun and
the place where the sun ought to be happen to coincide. The
remaining 361 days the sun is pothering around all over the
shop. Man, being more perfect than the sun, makes a clock
that keeps regular time. Also, he calculates how far the sun
is ahead of its schedule or behind. The difference between
the sun's position and the position where the sun ought to be
if it were a decent, self-respecting sun, man calls the Equation of Time. Thus, the navigator endeavoring to find his
ship's position on the sea, looks in his chronometer to see
where precisely the sun ought to be according to the Greenwich custodian of the sun. Then to that location he applies
the Equation of Time and finds out where the sun ought to
be and isn't. This latter location, along with several other
locations, enable him to find out what the man from Kansas
demanded to know some years ago.

The *Snark* sailed from Fiji on Saturday, June 6, and the
next day, Sunday, on the wide ocean, out of sight of land, I
proceeded to endeavor to find out my position by a chronometer sight for longitude and by a meridian observation

for latitude. The chronometer sight was taken in the morning, when the sun was some 21° above the horizon. I looked in the Nautical Almanac and found that on that very day, June 7, the sun was behind time 1 minute and 26 seconds, and that it was catching up at a rate of 14.67 seconds per hour. The chronometer said that at the precise moment of taking the sun's altitude it was twenty-five minutes after eight o'clock at Greenwich. From this date it would seem a schoolboy's task to correct the Equation of Time. Unfortunately, I was not a schoolboy. Obviously, at the middle of the day, at Greenwich, the sun was 1 minute and 26 seconds behind time. Equally obviously, if it were eleven o'clock in the morning, the sun would be 1 minute and 26 seconds behind time plus 14.67 seconds. If it were ten o'clock in the morning, twice 14.67 seconds would have to be added. And if it were 8:25 in the morning, then 3½ times 14.67 seconds would have to be added. Quite clearly, then, if, instead of being 8:25 A.M., it were 8:25 P.M., then 8½ times 14.67 seconds would have to be, not added, but *subtracted;* for, if, at noon, the sun were 1 minute and 26 seconds behind time, and if it were catching up with where it ought to be at the rate of 14.67 seconds per hour, then at 8:25 P.M. it would be much nearer where it ought to be than it had been at noon.

So far, so good. But was that 8:25 of the chronometer A.M. or P.M.? I looked at the *Snark's* clock. It marked 8:9, and it was certainly A.M., for I had just finished breakfast. Therefore, if it was eight in the morning on board the *Snark,* the eight o'clock of the chronometer (which was the time of the day at Greenwich) must be a different eight o'clock from the *Snark's* eight o'clock. But what eight o'clock was it? It can't be the eight o'clock of this morning, I reasoned; therefore, it must be either eight o'clock this evening or eight o'clock last night.

It was at this juncture that I fell into the bottomless pit of intellectual chaos. We are in east longitude, I reasoned, therefore we are ahead of Greenwich. If we are behind Greenwich, then to-day is yesterday; if we are ahead of Greenwich, then yesterday is to-day, but if yesterday is to-day, what under the sun is to-day! — tomorrow? Absurd! Yet it must be correct. When I took the sun this morning at 8:25, the sun's custodians at Greenwich were just arising from dinner last night.

"Then correct the Equation of Time for yesterday," says my logical mind.

"But to-day is to-day," my literal mind insists. "I must correct the sun for to-day and not for yesterday."

"Yet to-day is yesterday," urges my logical mind.

"That's all very well," my literal mind continues. "If I were in Greenwich I might be in yesterday. Strange things happen in Greenwich. But I know as sure as I am living that I am here, now, in to-day, June 7, and that I took the sun here, now, to-day, June 7. Therefore, I must correct the sun here, now, to-day, June 7."

"Bosh!" snaps my logical mind. "Lecky says —"

"Never mind what Lecky says," interrupts my literal mind. "Let me tell you what the Nautical Almanac says. The Nautical Almanac says that to-day, June 7, the sun was 1 minute and 26 seconds behind time and catching up at the rate of 14.67 seconds per hour. It says that yesterday, June 6, the sun was 1 minute and 36 seconds behind time and catching up at the rate of 15.66 seconds per hour. You see, it is preposterous to think of correcting to-day's sun by yesterday's time-table."

"Fool!"

"Idiot!"

Back and forth they wrangle until my head is whirling around and I am ready to believe that I am in the day after the last week before next.

I remembered a parting caution of the Suva harbormaster: *"In east longitude take from the Nautical Almanac the elements for the preceding day."*

Then a new thought came to me. I corrected the Equation of Time for Sunday and for Saturday, making two separate operations of it, and lo, when the results were compared, there was a difference only of four-tenths of a second. I was a changed man. I had found my way out of the crypt. The *Snark* was scarcely big enough to hold me and my experience. Four-tenths of a second would make a difference of only one-tenth of a mile — a cable-length!

All went merrily for ten minutes, when I chanced upon the following rhyme for navigators:

> *Greenwich time least*
> *Longitude east;*
> *Greenwich best,*
> *Longitude west.*

Heavens! The *Snark's* time was not as good as Greenwich time. When it was 8:25 at Greenwich, on board the *Snark* it was only 8:9. "Greenwich time best, longitude west." There I was. In west longitude beyond a doubt.

"Silly!" cries my literal mind. "You are 8:9 A.M. and Greenwich is 8:25 P.M."

"Very well," answers my logical mind. "To be correct, 8:25 P.M. is really twenty hours and twenty-five minutes, and that is certainly better than eight hours and nine minutes. No, there is no discussion; you are in west longitude."

Then my literal mind triumphs.

"We sailed from Suva, in the Fijis, didn't we?" it demands, and logical mind agrees. "And Suva is in east longitude?" Again logical mind agrees. "And we sailed west (which would take us deeper into east longitude), didn't we? Therefore, and you can't escape it, we are in east longitude."

"Greenwich time best, longitude west," chants my logical mind; "and you must grant that twenty hours and twenty-five minutes is better than eight hours and nine minutes."

"All right," I break in upon the squabble; "we'll work up the sight and then we'll see."

And work it up I did, only to find that my longitude was 184° west.

"I told you so," snorts my logical mind.

I am dumbfounded. So is my literal mind, for several minutes. Then it enounces:

"But there is no 184° west longitude, nor east longitude, nor any other longitude. The largest meridian is 180° as you ought to know very well."

Having got this far, literal mind collapses from the brain strain, logical mind is dumb flabbergasted; and as for me, I get a bleak and wintery look in my eyes and go around wondering whether I am sailing toward the China coast or the Gulf of Darien.

Then a thin small voice, which I do not recognize, coming from nowhere in particular in my consciousness, says:

"The total number of degrees is 360. Subtract the 184° west longitude from 360°, and you will get 176° east longitude."

"That is sheer speculation," objects literal mind; and logical mind remonstrates. "There is no rule for it."

"Darn the rules!" I exclaim. "Ain't I here?"

"The thing is self-evident," I continue. "184° west longitude means a lapping over in east longitude of four degrees. Besides I have been in east longitude all the time. I sailed from Fiji, and Fiji is in east longitude. Now I shall chart my position and prove it by dead reckoning."

But other troubles and doubts awaited me. Here is a sample of one. In south latitude, when the sun is in northern declination, chronometer sights may be taken early in the morning. I took mine at eight o'clock. Now, one of the necessary elements in working up such a sight is latitude. But one gets latitude at twelve o'clock, noon, by a meridian observation. It is clear that in order to work up my eight o'clock chronometer sight I must have my eight o'clock latitude. Of course, if the *Snark* were sailing due west at six knots per hour, for the intervening four hours her latitude would not change. But if she were sailing due south, her latitude would change to the tune of twenty-four miles. In which case a simple addition or subtraction would convert the twelve o'clock latitude into eight o'clock latitude. But suppose the *Snark* were sailing southwest. Then the traverse tables must be consulted.

This is the illustration. At eight A.M. I took my chronometer sight. At the same moment the distance recorded on the log was noted. At twelve P.M., when the sight for latitude was taken, I again noted the log, which showed me that since eight o'clock the *Snark* had run 24 miles. Her true course had been west ¾ south. I entered Table 1, in the distance column, on the page for ¾ point courses, and stopped at 24, the number of miles run. Opposite, in the next two columns, I found that the *Snark* had made 3.5 miles of southing or latitude, and that she had made 23.7 miles of westing. To find my eight o'clock latitude was easy. I had but to subtract

3.5 miles from my noon latitude. All the elements being present, I worked up my longitude.

But this was my eight o'clock longitude. Since then, and up till noon, I had made 23.7 miles of westing. What was my noon longitude? I followed the rule, turning to Traverse Table No. II. Entering the table, according to rule, and going through every detail, according to rule, I found the difference of longitude for the four hours to be 25 miles. I was aghast. I entered the table again, according to rule; I entered the table half a dozen times, according to rule, and every time found that my difference of longitude was 25 miles. I leave it to you, gentle reader. Suppose you had sailed due west 24 miles, and not changed your latitude, how could you have changed your longitude 25 miles? In the name of human reason, how could you cover one mile more of longitude than the total number of miles you had sailed?

It was a reputable traverse table, being none other than Bowditch's. The rule was simple (as navigators' rules go); I had made no error. I spent an hour over it, and at the end still faced the glaring impossibility of having sailed 24 miles, in the course of which I changed my latitude 3.5 miles and my longitude 25 miles. The worst of it was that there was nobody to help me out. Neither Charmian nor Martin knew as much as I knew about navigation. And all the time the *Snark* was rushing madly along toward Tanna, in the New Hebrides. Something had to be done.

How it came to me I know not — call it an inspiration if you will; but the thought arose in me: if southing is latitude, why isn't westing longitude? Why should I have to change westing into longitude? And then the whole beautiful situation dawned on me. The meridians of longitude are 60 miles (nautical) apart at the equator. At the poles they run together. Thus, if I should travel up the 180° meridian of longitude until I reached the North Pole, and if the astronomer at Greenwich travelled up the 0° meridian of longitude to the North Pole, then, at the North Pole, we could shake hands with each other, though before we started for the North Pole we had been some thousands of miles apart. Again: if a degree of longitude was 60 miles wide at the equator, and if the same degree, at the point of the Pole, had no width, then somewhere between the Pole and the equator that degree would be half a mile wide, and at other places a mile wide, two miles wide, ten miles wide, thirty miles wide, ay, and sixty miles wide.

All was plain again. The *Snark* was in 19° south latitude. The world wasn't as big around there as at the equator. Therefore, every mile of westing at 19° south was more than a minute of longitude; for sixty miles were sixty miles, but sixty minutes are sixty miles only at the equator. George Francis Train broke Jules Verne's record of around the world. But any man that wants can break George Francis Train's record. Such a man would need only to go, in a fast steamer, to the latitude of Cape Horn, and sail due east all the way around. The world is very small in that latitude, and there is no land in the way to turn him out of his course. If his steamer maintained sixteen knots, he would circumnavigate the globe in just about forty days.

But there are compensations. On Wednesday evening, June 10, I brought up my noon position by dead reckoning to eight P.M. Then I projected the *Snark's* course and saw that she would strike Futuna, one of the easternmost of the New Hebrides, a volcanic cone two thousand feet high that rose out of the deep ocean. I altered the course so that the *Snark* would pass ten miles to the northward. Then I spoke to Wada, the cook, who had the wheel every morning from four to six.

"Wada San, to-morrow morning, your watch, you look sharp on weather-bow you see land."

And then I went to bed. The die was cast. I had staked my reputation as a navigator. Suppose, just suppose, that at daybreak there was no land. Then, where would my navigation be? And where would we be? And how would we ever find ourselves? or find any land? I caught ghastly visions of the *Snark* sailing for months through ocean solitudes and seeking vainly for land while we consumed our provisions and sat down with haggard faces to stare cannibalism in the face.

I confess my sleep was not

> . . . *like a summer sky*
> *That held the music of a lark.*

Rather did "I waken to the voiceless dark," and listen to the creaking of the bulkheads and the rippling of the sea alongside as the *Snark* logged steadily her six knots an hour. I went over my calculations again and again, striving to find some mistake, until my brain was in such fever that it discovered dozens of mistakes. Suppose, instead of being sixty miles off Futuna, that my navigation was all wrong and that I was only six miles off? In which case my course would be wrong, too, and for all I knew the *Snark* might be running straight at Futuna. For all I knew the *Snark* might strike Futuna the next moment. I almost sprang from the bunk at that thought; and, though I restrained myself, I know that I lay for a moment, nervous and tense, waiting for the shock.

My sleep was broken by miserable nightmares. Earthquake seemed the favorite affliction, though there was one man, with a bill, who persisted in dunning me throughout the night. Also, he wanted to fight; and Charmian continually persuaded me to let him alone. Finally, however, the man with the everlasting dun ventured into a dream from which Charmian was absent. It was my opportunity, and we went at it, gloriously, all over the sidewalk and street, until he cried enough. Then I said, "Now how about that bill?" Having conquered, I was willing to pay. But the man looked at me and groaned. "It was all a mistake," he said; "the bill is for the house next door."

That settled him, for he worried my dreams no more; and it settled me, too, for I woke up chuckling at the episode. It was three in the morning. I went up on deck. Henry, the Rapa islander, was steering. I looked at the log. It recorded forty-two miles. The *Snark* had not abated her six-knot gait, and she had not struck Futuna yet. At half-past five I was again on deck. Wada, at the wheel, had seen no land. I sat on the cockpit rail, a prey to morbid doubt for a quarter of an hour. Then I saw land, a small, high piece of land, just where it ought to be, rising from the water on the weather-bow. At six o'clock I could clearly make it out to be the beautiful volcanic cone of Futuna. At eight o'clock, when it was abreast, I took its distance by the sextant and found it to be 9.3 miles away. And I had elected to pass it 10 miles away!

Then, to the south, Aneiteum rose out of the sea, to the north, Aniwa, and, dead ahead, Tanna. There was no mis-taking Tanna, for the smoke of its volcano was towering high in the sky. It was forty miles away, and by afternoon, as we drew close, never ceasing to log our six knots, we saw that it was a mountainous, hazy land, with no apparent openings in its coast-line. I was looking for Port Resolution, though I was quite prepared to find that as an anchorage, it had been destroyed. Volcanic earthquakes had lifted its bottom dur-ing the last forty years, so that where once the largest ships rode at anchor there was now, by last reports, scarcely space and depth sufficient for the *Snark*. And why should not another convulsion, since the last report, have closed the harbor completely?

I ran in close to the unbroken coast, fringed with rocks awash upon which the crashing trade-wind sea burst white and high. I searched with my glasses for miles, but could see no entrance. I took a compass bearing of Futuna, another of Aniwa, and laid them off on the chart. Where the two bearings crossed was bound to be the position of the *Snark*. Then, with my parallel rulers, I laid down a course from the *Snark's* position to Port Resolution. Having corrected this course for variation and deviation, I went on deck, and lo, the course directed me towards that unbroken coast-line of bursting seas. To my Rapa islander's great concern, I held on till the rocks awash were an eighth of a mile away.

"No harbor this place," he announced, shaking his head ominously.

But I altered the course and ran along parallel with the coast. Charmian was at the wheel. Martin was at the engine, ready to throw on the propeller. A narrow slit of an opening showed up suddenly. Through the glasses I could see the seas breaking clear across. Henry, the Rapa man, looked with troubled eyes; so did Tehei, the Tahaa man.

"No passage there," said Henry. "We go there, we finish quick, sure."

I confess I thought so, too; but I ran on abreast, watching to see if the line of breakers from one side the entrance did not overlap the line from the other side. Sure enough, it did. A narrow place where the sea ran smooth appeared. Charmian put down the wheel and steadied for the entrance. Martin threw on the engine, while all hands and the cook sprang to take in sail.

A trader's house showed up in the bight of the bay. A geyser, on the shore, a hundred yards away, spouted a column of steam. To port, as we rounded a tiny point, the mission station appeared.

"Three fathoms," cried Wada at the lead-line.

"Three fathoms," "two fathoms," came in quick succession.

Charmian put the wheel down, Martin stopped the engine, and the *Snark* rounded to and the anchor rumbled down in three fathoms. Before we could catch our breaths a swarm of black Tannese was alongside and aboard — grinning, apelike creatures, with kinky hair and troubled eyes, wearing safety-pins and clay-pipes in their slitted ears: and as for the rest, wearing nothing behind and less than that before. And I don't mind telling that that night, when everybody was asleep, I sneaked up on deck, looked out over the quiet scene, and gloated — yes, gloated — over my navigation.

# 10

HAVING PLACED HIS crew on alert for a possible rescue attempt, the captain of the Number Nine outrigger at Waikiki Beach has every reason to be worried. Through his binoculars, he observes the progress of a couple apparently drifting toward disaster in the awesome waves of the Kanaka surf.

Unknown to the captain is the fact that the two "damned malihinis" he watches are in reality Lee and Ida Barton, two of the most skilled and audacious water athletes in the Islands.

Despite all their daring proficiency, however, the Bartons play a dangerous game in attempting to go "adventuring among the blind elemental forces, daring the titanic buffets of the sea." Any one of those mighty buffets may descend like the hand of God, slapping a careless or luckless swimmer down to smash like pulp on the sea's coral floor.

On the beach below the nervous captain's vantage point, a lolling public sunbathes and wades, unaware of the potential tragedy far offshore. The crew of Number Nine languidly await a signal for a rescue try, but the captain knows that Number Nine can neither arrive in time to save the bodysurfing daredevils nor depart without being capsized by the heavy swells. Any rescue attempt would be a gallant, but futile, gesture.

Riding out on the biggest waves in the world, the Bartons are alone. If they succeed in their dangerous sport, they will have known a few godlike moments and won the captain's reluctant approbation.

If they fail, they will be meat for the sharks.

# The Captain of Number Nine

THERE ARE TWO surfs at Waikiki: the big, bearded-man surf that roars far out beyond the diving stage; the smaller, gentler, wahine, or woman, surf that breaks upon the shore itself. Here is a great shallowness, where one may wade a hundred or several hundred feet to get beyond depth. Yet, with a good surf on outside, the wahine surf can break three or four feet, so that, close in against the shore, the hard-sand bottom may be three feet or three inches under the welter of surface foam. To dive from the beach into this, to fly into the air off racing feet, turn in mid-flight so that heels are up and head is down, and so to enter the water headfirst, requires wisdom of waves, timing of waves, and a trained deftness in entering such unstable depths of water with pretty, unapprehensive, headfirst cleavage while at the same time making the shallowest possible of dives.

It is a sweet and pretty and daring trick, not learned in a day nor learned at all without many a mild bump on the bottom or close shave of fractured skull or broken neck. Here, on the spot where the Bartons so beautifully dived, two days earlier a Stanford track athlete had broken his neck. His had been an error in timing the rise and subsidence of a wahine wave.

"A professional," Mrs. Hanley Black sneered to her husband at Ida Barton's feat.

"Some vaudeville tank girl," was one of the similar remarks with which the women in the shade complacently reassured one another; finding, by way of the weird mental processes of self-illusion, a great satisfaction in the money caste distinction between one who worked for what she ate and themselves who did not work for what they ate.

It was a day of heavy surf on Waikiki. In the wahine surf it was boisterous enough for good swimmers. But out beyond, in the *Kanaka,* or man, surf, no one ventured. Not that the score or more of young surf-riders, loafing on the beach, could not venture there, or were afraid to venture there; but because their biggest outrigger canoes would have been swamped, and their surfboards would have been overwhelmed in the too-immense overtopple and downfall of the thundering monsters. They themselves, most of them, could have swum, for man can swim through breakers which canoes and surfboards cannot surmount; but to ride the backs of the waves, rise out of the foam to stand full length in the air above and with heels winged with the swiftness of horses to fly shoreward, was what made sport for them and brought out from Honolulu to Waikiki.

The captain of Number Nine canoe, himself a charter member of the Outrigger and a many-times medalist in long-distance swimming, had missed seeing the Bartons take the water and first glimpsed them beyond the last festoon of bathers who clung to the life lines. From then on, from his vantage of the upstairs lanai, he kept his eyes on them. When they continued out past the steel diving stage where a few of the hardiest divers disported, he muttered vexedly under his breath, "damned malihinis!"

Now malihini means newcomer, tenderfoot; and, despite the prettiness of their stroke, he knew that none except malihinis would venture into the racing channel beyond the diving stage. Hence, the vexation of the captain of Number Nine. He descended to the beach, with a low word here and there picked a crew of the strongest surfers, and returned to the lanai with a pair of binoculars. Quite casually, the crew, six of them, carried Number Nine to the water's edge, saw paddles and everything in order for a quick launching, and lolled about carelessly on the sand. They were guilty of not advertising that anything untoward was afoot, although they did steal glances up to their captain straining through the binoculars.

What made the channel was the fresh-water stream. Coral cannot abide fresh water. What made the channel race was the immense shoreward surf-fling of the sea. Unable to remain flung up on the beach, pounded ever back toward the beach by the perpetual shoreward rush of the Kanaka surf, the up-piled water escaped to the sea by way of the channel and in the form of undertow along the bottom under the breakers. Even in the channel the waves broke big, but not with the magnificent bigness of terror as to right and left. So it was that a canoe or a comparatively strong swimmer could dare the channel. But the swimmer must be a strong swimmer indeed who could successfully buck the current in. Wherefore the captain of Number Nine continued his vigil and his muttered damnation of malihinis, disgustedly sure that these two malihinis would compel him to launch Number Nine and go after them when they found the current too strong to swim in against. As for himself, caught in their predicament, he would have veered to the left toward Diamond Head and come in on the shoreward fling of the Kanaka surf. But then, he was no one other than himself, a bronze Hercules of twenty-two, the whitest blood man ever burned to mahogany brown by a subtropic sun, with body and lines and muscles very much resembling the wonderful ones of Duke Kahanamoku. In a hundred yards the world champion could invariably beat him a second flat;

but over a distance of miles he could swim circles around the champion.

No one of the many hundreds on the beach, with the exception of the captain and his crew, knew that the Bartons had passed beyond the diving stage. All who had watched them start to swim out had taken for granted that they had joined the others on the stage.

The captain suddenly sprang upon the railing of the lanai, held on to a pillar with one hand, and again picked up the two specks of heads through the glasses. His surmise was verified. The two fools had veered out of the channel toward Diamond Head and were directly seaward of the Kanaka surf. Worse, as he looked, they were starting to come in through the Kanaka surf.

He glanced down quickly to the canoe, and even as he glanced, and as the apparently loafing members quietly arose and took their places by the canoe for the launching, he achieved judgment. Before the canoe could get abreast in the channel, all would be over with the man and woman. And, granted that it could get abreast of them, the moment it ventured into the Kanaka surf it would be swamped, and a sorry chance would the strongest swimmer of them have of rescuing a person pounding to pulp on the bottom under the smashes of the great bearded ones.

The captain saw the first Kanaka wave, large of itself but small among its fellow, lift seaward behind the two speck swimmers. Then he saw them strike a crawl stroke, side by side, faces downward, full lengths outstretched on surface, their feet sculling like propellers and their arms flailing in rapid overhand strokes as they spurted speed to approximate the speed of the overtaking wave, so that, when overtaken, they would become part of the wave and travel with it in-

stead of being left behind it. Thus, if they were coolly skilled
enough to ride outstretched on the surface and the forward
face of the crest instead of being flung and crumpled or
driven headfirst to bottom, they would dash shoreward, not
propelled by their own energy but by the energy of the wave
into which they had become incorporated.

And they did it! "*Some* swimmers," the captain of Number Nine made announcement to himself under his breath.
He continued to gaze eagerly. The best of swimmers could
hold such a wave for several hundred feet. But could they?
If they did, they would be a third of the way through the
perils they had challenged. But, not unexpected by him,
the woman failed first, her body not presenting the larger
surfaces that her husband's did. At the end of seventy feet
she was overwhelmed, being driven downward and out of
sight by the tons of water in the overtopple. Her husband
followed, and both appeared swimming beyond the wave
they had lost.

The captain saw the next wave first. "If they try to body-
surf on that, *good* night," he muttered; for he knew the
swimmer did not live who would tackle it. Beardless itself, it
was father of all bearded ones, a mile long, rising up far out
beyond where the others rose, towering its solid bulk higher
and higher till it blotted out the horizon and was a giant
among its fellows ere its beard began to grow as it thinned its
crest to the overcurl.

But it was evident that the man and woman knew big
water. No racing stroke did they make in advance of the
wave. The captain inwardly applauded as he saw them turn
and face the wave and wait for it. It was a picture that of all
on the beach he alone saw, wonderfully distinct and vivid in
the magnification of the binoculars. The wall of the wave
was truly a wall, mounting, ever mounting, and thinning,

far up, to a transparency of the colors of the setting sun shooting athwart all the green and blue of it. The green thinned to lighter green that merged blue even as he looked. But it was a blue gem brilliant with innumerable sparkle points of rose and gold flashed through it by the sun. On and up, to the sprouting beard of growing crest, the color orgy increased until it was a kaleidoscopic effervescence of transfusing rainbows.

Against the face of the wave showed the heads of the man and woman like two sheer specks. Specks they were, of the quick, adventuring among the blind elemental forces, daring the Titanic buffets of the sea. The weight of the downfall of that father of waves, even then imminent above their heads, could stun a man or break the fragile bones of a woman. The captain of Number Nine was unconscious that he was holding his breath. He was oblivious of the man. It was the woman. Did she lose her head or courage, or misplay her muscular part for a moment, she could be hurled a hundred feet by that giant buffet and left wrenched, helpless, and breathless to be pulped on the coral bottom and sucked out by the undertow to be battened on by the fish sharks too cowardly to take their human meat alive.

Why didn't they dive deep, and with plenty of time, the captain wanted to know, instead of waiting till the last tick of safety and the first tick of peril were one? He saw the woman turn her head and laugh to the man, and his head turn in response. Above them, overhanging them, as they mounted the body of the wave, the beard, creaming white, then frothing into rose and gold, tossed upward into a spray of jewels. The crisp offshore trade wind caught the beard's fringes and blew them backward and upward yards and yards into the air. It was then, side by side, and six feet apart, that they dived straight under the overcurl even then disintegrating to chaos and falling. Like insects disappearing into the convolutions of some gorgeous, gigantic orchid, so they disappeared, as beard and crest and spray and jewels, in many tons, crashed and thundered down just where they had disappeared the moment before but where they were no longer.

Beyond the wave they had gone through they finally showed, side by side, still six feet apart, swimming shoreward with a steady stroke until the next wave should make them body-surf it or face and pierce it. The captain of Number Nine waved his hand to his crew in dismissal and sat down on the lanai railing, feeling vaguely tired, and still watching the swimmers through his glasses.

"Whoever and whatever they are," he murmured, "they aren't malihinis. They simply can't be malihinis."

**11** SOME OF THE most exciting contests never take place in stadiums and never appear in the box scores of sports sections. Here is one example, drawn from Jack London's tramp days as an "easy rider" across the American continent.

Riding by rail, seeking to keep his place as an unpaid passenger, and trying always to outwit the brakemen and detectives who dispute his progress, London invents a game of cross-country survival skills which has all the pace, suspense, and style of conventional sport.

The game is played out at sixty miles per hour along an unending line of track. Testing himself for fitness and fearlessness, a lone player battles man and machine. One slip can mean the sudden end of the contest — and of the contestant himself.

More than an essay in open road autobiography, here is a definition of an entirely new kind of sport and a glimpse at a strange kind of sportsman who is a combination of competitor, spectator, scorekeeper, and survivor. Surely part of the appeal of this dangerous game to London was the way it enabled him to play these various roles and to risk, if he so chose, the ultimate stake.

*"Cross-Country: King of the Road"*
*(originally entitled "Holding Her Down")*
*is reprinted from* The Road.
*Copyright 1907 by The Macmillan Company;*
*renewed 1947 by Charmian K. London.*

# Cross-Country:
# King of the Road

B ARRING ACCIDENTS, a good hobo, with youth and
agility, can hold a train down despite all the efforts of
the train-crew to "ditch" him — given, of course, night-time
as an essential condition. When such a hobo, under such
conditions, makes up his mind that he is going to hold her
down, either he does hold her down, or chance trips him up.
There is no legitimate way, short of murder, whereby the
train-crew can ditch him. That train-crews have not stopped
short of murder is a current belief in the tramp world. Not
having had that particular experience in my tramp days I
cannot vouch for it personally.

But this I have heard of the "bad" roads. When a tramp
has "gone underneath," on the rods, and the train is in
motion, there is apparently no way of dislodging him until
the train stops. The tramp, snugly ensconced inside the
truck, with the four wheels and all the framework around
him, has the "cinch" on the crew — or so he thinks, until
some day he rides the rods on a bad road. A bad road is
usually one on which a short time previously one or several
trainmen have been killed by tramps. Heaven pity the tramp
who is caught "underneath" on such a road — for caught he
is, though the train be going sixty miles an hour.

The "shack" (brakeman) takes a coupling-pin and a
length of bell-cord to the platform in front of the truck in
which the tramp is riding. The shack fastens the coupling-

pin to the bell-cord, drops the former down between the platforms, and pays out the latter. The coupling-pin strikes the ties between the rails, rebounds against the bottom of the car, and again strikes the ties. The shack plays it back and forth, now to this side, now to the other, lets it out a bit and hauls it in a bit, giving his weapon opportunity for every variety of impact and rebound. Every blow of that flying coupling-pin is freighted with death, and at sixty miles an hour it beats a veritable tattoo of death. The next day the remains of that tramp are gathered up along the right of way, and a line in the local paper mentions the unknown man, undoubtedly a tramp, assumably drunk, who had probably fallen asleep on the track.

As a characteristic illustration of how a capable hobo can hold her down, I am minded to give the following experience. I was in Ottawa, bound west over the Canadian Pacific. Three thousand miles of that road stretched before me; it was the fall of the year, and I had to cross Manitoba and the Rocky Mountains. I could expect "crimpy" weather, and every moment of delay increased the frigid hardships of the journey. Furthermore, I was disgusted. The distance between Montreal and Ottawa is one hundred and twenty miles. I ought to know, for I had just come over it and it had taken me six days. By mistake I had missed the main line and come over a small "jerk" with only two locals a day on it. And during these six days I had lived on dry crusts, and not enough of them, begged from the French peasants.

Furthermore, my disgust had been heightened by the one day I had spent in Ottawa trying to get an outfit of clothing for my long journey. Let me put it on record right here that Ottawa, with one exception, is the hardest town in the United States and Canada to beg clothes in; the one exception is Washington, D.C. The latter fair city is the limit. I spent two weeks there trying to beg a pair of shoes, and then had to go on to Jersey City before I got them.

But to return to Ottawa. At eight sharp in the morning I started out after clothes. I worked energetically all day. I swear I walked forty miles. I interviewed the housewives of a thousand homes. I did not even knock off work for dinner. And at six in the afternoon, after ten hours of unremitting and depressing toil, I was still shy one shirt, while the pair of trousers I had managed to acquire was tight and, moreover, was showing all the signs of an early disintegration.

At six I quit work and headed for the railroad yards, expecting to pick up something to eat on the way. But my hard luck was still with me. I was refused food at house after house. Then I got a "hand-out." My spirits soared, for it was the largest hand-out I had ever seen in a long and varied experience. It was a parcel wrapped in newspapers and as big as a mature suit-case. I hurried to a vacant lot and opened it. First, I saw cake, then more cake, all kinds and makes of cake, and then some. It was all cake. No bread and butter with thick firm slices of meat between — nothing but cake; and I who of all things abhorred cake most! In another age and clime they sat down by the waters of Babylon and wept. And in a vacant lot in Canada's proud capital, I, too, sat down and wept . . . over a mountain of cake. As one looks upon the face of his dead son, so looked I upon that multitudinous pastry. I suppose I was an ungrateful tramp, for I refused to partake of the bounteousness of the house that had had a party the night before. Evidently the guests hadn't liked cake either.

That cake marked the crisis in my fortunes. Than it nothing could be worse; therefore things must begin to mend. And they did. At the very next house I was given a "set-down." Now a "set-down" is the height of bliss. One is taken inside, very often is given a chance to wash, and is then "set-down" at a table. Tramps love to throw their legs under a table. The house was large and comfortable, in the midst of spacious grounds and fine trees, and sat well back from the street. They had just finished eating, and I was taken right into the dining room — in itself a most unusual happening, for the tramp who is lucky enough to win a set-down usually receives it in the kitchen. A grizzled and gracious Englishman, his matronly wife, and a beautiful young Frenchwoman talked with me while I ate.

I wonder if that beautiful young Frenchwoman would remember, at this late day, the laugh I gave her when I uttered the barbaric phrase, "two-bits." You see, I was trying to hit them for a "light piece." That was how the sum of money came to be mentioned. "What?" she said. "Two-bits," said I. Her mouth was twitching as she again said, "What?" "Two-bits," said I. Whereat she burst into laughter. "Won't you repeat it?" she said, when she had regained control of herself. "Two-bits," said I. And once more she rippled into uncontrollable silvery laughter. "I beg your pardon," said she; "but what . . . what was it you said?" "Two-bits," said I; "is there anything wrong about it?" "Not that I know of," she gurgled between gasps; "but what does it mean?" I explained, but I do not remember now whether or not I got that two-bits out of her; but I have often wondered since as to which of us was the provincial.

When I arrived at the depot, I found, much to my disgust, a bunch of at least twenty tramps that were waiting to ride out the blind baggages of the overland. Now two or three tramps on the blind baggage are all right. They are inconspicuous. But a score! That meant trouble. No train-crew would ever let all of us ride.

I may as well explain here what a blind baggage is. Some mail-cars are built without doors in the ends; hence, such a car is "blind." The mail-cars that possess end doors, have those doors always locked. Suppose, after the train has started, that a tramp gets on to the platform of one of these blind cars. There is no door, or the door is locked. No conductor or brakeman can get to him to collect fare or throw him off. It is clear that the tramp is safe until the next time the train stops. Then he must get off, run ahead in the darkness, and when the train pulls by, jump on to the blind again. But there are ways and ways, as you shall see.

When the train pulled out, those twenty tramps swarmed upon the three blinds. Some climbed on before the train had run a car-length. They were awkward dubs, and I saw their speedy finish. Of course, the train-crew was "on," and at the first stop the trouble began. I jumped off and ran forward along the track. I noticed that I was accompanied by a number of the tramps. They evidently knew their business. When one is beating an overland, he must always keep well ahead of the train at the stops. I ran ahead, and as I ran, one by one those that accompanied me dropped out. This dropping out was the measure of their skill and nerve in boarding a train.

For this is the way it works. When the train starts, the shack rides out the blind. There is no way for him to get back into the train proper except by jumping off the blind and catching a platform where the car-ends are not "blind." When the train is going as fast as the shack cares to risk, he therefore jumps off the blind, lets several cars go by, and gets on to the train. So it is up to the tramp to run so far ahead that before the blind is opposite him the shack will have already vacated it.

I dropped the last tramp by about fifty feet, and waited. The train started. I saw the lantern of the shack on the first blind. He was riding her out. And I saw the dubs stand forlornly by the track as the blind went by. They made no

attempt to get on. They were beaten by their own ineffi-
ciency at the very start. After them, in the line-up, came the
tramps that knew a little something about the game. They
let the first blind, occupied by the shack, go by, and jumped
on the second and third blinds. Of course, the shack jumped
off the first and on to the second as it went by, and scrambled around there, throwing off the men who had boarded
it. But the point is that I was so far ahead than when the first
blind came opposite me, the shack had already left it and
was tangled up with the tramps on the second blind. A half
dozen of the more skilful tramps, who had run far enough
ahead, made the first blind, too.

At the next stop, as we ran forward along the track, I
counted but fifteen of us. Five had been ditched. The
weeding-out process had begun nobly, and it continued station by station. Now we were fourteen, now twelve, now
eleven, now nine, now eight. It reminded me of the ten little
niggers of the nursery rhyme. I was resolved that I should be
the last little nigger of all. And why not? Was I not blessed
with strength, agility, and youth? (I was eighteen, and in
perfect condition.) And didn't I have my "nerve" with me?
And furthermore, was I not a tramp-royal? Were not these
other tramps mere dubs and "gay-cats" and amateurs alongside of me? If I weren't the last little nigger, I might as well
quit the game and get a job on an alfalfa farm somewhere.

By the time our number had been reduced to four, the
whole train-crew had become interested. From then on it
was a contest of skill and wits, with the odds in favor of the
crew. One by one the three other survivors turned up missing, until I alone remained. My, but I was proud of myself!
No Crœsus was ever prouder of his first million. I was holding her down in spite of two brakemen, a conductor, a fireman, and an engineer.

And here are a few samples of the way I held her down. Out ahead, in the darkness, — so far ahead that the shack riding out the blind must perforce get off before it reaches me, — I get on. Very well. I am good for another station. When that station is reached, I dart ahead again to repeat the manœuvre. The train pulls out. I watch her coming. There is no light of a lantern on the blind. Has the crew abandoned the fight? I do not know. One never knows, and one must be prepared every moment for anything. As the first blind comes opposite me, and I run to leap aboard, I strain my eyes to see if the shack is on the platform. For all I know he may be there, with his lantern doused, and even as I spring upon the steps that lantern may smash down upon my head. I ought to know. I have been hit by lanterns two or three times.

But no, the first blind is empty. The train is gathering speed. I am safe for another station. But am I? I feel the train slacken speed. On the instant I am alert. A manœuvre is being executed against me, and I do not know what it is. I try to watch on both sides at once, not forgetting to keep track of the tender in front of me. From any one, or all, of these three directions, I may be assailed.

Ah, there it comes. The shack has ridden out the engine. My first warning is when his feet strike the steps of the right-hand side of the blind. Like a flash I am off the blind to the left and running ahead past the engine. I lose myself in the darkness. The situation is where it has been ever since the train left Ottawa. I am ahead, and the train must come past me if it is to proceed on its journey. I have as good a chance as ever for boarding her.

I watch carefully. I see a lantern come forward to the engine, and I do not see it go back from the engine. It must therefore be still on the engine, and it is a fair assumption that attached to the handle of that lantern is a shack. That shack was lazy, or else he would have put out his lantern instead of trying to shield it as he came forward. The train pulls out. The first blind is empty, and I gain it. As before the train slackens, the shack from the engine boards the blind from one side, and I go off the other side and run forward.

As I wait in the darkness I am conscious of a big thrill of pride. The overland has stopped twice for me — for me, a poor hobo on the bum. I alone have twice stopped the overland with its many passengers and coaches, its government mail, and its two thousand steam horses straining in the engine. And I weigh only one hundred and sixty pounds, and I haven't a five-cent piece in my pocket!

Again I see the lantern come forward to the engine. But this time it comes conspicuously. A bit too conspicuously to suit me, and I wonder what is up. At any rate I have something else to be afraid of than the shack on the engine. The train pulls by. Just in time, before I make my spring, I see the dark form of a shack, without a lantern, on the first blind. I let it go by, and prepare to board the second blind. But the shack on the first blind has jumped off and is at my heels. Also, I have a fleeting glimpse of the lantern of the shack who rode out the engine. He has jumped off, and now both shacks are on the ground on the same side with me. The next moment the second blind comes by and I am aboard it. But I do not linger. I have figured out my counter-move. As I dash across the platform I hear the impact of the shack's feet across the steps as he boards. I jump off the other side and run forward with the train. My plan is to run forward and get on the first blind. It is nip and tuck, for the train is gathering speed. Also, the shack is behind me and running after me. I guess I am the better sprinter, for I make the first blind. I stand on the steps and watch my pursuer. He is only about ten feet back and running hard; but now the train has approximated his own speed, and, relative to me, he is standing still. I encourage him, hold out my hand to him; but he explodes in a mighty oath, gives up and makes the train several cars back.

The train is speeding along, and I am still chuckling to myself, when, without warning, a spray of water strikes me. The fireman is playing the hose on me from the engine. I step forward from the car-platform to the rear of the tender, where I am sheltered under the overhang. The water flies harmlessly over my head. My fingers itch to climb up on the tender and lam that fireman with a chunk of coal; but I know if I do that, I'll be massacred by him and the engineer, and I refrain.

At the next stop I am off and ahead in the darkness. This time, when the train pulls out, both shacks are on the first blind. I divine their game. They have blocked the repetition of my previous play. I cannot again take the second blind, cross over, and run forward to the first. As soon as the first blind passes and I do not get on, they swing off, and as I do so I know that a moment later, simultaneously, those two shacks will arrive on both sides of me. It is like a trap. Both ways are blocked. Yet there is another way out, and that way is up.

So I do not wait for my pursuers to arrive. I climb upon the upright ironwork of the platform and stand upon the wheel of the hand-brake. This has taken up the moment of grace and I hear the shacks strike the steps on either side. I don't stop to look. I raise my arms overhead until my hands rest against the down-curving ends of the roofs of the two cars. One hand, of course, is on the curved roof of one car, the other hand on the curved roof of the other car. By this time both shacks are coming up the steps. I know it, though I am too busy to see them. All this is happening in the space of only several seconds. I make a spring with my legs and "muscle" myself up with my arms. As I draw up my legs, both shacks reach for me and clutch empty air. I know this, for I look down and see them. Also I hear them swear.

I am now in a precarious position, riding the ends of the down-curving roofs of two cars at the same time. With a quick, tense movement, I transfer both legs to the curve of one roof and both hands to the curve of the other roof. Then, gripping the edge of that curving roof, I climb over the curve to the level roof above, where I sit down to catch my breath, holding on the while to a ventilator that projects above the surface. I am on top of the train — on the "decks," as the tramps call it, and this process I have described is by them called "decking her." And let me say right here that only a young and vigorous tramp is able to deck a passenger train, and also, that the young and vigorous tramp must have his nerve with him as well.

The train goes on gathering speed, and I know I am safe until the next stop — but only until the next stop. If I remain on the roof after the train stops, I know those shacks will fusillade me with rocks. A healthy shack can "dewdrop" a pretty heavy chunk of stone on top of a car — say anywhere from five to twenty pounds. On the other hand, the chances are large that at the next stop the shacks will be waiting for me to descend at the place I climbed up. It is up to me to climb down at some other platform.

Registering a fervent hope that there are no tunnels in the next half mile, I rise to my feet and walk down the train half a dozen cars. And let me say that one must leave timidity behind him on such a *passear*. The roofs of passenger coaches are not made for midnight promenades. And if any one thinks they are, let me advise him to try it. Just let him walk along the roof of a jolting, lurching car, with nothing to hold on to but the black and empty air, and when he comes to the down-curving end of the roof, all wet and slippery with dew, let him accelerate his speed so as to step across to the next roof, down-curving and wet and slippery. Believe me, he will learn whether his heart is weak or his head is giddy.

As the train slows down for a stop, half a dozen platforms from where I had decked her I come down. No one is on the platform. When the train comes to a standstill, I slip off to the ground. Ahead, and between me and the engine, are two moving lanterns. The shacks are looking for me on the roofs of the cars. I note that the car beside which I am standing is a "four-wheeler" — by which is meant that it has only four wheels to each truck. (When you go underneath on the rods, be sure to avoid the "six-wheelers," — they lead to disasters.)

I duck under the train and make for the rods, and I can tell you I am mighty glad that the train is standing still. It is the first time I have ever gone underneath on the Canadian Pacific, and the internal arrangements are new to me. I try to crawl over the top of the truck, between the truck and the bottom of the car. But the space is not large enough for me to squeeze through. This is new to me. Down in the United States I am accustomed to going underneath on rapidly moving trains, seizing a gunnel and swinging my feet under to the brake-beam, and from there crawling over the top of the truck and down inside the truck to a seat on the cross-rod.

Feeling with my hands in the darkness, I learn that there is room between the brake-beam and the ground. It is a tight squeeze. I have to lie flat and worm my way through. Once inside the truck, I take my seat on the rod and wonder what the shacks are thinking has become of me. The train gets under way. They have given me up at last.

But have they? At the very next stop, I see a lantern thrust under the next truck to mine at the other end of the car. They are searching the rods for me. I must make my get-away pretty lively. I crawl on my stomach under the brake-beam. They see me and run for me, but I crawl on hands and knees across the rail on the opposite side and gain my feet. Then away I go for the head of the train. I run past the engine and hide in the sheltering darkness. It is the same old situation. I am ahead of the train, and the train must go past me.

The train pulls out. There is a lantern on the first blind. I lie low, and see the peering shack go by. But there is also a lantern on the second blind. That shack spots me and calls to the shack who has gone on past the first blind. Both jump off. Never mind, I'll take the third blind and deck her. But heavens, there is a lantern on the third blind, too. It is the conductor. I let it go by. At any rate I have now the full train-crew in front of me. I turn and run back in the opposite direction to what the train is going. I look over my shoulder. All three lanterns are on the ground and wobbling along in pursuit. I sprint. Half the train has gone by, and it is going fast, when I spring aboard. I know that the two shacks and the conductor will arrive like ravening wolves in about two seconds. I spring upon the wheel of the hand-brake, get my hands on the curved ends of the roofs, and muscle myself up to the decks; while my disappointed pursuers, clustering on the platform beneath like dogs that have treed a fox, howl curses up at me and say unsocial things about my ancestors.

But what does it matter? It is five to one, including the engineer and fireman, and the majesty of the law and the might of a great corporation are behind them, and I am beating them out. I am too far down the train, and I run ahead over the roofs of the coaches until I am over the fifth or sixth platform from the engine. I peer down cautiously. A shack is on that platform. That he has caught sight of me, I know from the way he makes a swift sneak inside the car; and I know, also, that he is waiting inside the door, all ready to pounce out on me when I climb down. But I make believe that I don't know, and I remain there to encourage him in his error. I do not see, yet I know that he opens the door once and peeps up to assure himself that I am still there.

The train slows down for a station. I dangle my legs down in a tentative way. The train stops. My legs are still dangling. I hear the door unlatch softly. He is all ready for me. Suddenly I spring up and run forward over the roof. This is right over his head, where he lurks inside the door. The train is standing still; the night is quiet, and I take care to make plenty of noise on the metal roof with my feet. I don't know, but my assumption is that he is now running forward to catch me as I descend at the next platform. But I don't descend there. Halfway along the roof of the coach, I turn, retrace my way softly, and quickly to the platform both the shack and I have just abandoned. The coast is clear. I descend to the ground on the off-side of the train and hide in the darkness. Not a soul has seen me.

I go over to the fence, at the edge of the right of way, and watch. Ah, ha! What's that? I see a lantern on top of the train, moving along from front to rear. They think I haven't come down, and they are searching the roofs for me. And better than that — on the ground on each side of the train, moving abreast with the lantern on top, are two other lanterns. It is a rabbit-drive, and I am the rabbit. When the shack on top flushes me, the ones on each side will nab me. I roll a cigarette and watch the procession go by. Once past me, I am safe to proceed to the front of the train. She pulls out, and I make the front blind without opposition. But before she is fully under way and just as I am lighting my cigarette, I am aware that the fireman has climbed over the coal to the back of the tender and is looking down at me. I am filled with apprehension. From his position he can mash me to a jelly with lumps of coal. Instead of which he addresses me, and I note with relief the admiration in his voice.

"You son-of-a-gun," is what he says.

It is a high compliment, and I thrill as a schoolboy thrills on receiving a reward of merit.

"Say," I call up to him, "don't you play the hose on me any more."

"All right," he answers, and goes back to his work.

I have made friends with the engine, but the shacks are still looking for me. At the next stop, the shacks ride out all three blinds, and as before, I let them go by and deck in the middle of the train. The crew is on its mettle by now, and the train stops. The shacks are going to ditch me or know the reason why. Three times the mighty overland stops for me at that station, and each time I elude the shacks and make the decks. But it is hopeless, for they have finally come to an understanding of the situation. I have taught them that they cannot guard the train from me. They must do something else.

And they do it. When the train stops that last time, they take after me hot-footed. Ah, I see their game. They are trying to run me down. At first they herd me back toward the rear of the train. I know my peril. Once to the rear of the train, it will pull out with me left behind. I double, and twist, and turn, dodge through my pursuers, and gain the front of the train. One shack still hangs on after me. All right, I'll give him the run of his life, for my wind is good. I run straight ahead along the track. It doesn't matter. If he chases me ten miles, he'll nevertheless have to catch the train, and I can board her at any speed that he can.

So I run on, keeping just comfortably ahead of him and straining my eyes in the gloom for cattle-guards and switches that may bring me to grief. Alas! I strain my eyes too far ahead, and trip over something just under my feet, I know not what, some little thing, and go down to earth in a long, stumbling fall. The next moment I am on my feet, but the shack has me by the collar. I do not struggle. I am busy with breathing deeply and with sizing him up. He is narrow-shouldered, and I have at least thirty pounds the better of him in weight. Besides, he is just as tired as I am, and if he tries to slug me, I'll teach him a few things.

But he doesn't try to slug me, and that problem is settled. Instead, he starts to lead me back toward the train, and another possible problem arises. I see the lanterns of the conductor and the other shack. We are approaching them. Not for nothing have I made the acquaintance of the New York police. Not for nothing, in box-cars, by water-tanks, and in prison-cells, have I listened to bloody tales of man-handling. What if these three men are about to man-handle me? Heaven knows I have given them provocation enough. I think quickly. We are drawing nearer and nearer to the other two trainmen. I line up the stomach and the jaw of my captor, and plan the right and left I'll give him at the first sign of trouble.

Pshaw! I know another trick I'd like to work on him, and I almost regret that I did not do it at the moment I was captured. I could make him sick, what of his clutch on my collar. His fingers, tight-gripping, are buried inside my collar. My coat is tightly buttoned. Did you ever see a tourni-quet? Well, this is one. All I have to do is to duck my head under his arm and begin to twist. I must twist rapidly — very rapidly. I know how to do it; twisting in a violent, jerky way, ducking my head under his arm with each revolution. Before he knows it, those detaining fingers of his will be detained. He will be unable to withdraw them. It is a powerful leverage. Twenty seconds after I have started revolving, the blood will be bursting out of his finger-ends, the delicate tendons will be rupturing, and all the muscles and nerves will be mashing and crushing together in a shrieking mass. Try it sometime when somebody has you by the collar. But be quick — quick as lightning. Also, be sure to hug yourself while you are revolving — hug your face with your left arm and your abdomen with your right. You see, the other fellow might try to stop you with a punch from his free arm. It would be a good idea, too, to revolve away from that free arm rather than toward it. A punch going is never so bad as a punch coming.

That shack will never know how near he was to being made very, very sick. All that saves him is that it is not in their plan to man-handle me. When we draw near enough, he calls out that he has me, and they signal the train to come on. The engine passes us, and the three blinds. After that, the conductor and the other shack swing aboard. But still my captor holds on to me. I see the plan. He is going to hold me until the rear of the train goes by. Then he will hop on, and I shall be left behind — ditched.

But the train has pulled out fast, the engineer trying to make up for lost time. Also, it is a long train. It is going very lively, and I know the shack is measuring its speed with apprehension.

"Think you can make it?" I query innocently.

He releases my collar, makes a quick run, and swings aboard. A number of coaches are yet to pass by. He knows it, and remains on the steps, his head poked out and watching me. In that moment my next move comes to me. I'll make the last platform. I know she's going fast and faster, but I'll only get a roll in the dirt if I fail, and the optimism of youth is mine. I do not give myself away. I stand with a dejected droop of shoulder, advertising that I have abandoned hope. But at the same time I am feeling with my feet the good gravel. It is perfect footing. Also I am watching the poked-out head of the shack. I see it withdrawn. He is confident that the train is going too fast for me ever to make it.

And the train *is* going fast — faster than any train I have ever tackled. As the last coach comes by I sprint in the same direction with it. It is a swift, short sprint. I cannot hope to equal the speed of the train, but I can reduce the difference of our speed to the minimum, and, hence, reduce the shock of impact, when I leap on board. In the fleeting instant of darkness I do not see the iron hand-rail of the last platform; nor is there time for me to locate it. I reach for where I think it ought to be, and at the same instant my feet leave the ground. It is all in the toss. The next moment I may be rolling in the gravel with broken ribs, or arms, or head. But my fingers grip the hand-hold, there is a jerk on my arms that slightly pivots my body, and my feet land on the steps with sharp violence.

I sit down, feeling very proud of myself. In all my hoboing it is the best bit of train-jumping I have done. I know that late at night one is always good for several stations on the last platform, but I do not care to trust myself at the rear of the train. At the first stop I run forward on the off-side of the train, pass the Pullmans, and duck under and take a rod under a day-coach. At the next stop I run forward again and take another rod.

I am now comparatively safe. The shacks think I am ditched. But the long day and the strenuous night are beginning to tell on me. Also, it is not so windy nor cold underneath, and I begin to doze. This will never do. Sleep on the rods spells death, so I crawl out at a station and go forward to the second blind. Here I can lie down and sleep; and here I do sleep — how long I do not know — for I am awakened by a lantern thrust into my face. The two shacks are staring at me. I scramble up on the defensive, wondering as to which one is going to make the first "pass" at me. But slugging is far from their minds.

"I thought you was ditched," says the shack who had held me by the collar.

"If you hadn't let go of me when you did, you'd have been ditched along with me," I answer.

"How's that?" he asks.

"I'd have gone into a clinch with you, that's all," is my reply.

They hold a consultation, and their verdict is summed up in: —

"Well, I guess you can ride, Bo. There's no use trying to keep you off."

And they go away and leave me in peace to the end of their division.

I have given the foregoing as a sample of what "holding her down" means. Of course, I have selected a fortunate night out of my experiences, and said nothing of the nights — and many of them — when I was tripped up by accident and ditched.

In conclusion, I want to tell of what happened when I reached the end of the division. On single-track, transcontinental lines, the freight trains wait at the divisions and follow out after the passenger trains. When the division was reached, I left my train, and looked for the freight that would pull out behind it. I found the freight, made up on a side-track and waiting. I climbed into a box-car half full of coal and lay down. In no time I was asleep.

I was awakened by the sliding open of the door. Day was just dawning, cold and gray, and the freight had not yet started. A "con" (conductor) was poking his head inside the door.

"Get out of that, you blankety-blank-blank!" he roared at me.

I got, and outside I watched him go down the line inspecting every car in the train. When he got out of sight I thought to myself that he would never think I'd have the nerve to climb back into the very car out of which he had fired me. So back I climbed and lay down again.

Now that con's mental processes must have been paralleling mine, for he reasoned that it was the very thing I would do. For back he came and fired me out.

Now, surely, I reasoned, he will never dream that I'd do it a third time. Back I went, into the very same car. But I decided to make sure. Only one side-door could be opened. The other side-door was nailed up. Beginning at the top of the coal, I dug a hole alongside of that door and lay down in it. I heard the other door open. The con climbed up and looked in over the top of the coal. He couldn't see me. He called to me to get out. I tried to fool him by remaining quiet. But when he began tossing chunks of coal into the hole on top of me, I gave up and for the third time was fired out. Also, he informed me in warm terms of what would happen to me if he caught me in there again.

I changed my tactics. When a man is paralleling your mental processes, ditch him. Abruptly break off your line of reasoning, and go off on a new line. This I did. I hid between some cars on an adjacent side-track, and watched. Sure enough, that con came back again to the car. He opened the door, he climbed up, he called, he threw coal into the hole I had made. He even crawled over the coal and looked into the hole. That satisfied him. Five minutes later the freight was pulling out, and he was not in sight. I ran alongside the car, pulled the door open, and climbed in. He never looked for me again, and I rode that coal-car precisely one thousand and twenty-two miles, sleeping most of the time and getting out at divisions (where the freights always stop for an hour or so) to beg my food. And at the end of the thousand and twenty-two miles I lost that car through a happy incident. I got a "set-down," and the tramp doesn't live who won't miss a train for a set-down any time.

# 12

IT IS A fair certainty that the man who broke the bank at Monte Carlo never risked a red chip at the roulette table of the Elkhorn Saloon. But it was there that an enterprising amateur gambler named Smoke Bellew once devised a winning system so foolproof that every saloon owner in Dawson had to buy him off to learn his secret. The main character in the following tale is not the bank-breaking, odds-defying Mr. Bellew, however, but his partner, confidant, and alter ego, Jack Short.

Caught up in the grip of Smoke's tall winning streak, "Shorty" passes from initial skepticism to giddy incredulity in less time than it takes the wheel of the Elkhorn to complete one revolution. Even after Smoke's surprising explanation at the end of the story, the astonished Mr. Short shows no sign of desiring to be awakened from his fantastic dream of easy and sudden riches.

It was just such a dream to which many similar Klondike fortune-seekers were drawn, and from which many were rudely awakened by the hardship and privation of the Alaskan trail. Even the impossible odds of the roulette table were better than the odds of finding gold, especially when, as in "Shorty Dreams," the player knew how to make the game play for him.

# Shorty Dreams

"F"UNNY YOU DON'T gamble none," Shorty said to Smoke one night in the Elkhorn. "Ain't it in your blood?"

"It is," Smoke answered. "But the statistics are in my head. I like an even break for my money."

All about them, in the huge barroom, arose the click and rattle and rumble of a dozen games, at which fur-clad, moccasined men tried their luck. Smoke waved his hand to include them all.

"Look at them," he said. "It's cold mathematics that they will lose more than they win to-night, that the big proportion are losing right now."

"You're sure strong on figgers," Shorty murmured admiringly. "An' in the main you're right. But they's such a thing as facts. An' one fact is streaks of luck. They's times when every geezer playin' wins, as I know, for I've sat in such games an' saw more'n one bank busted. The only way to win at gamblin' is, wait for a hunch that you've got a lucky streak comin' and then play it to the roof."

"It sounds simple," Smoke criticised, "so simple I can't see how men lose."

"The trouble is," Shorty admitted, "that most men gets fooled on their hunches. On occasion I sure get fooled on mine. The thing is to try an' find out."

Smoke shook his head. "That's a statistic, too, Shorty. Most men prove wrong on their hunches."

"But don't you ever get one of them streaky feelin's that all you got to do is put your money down an' pick a winner?"

Smoke laughed. "I'm too scared of the percentage against me. But I'll tell you what, Shorty, I'll throw a dollar on the 'high card' right now, and see if it will buy us a drink." Smoke was edging his way in to the faro-table when Shorty caught his arm.

"Hold on! I'm getting one of them hunches now. You put that dollar on roulette."

They went over to the roulette-table near the bar.

"Wait till I give the word," Shorty counseled.

"What number?" Smoke asked.

"Pick it yourself. But wait till I say let her go."

"You don't mean to say I've got an even chance on that table?" Smoke argued.

"As good as the next geezer's."

"But not as good as the bank's."

"Wait an' see," Shorty urged. "Now! Let her go!"

The game-keeper had just sent the little ivory ball whirling around the smooth rim above the revolving, many-slotted wheel. Smoke, at the lower end of the table, reached over a player, and blindly tossed the dollar. It slid along the smooth, green cloth and stopped fairly in the center of "34."

The ball came to a rest, and the game-keeper announced, "Thirty-four wins!" He swept the table, and alongside of Smoke's dollar stacked thirty-five dollars. Smoke drew the money in, and Shorty slapped him on the shoulder.

"Now that was the real goods of a hunch, Smoke! How'd I know it? There's no tellin'. I just knew you'd win. Why, if that dollar of yourn'd fell on any other number it'd won just the same. When the hunch is right, you just can't help winnin'."

"Suppose it had come double naught?" Smoke queried, as they made their way to the bar.

"Then your dollar'd been on double naught," was Shorty's answer. "They's no gettin' away from it. A hunch is a hunch. Here's how. Come on back to the table. I got a hunch, after pickin' you for a winner, that I can pick some few numbers myself."

"Are you playing a system?" Smoke asked, at the end of ten minutes, when his partner had dropped a hundred dollars.

Shorty shook his head indignantly, as he spread his chips out in the vicinities of "3," "11," and "17," and tossed a spare chip on the green. "Hell is sure cluttered with geezers that played systems," he exposited, as the keeper raked the table.

From idly watching, Smoke became fascinated, following closely every detail of the game from the whirling of the ball to the making and the paying of bets. He made no plays, however, merely contenting himself with looking on. Yet so interested was he that Shorty, announcing that he had had enough, with difficulty drew Smoke away from the table.

The game-keeper returned Shorty the gold-sack he had deposited as a credential for playing, and with it went a slip of paper on which was scribbled, "Out — $350.00." Shorty carried the sack and the paper across the room and handed them to the weigher, who sat behind a large pair of gold-scales. Out of Shorty's sack he weighed three hundred and fifty dollars, which he poured into the coffer of the house.

"That hunch of yours was another one of those statistics," Shorty jeered.

"I had to play it, didn't I, in order to find out?" Shorty retorted. "I reckon I was crowdin' some just on account of tryin' to convince you they's such a thing as hunches."

"Never mind, Shorty," Smoke laughed. "I've got a hunch right now —"

Shorty's eyes sparkled as he cried eagerly: "What is it? Kick in and play it pronto."

"It's not that kind, Shorty. Now what I've got is a hunch that some day I'll work out a system that will beat the spots off that table."

"System!" Shorty groaned, then surveyed his partner with a vast ptiy. "Smoke, listen to your sidekicker an' leave system alone. Systems is sure losers. They ain't no hunches in systems."

"That's why I like them," Smoke answered. "A system is statistical. When you get the right system you can't lose and that's the difference between it and a hunch. You never know when the right hunch is going wrong."

"But I know a lot of systems that went wrong, an' I never seen a system win." Shorty paused and sighed. "Look here, Smoke, if you're gettin' cracked on systems this ain't no place for you, an' it's about time we hit the trail again."

During the several following weeks, the two partners played at cross-purposes. Smoke was bent on spending his time watching the roulette game in the Elkhorn, while Shorty was equally bent on traveling trail. At last Smoke put his foot down when a stampede was proposed for two hundred miles down the Yukon.

"Look here, Shorty," he said, "I'm not going. That trip will take ten days, and before that time I hope to have my system in proper working order. I could almost win with it now. What are you dragging me around the country this way for, anyway?"

"Smoke, I got to take care of you," was Shorty's reply. "You're getting nutty. I'd drag you stampedin' to Jericho or the north pole if I could keep you away from that table."

"It's all right, Shorty. But just remember I've reached full man-grown, meat-eating size. The only dragging you'll do will be dragging home the dust I'm going to win with that system of mine, and you'll most likely have to do it with a dog-team."

Shorty's response was a groan.

"And I don't want you to be bucking any games on your own," Smoke went on. "We're going to divide the winnings, and I'll need all our money to get started. That system's young yet, and it's liable to trip me for a few falls before I get it lined up."

At last, after long hours and days spent at watching the table, the night came when Smoke proclaimed that he was ready, and Shorty, glum and pessimistic, with all the seeming of one attending a funeral, accompanied his partner to the Elkhorn. Smoke bought a stack of chips and stationed himself at the game-keeper's end of the table. Again and again the ball was whirled, and the other players won or lost, but Smoke did not venture a chip. Shorty waxed impatient.

"Buck in, buck in," he urged. "Let's get this funeral over. What's the matter? Got cold feet?"

Smoke shook his head and waited. A dozen plays went by, and then, suddenly, he placed ten one-dollar chips on "26." The number won, and the keeper paid Smoke three hundred and fifty dollars. A dozen plays went by, twenty plays, and thirty, when Smoke placed ten dollars on "32." Again he received three hundred and fifty dollars.

"It's a hunch!" Shorty whispered vociferously in his ear. "Ride it! Ride it!"

Half an hour went by, during which Smoke was inactive, then he placed ten dollars on "34" and won.

"A hunch!" Shorty whispered.

"Nothing of the sort," Smoke whispered back. "It's the system. Isn't she a dandy?"

"You can't tell me," Shorty contended. "Hunches comes in mighty funny ways. You might think it's a system, but it ain't. Systems is impossible. They can't happen. It's a sure hunch you're playin'."

Smoke now altered his play. He bet more frequently, with single chips, scattered here and there, and he lost more often than he won.

"Quit it," Shorty advised. "Cash in. You've rung the bulls-eye three times, an' you're ahead a thousand. You can't keep it up."

At this moment the ball started whirling, and Smoke dropped ten chips on "26." The ball fell into the slot of "26," and the keeper again paid him three hundred and fifty dollars.

"If you're plumb crazy an' got the immortal cinch, bet 'em the limit," Shorty said. "Put down twenty-five next time."

A quarter of an hour passed, during which Smoke won and lost on small scattering bets. Then, with the abruptness that characterized his big betting, he placed twenty-five dollars on "00," and the keeper paid him eight hundred and seventy-five dollars.

"Wake me up, Smoke, I'm dreamin'," Shorty moaned.

Smoke smiled, consulted his notebook, and became absorbed in calculation. He continually drew the notebook from his pocket, and from time to time jotted down figures.

A crowd had packed densely around the table, while the players themselves were attempting to cover the same numbers he covered. It was then that a change came over his play. Ten times in succession he placed ten dollars on "18" and lost. At this stage he was deserted by the hardiest. He changed his number and won another three hundred and fifty dollars. Immediately the players were back with him, deserting again after a series of losing bets.

"Quit it, Smoke, quit it," Shorty advised. "The longest string of hunches is only so long, an' your string's finished. No more bull's-eyes for you."

"I'm going to ring her once again before I cash in," Smoke answered.

For a few minutes, with varying luck, he played scattering chips over the table, and then dropped twenty-five dollars on "00."

"I'll take my slip now," he said to the dealer, as he won.

"Oh, you don't need to show it to me," Shorty said, as they walked to the weigher. "I been keepin' track. You're something like thirty-six hundred to the good. How near am I?"

"Thirty-six sixty," Smoke replied. "And now you've got to pack the dust home. That was the agreement."

"Don't crowd your luck," Shorty pleaded with Smoke, the next night, in the cabin, as he evidenced preparations to return to the Elkhorn. "You played a mighty long string of hunches, but you played it out. If you go back you'll sure drop all your winnings."

"But I tell you it isn't hunches, Shorty. It's statistics. It's a system. It can't lose."

"System the devil. They ain't no such a thing as system. I made seventeen straight passes at a crap-table once. Was it system? Nope. It was fool luck, only I had cold feet an' didn't dast let it ride. If it'd rid, instead of me drawin' down after the third pass I'd 'a' won over thirty thousan' on the original two-bit piece."

"Just the same, Shorty, this is a real system."

"Huh! You got to show me."

"I did show you. Come on with me now, and I'll show you again."

When they entered the Elkhorn all eyes centered on Smoke, and those about the table made way for him as he took up his old place at the keeper's end. His play was quite unlike that of the previous night. In the course of an hour and a half he made only four bets, but each bet was for twenty-five hundred dollars, and Shorty carried the dust home to the cabin.

"Now's the time to jump the game," Shorty advised, as he sat on the edge of his bunk and shook off his moccasins. "You're seven thousan' ahead. A man's a fool that'd crowd his luck harder."

"Shorty, a man would be a blithering lunatic if he didn't keep on backing a winning system like mine."

"Smoke, you're a sure bright boy. You're college-learnt. You know more'n a minute than I could know in forty thousan' years. But just the same you're dead wrong when you call your luck a system. I've been around some, an' seen a few, an' I tell you straight an' confidential an' all-assurin', a system to beat a bankin' game ain't possible."

"But I'm showing you this one. It's a pipe."

"No, you're not, Smoke. It's a pipe-dream. I'm asleep. Bimeby I'll wake up, an' build the fire, an' start breakfast."

"Well, my unbelieving friend, there's the dust. Heft it."

So saying, Smoke tossed the bulging gold-sack upon his partner's knees. It weighed thirty-five pounds, and Shorty was fully aware of the crush of its impact on his flesh.

"It's real," Smoke hammered his point home.

"Huh! I've saw some mighty real dreams in my time. In a dream all things is possible. In real life a system ain't possible. Now I ain't never been to college, but I'm plumb justified in sizin' up this gamblin' orgy of ourn as a sure-enough dream."

"Hamilton's 'Law of Parsimony,' " Smoke laughed.

"I ain't never heard of the geezer, but his dope's sure right. I'm dreamin', Smoke, an' you're just snoopin' around in my dream an' tormentin' me with system. If you love me, if you sure do love me, you'll just yell: 'Shorty! Wake up!' An' I'll wake up an' start breakfast."

The third night of play, as Smoke laid his first bet, the game-keeper shoved fifteen dollars back to him.

"Ten's all you can play," he said. "The limit's come down."

"Gettin' picayune," Shorty sneered.

"No one has to play at this table that don't want to," the keeper retorted. "And I'm willing to say straight out in meeting that we'd sooner your pardner didn't play at our table."

"Scared of his system, eh?" Shorty challenged, as the keeper paid over three hundred and fifty dollars.

"I ain't saying I believe in system, because I don't. There never was a system that'd beat roulette or any percentage game. But just the same I've seen some queer strings of luck, and I ain't going to let this bank go bust if I can help it."

"Cold feet."

"Gambling is just as much business, my friend, as any other business. We ain't philanthropists."

Night by night, Smoke continued to win. His method of play varied. Expert after expert, in the jam about the table, scribbled down his bets and numbers in vain attempts to work out his system. They complained of their inability to get a clue to start with, and swore that it was pure luck, though the most colossal streak of it they had ever seen.

It was Smoke's varied play that obfuscated them. Sometimes, consulting his notebook or engaging in long calculations, an hour elapsed without his staking a chip. At other times he would win three limit-bets and clean up a thousand dollars and odd, in five or ten minutes. At still other times, his tactics would be to scatter single chips prodigally and amazingly over the table. This would continue for from ten to thirty minutes of play, when, abruptly, as the ball whirled through the last few of its circles, he would play the limit on column, color, and number, and win all three. Once, to complete confusion in the minds of those that strove to divine his secret, he lost forty straight bets, each at the limit. But each night, play no matter how diversely, Shorty carried home thirty-five hundred dollars for him.

"It ain't no system," Shorty expounded at one of their bed-going discussions. "I follow you, an' follow you, but they ain't no figgerin' out. You never play twice the same. All you do is pick winners when you want to, an' when you don't want to you just on purpose don't."

"Maybe you're nearer right than you think, Shorty. I've just got to pick losers sometimes. It's part of the system."

"System the devil! I've talked with every gambler in town, an' the last one is agreed they ain't no such thing as system."

"Yet I'm showing them one all the time."

"Look here, Smoke." Shorty paused over the candle, in the act of blowing it out. "I'm real irritated. Maybe you think this is a candle. It ain't. No, sir! An' this ain't me neither. I'm out on trail somewheres, in my blankets, lyin' flat on my back with my mouth open, an' dreamin' all this. And that ain't you talkin', any more than this candle is a candle."

"It's funny how I happen to be dreaming along with you then," Smoke persisted.

"No, it ain't. You're part of my dream, that's all. I've heard many a man talk in my dreams. I want to tell you one thing, Smoke, I'm gettin' mangy an' mad. If this here dream keeps up much more I'm goin' to bite my veins and howl."

On the sixth night of play at the Elkhorn, the limit was reduced to five dollars.

"It's all right," Smoke assured the game-keeper. "I want thirty-five hundred to-night, as usual, and you only compel me to play longer. I've got to pick twice as many winners, that's all."

"Why don't you buck somebody else's table?" the keeper demanded wrathfully.

"Because I like this one." Smoke glanced over at the roaring stove only a few feet away. "Besides, there are no drafts here, and it is warm and comfortable."

On the ninth night, when Shorty had carried the dust home, he had a fit. "I quit, Smoke, I quit," he began. "I know when I got enough. I ain't dreamin'. I'm wide awake. A system can't be, but you got one just the same. There's nothing in the rule o' three. The almanac's clean out. The world's gone smash. There's nothin' regular an' uniform no more. The multiplication table's gone loco. Two is eight, nine is eleven, and two-times-two is eight hundred an' forty-six — an' — an' a half. Anything is everything, an' nothing's all, an' twice all is cold-cream, milk-shakes, an' calico horses. You've got a system. Figgers beat the figgerin'. What ain't is, an' what isn't has to be. The sun rises in the west, the moon's a pay-streak, the stars is canned corn-beef, scurvy's the blessin' of God, him that dies kicks again, rocks floats, water's gas, I ain't me, you're somebody else, an' mebbe we're twins if we ain't hashed-brown potatoes fried in verdigris. Wake me up, somebody! Oh, wake me up!"

The next morning a visitor came to the cabin. Smoke

knew him, Harvey Moran, the owner of all the games in the Tivoli. There was a note of appeal in his deep gruff voice as he plunged into his business.

"It's like this, Smoke," he began. "You've got us all guessing. I'm representing nine other game-owners and myself from all the saloons in town. We don't understand. We know that no system ever worked against roulette. All the mathematic sharps in the colleges have told us gamblers the same thing. They say that roulette itself is the system, the one and only system, and therefore that no system can beat it, for that would mean arithmetic has gone bug-house." Shorty nodded his head violently.

"If a system can beat a system, then there's no such thing as system," the gambler went on. "In such a case anything could be possible—a thing could be in two different places at once, or two things could be in the same place that's only large enough for one at the same time."

"Well, you've seen me play," Smoke answered defiantly; "and if you think it's only a string of luck on my part, why worry?"

"That's the trouble. We can't help worrying. It's a system you've got, and all the time we know it can't be. I've watched you five nights now, and all I can make out is that you favor certain numbers and keep winning. Now the ten of us game-owners have got together, and we want to make a friendly proposition. We'll put a roulette-table in a back room of the Elkhorn, pool the bank against you, and have you buck us. It will be all quiet and private. Just you and Shorty and us. What do you say?"

"I think it's the other way around," Smoke answered. "It's up to you to come and see me. I'll be playing in the barroom of the Elkhorn to-night. You can watch me there just as well."

That night, when Smoke took up his customary place at the table, the keeper shut down the game. "The game's closed," he said. "Boss's orders."

But the assembled game-owners were not to be balked. In a few minutes they arranged a pool, each putting in a thousand, and took over the table.

"Come on and buck us," Harvey Moran challenged, as the keeper sent the ball on its first whirl around.

"Give me the twenty-five limit?" Smoke suggested.

"Sure; go to it."

Smoke immediately placed twenty-five chips on "00" and won.

Moran wiped the sweat from his forehead. "Go on," he said. "We got ten thousand in this bank."

At the end of an hour and a half, the ten thousand was Smoke's.

"The bank's bust," the keeper announced.

"Got enough?" Smoke asked.

The game-owners looked at one another. They were awed. They, the fatted protégés of the laws of chance, were undone. They were up against the one who had more intimate access to those laws, or who had invoked higher and undreamed laws.

"We quit," Moran said. "Ain't that right, Burke?"

Big Burke, who owned the games in the M. and G. Saloon, nodded. "The impossible has happened," he said. "This Smoke here has got a system all right. If we let him go on we'll all bust. All I can see, if we're goin' to keep our tables running, is to cut down the limit to a dollar, or to ten cents, or a cent. He won't win much in a night with such stakes."

All looked at Smoke.

He shrugged his shoulders. "In that case, gentlemen, I'll

have to hire a gang of men to play at all your tables. I can pay them ten dollars for a four-hour shift and make money."

"Then we'll shut down our tables," Big Burke replied. "Unless—" He hesitated and ran his eye over his fellows to see that they were with him. "Unless you're willing to talk business. What will you sell the system for?"

"Thirty thousand dollars," Smoke answered. "That's a tax of three thousand apiece."

They debated and nodded. "And you'll tell us your system?"

"Surely."

"And you'll promise not to play roulette in Dawson ever again?"

"No, sir," Smoke said positively. "I'll promise not to play this system again."

"My God!" Moran exploded. "You haven't got other systems, have you?"

"Hold on!" Shorty cried. "I want to talk to my pardner. Come over here, Smoke, on the side."

Smoke followed into a quiet corner of the room, while hundreds of curious eyes centered on him and Shorty.

"Look here, Smoke," Shorty whispered hoarsely. "Mebbe it ain't a dream. In which case you're sellin' out almighty cheap. You're sure got the world by the slack of its pants. They's millions in it. Shake it! Shake it hard!"

"But if it's a dream?" Smoke queried softly.

"Then, for the sake of the dream an' the love of Mike, stick them gamblers up good an' plenty. What's the good of dreamin' if you can't dream to the real right, dead sure, eternal finish?"

"Fortunately, this isn't a dream, Shorty."

"Then if you sell out for thirty thousan', I'll never forgive you."

"When I sell out for thirty thousand, you'll fall on my neck an' wake up to find out that you haven't been dreaming at all. This is no dream, Shorty. In about two minutes you'll see you have been wide awake all the time. Let me tell you that when I sell out it's because I've got to sell out."

Back at the table, Smoke informed the game-owners that his offer still held. They proffered him their paper to the extent of three thousand each.

"Hold out for the dust," Shorty cautioned.

"I was about to intimate that I'd take the money weighed out," Smoke said.

The owner of the Elkhorn cashed their paper, and Shorty took possession of the gold-dust.

"Now I don't want to wake up," he chortled, as he hefted the various sacks. "Toted up, it's a seventy-thousan' dream. It'd be too blamed expensive to open my eyes, roll out the blanket, an' start breakfast."

"What's your system?" Big Burke demanded. "We've paid for it, and we want it."

Smoke led the way to the table. "Now, gentlemen, bear with me a moment. This isn't an ordinary system. It can scarcely be called legitimate, but its only great virtue is that it works. I've got my suspicions, but I'm not saying anything. You watch. Mr. Keeper, be ready with the ball. Wait. I am going to pick '26.' Consider I've bet on it. Be ready, Mr. Keeper. Now!"

The ball whirled around.

"You observe," Smoke went on, "that '9' was directly opposite."

The ball finished in "26."

Big Burke swore deep in is chest, and all waited.

"For '00' to win, '11' must be opposite. Try it yourself and see."

"But the system?" Moran demanded impatiently. "We know you can pick winning numbers, and we know what those numbers are, but how do you do it?"

"By observed sequences. By accident I chanced twice to notice the ball whirled when '9' was opposite. Both times '26' won. After that I saw it happen again. Then I looked for other sequences, and found them. 'Double naught' opposite fetches '32,' and '11' fetches '00." It doesn't always happen, but it *usually* happens. You notice, I say 'usually.' As I said before, I have my suspicions, but I'm not saying anything."

Big Burke, with a sudden flash of comprehension, reached over, stopped the wheel, and examined it carefully. The heads of the nine other game-owners bent over and joined in the examination. Then Big Burke straightened up and cast a glance at the near-by stove.

"Hell," he said. "It wasn't any system at all. The table stood close to the fire, and the blamed wheel's warped. And we've been worked to a frazzle. No wonder he liked this table. He couldn't have bucked for sour apples at any other table."

Harvey Moran gave a great sigh of relief and wiped his forehead. "Well, anyway," he said, "it's cheap at the price just to find out that it wasn't a system." His face began to work, and then he broke into laughter and slapped Smoke on the shoulder. "Smoke, you had us going for a while, and we patting ourselves on the back because you were letting our tables alone! Say, I've got some real fizz I'll open if you'll all come over to the Tivoli with me."

Later, back in the cabin, Shorty silently overhauled and hefted the various bulging gold-sacks. He finally piled them on the table, sat down on the edge of his bunk, and began taking off his moccasins.

"Seventy thousan'," he calculated. "It weighs three hundred and fifty pounds. And all out of a warped wheel an' a quick eye. Smoke, you eat'm raw, you eat'm alive, you work under water, you've given me the jim-jams; but just the same I know it's a dream. It's only in dreams that the good things comes true. I'm almighty unanxious to wake up. I hope I never wake up."

"Cheer up," Smoke answered. "You won't. There are a lot of philosophy sharps that think men are sleep-walkers. You're in good company."

Shorty got up, went to the table, selected the heaviest sack, and cuddled it in his arms as if it were a baby. "I may be sleep-walkin'," he said, "but, as you say, I'm sure in mighty good company."

# 13

"THE RACE FOR Number Three" is based on an actual episode of Alaskan gold rush history, a no-holds-barred and winner-take-all night race by men atop dogsleds to stake and claim fields of suspected gold.

In real life, the claims actually proved to be worthless, the arduous and brutal race run in vain. London softens this irony in his story, but makes vivid the desperation and courage of the contestants, be they emperor's favorites or Arizona cowpokes, short-winded soldiers of fortune or long-striding Scandinavian giants.

Once under way, the momentum of this swift-paced adventure to end all adventures carries London's reader irresistibly along to the finish. No more exciting story of a race for riches exists in American literature.

# The Race for Number Three: Winner Take All

"**H**UH! GET ONTO the glad rags!"

Shorty surveyed his partner with simulated disapproval, and Smoke, vainly attempting to rub the wrinkles out of the pair of trousers he had just put on, was irritated.

"They sure fit you close for a second-hand buy," Shorty went on. "What was the tax?"

"One hundred and fifty for the suit," Smoke answered. "The man was nearly my own size. I thought it was remarkably reasonable. What are you kicking about?"

"Who? Me? Oh, nothin'. I was just thinkin' it was goin' some for a meat-eater that hit Dawson in an ice-jam, with no grub, one suit of underclothes, a pair of mangy moccasins, an' overalls that looked like they'd been through the wreck of the *Hesperus*. Pretty gay front, pardner. Say?"

"What do you want now?" Smoke demanded testily.

"What's her name?"

"There isn't any her, my friend. I'm to have dinner at Colonel Bowie's, if you want to know. The trouble with you, Shorty, is you're envious because I'm going into high society and you're not invited."

"Ain't you some late?" Shorty queried.

"What do you mean?"

"For dinner. They'll be eatin' supper when you get there."

Smoke was about to explain with crudely elaborate sarcasm when he caught the twinkle in the other's eye. He went on dressing, with fingers that had lost their deftness, tying a Windsor tie in a bow-knot at the throat of his soft cotton shirt.

"Wisht I hadn't sent all my starched shirts to the laundry," Shorty murmured sympathetically. "I might 'a' fitted you out."

By this time Smoke was straining at a pair of shoes. The woolen socks were too thick to go into them. He looked appealingly at Shorty, who shook his head.

"Nope. If I had thin ones I wouldn't lend 'em to you. Back to the moccasins, pardner. You'd sure freeze your toes in skimpy-fangled gear like that."

"I paid fifteen dollars for them, second hand," Smoke lamented.

"I reckon they won't be a man not in moccasins."

"But there are to be women, Shorty. I'm going to sit down and eat with real live women — Mrs. Bowie, and several others, so the colonel told me."

"Well, moccasins won't spoil their appetite none," was Shorty's comment. "Wonder what the colonel wants with you?"

"I don't know, unless he's heard about my finding Surprise Lake. It will take a fortune to drain it, and the Guggenheims are out for investment."

"Reckon that's it. That's right, stick to the moccasins. Gee! That coat is sure wrinkled, an' it fits you a mite too swift. Just peck around at your vittles. If you eat hearty you'll bust through. An' if them women folks gets to droppin' handkerchiefs, just let 'em lay. Don't do any pickin' up. Whatever you do, don't."

As became a high-salaried expert and the representative of the great house of Guggenheim, Colonel Bowie lived in one of the most magnificent cabins in Dawson. And there

Smoke met the social elect of Dawson — not the mere pick-handle millionaires, but the ultra-cream of a mining city whose population had been recruited from all over the world — men like Warburton Jones, the explorer and writer; Captain Consadine, of the Mounted Police; Haskell, gold commissioner of the Northwest Territory; and Baron Von Schroeder, an emperor's favorite with an international dueling reputation. And here, dazzling in evening gown, he met Joy Gastell, whom hitherto he had encountered only on trail, befurred and moccasined. At dinner he found himself beside her.

"I feel like a fish out of water," he confessed. "All you folks are so real grand, you know. Besides, I never dreamed such Oriental luxury existed in the Klondike. Look at Von Schroeder there. He's actually got a dinner-jacket, and Consadine's got a starched shirt. I noticed he wore moccasins just the same. How do you like *my* outfit?" He moved his shoulders about as if preening himself for Joy's approval.

"It looks as if you'd grown stout since you came over the pass," she laughed.

"Wrong. Guess again."

"It's somebody else's."

"You win. I bought it for a price from one of the clerks at the A. C. Company."

"It's a shame clerks are so narrow-shouldered," she sympathized. "And you haven't told me what you think of *my* outfit."

"I can't," he said. "I'm out of breath. I've been living on trail too long. This sort of thing comes to me with a shock, you know. I'd quite forgotten that women have arms and shoulders. To-morrow morning, like my friend Shorty, I'll wake up and know it's all a dream. Now the last time I saw you on Squaw Creek—"

"I was just a squaw," she broke in.

"I hadn't intended to say that. I was remembering that it was on Squaw Creek that I discovered you had feet."

"And I can never forget that you saved them for me," she said. "I've been wanting to see you ever since, to thank you." He shrugged his shoulders deprecatingly. "And that's why you are here to-night."

"You asked the colonel to invite me?"

"No; Mrs. Bowie. And I asked her to let me have you at table. And here's my chance. Everybody's talking. Listen. You know Mono Creek?"

"Yes."

"It has turned out rich, dreadfully rich. They estimated the claims as worth a million and more apiece. It was only located the other day."

"I remember the stampede."

"Well, the whole creek was staked to the sky-line, and all the feeders, too. And yet, right now, on the main creek, Number Three below Discovery is unrecorded. The creek was so far away from Dawson that the commissioner allowed sixty days for recording after location. Every claim was recorded except Number Three below. It was staked by Cyrus Johnson. And that was all. Cyrus Johnson has disappeared, and in six days the time for recording will be up. Then the man who stakes it, and reaches Dawson first and records it, gets it,"

"A million dollars," Smoke murmured.

"Gilchrist, who has the next claim below, has got six hundred dollars in a single pan of bedrock. He's burned one hole down. And the claim on the other side is even richer. I know."

"But why doesn't everybody know?" Smoke queried skeptically.

"They're beginning to know. They kept it secret for a long

time, and it is only now that it's coming out. Good dog-teams will be at a premium in another twenty-four hours. Now you've got to get away as decently as you can as soon as dinner is over. I've arranged it. An Indian will come with a message for you. You read it, let on that you're very much put out, make your excuses, and get away."

"I — er — I fail to follow."

"Ninny!" she exclaimed in a half-whisper. "What you must do is to get out to-night and hustle dog-teams. I know of two. There's Hanson's team, seven big Hudson Bay dogs — he's holding them at four hundred each. That's top price to-night, but it won't be to-morrow. And Sitka Charley has eight Malemutes he's asking thirty-five hundred for. To-morrow he'll laugh at an offer of five thousand. Then you've got your own team of dogs. And you'll have to buy several more teams. That's your work to-night. Get the best. It's dogs as well as men that will win this race. It's a hundred and ten miles, and you'll have to relay as frequently as you can."

"Oh, I see, you want me to go in for it," Smoke drawled.

"If you haven't the money for the dogs, I'll — " She faltered, but before she could continue, Smoke was speaking.

"I can buy the dogs. But aren't you afraid this is gambling?"

"After your exploits at roulette in the Elkhorn," she retorted, "I'm not afraid that you're afraid. It's a sporting proposition, if that's what you mean. A race for a million and with some of the stiffest dog-mushers and travelers in the country entered against you. They haven't entered yet, but by this time to-morrow they will, and dogs will be worth what the richest man can afford to pay. Big Olaf is in town. He came up from Circle City last month. He is one of the most terrible dog-mushers in the country, and if he enters he will be your most dangerous man. Arizona Bill is another. He's been a professional freighter and mail-carrier for years. If he goes in, interest will be centered on him and Big Olaf."

"And you intend me to come along as a sort of dark horse?"

"Exactly. And it will have its advantages. You will not be supposed to stand a show. After all, you know, you are still classed as a chekako. You haven't seen the four seasons go around. Nobody will take notice of you until you come into the home stretch in the lead."

"It's on the home stretch the dark horse is to show up its classy form, eh?"

She nodded, and continued earnestly: "Remember, I shall never forgive myself for the trick I played on the Squaw Creek stampede unless you win this Mono claim. And if any man can win this race against the old-timers, it's you."

It was the way she said it. He felt warm all over, and in his heart and head. He gave her a quick, searching look, involuntary and serious, and for the moment that her eyes met his steadily ere they fell, it seemed to him that he read something of vaster import than the claim Cyrus Johnson had failed to record.

"I'll do it," he said, "I'll win it."

The glad light in her eyes seemed to promise a greater meed than all the gold in the Mono claim. He was aware of a movement of her hand in her lap. Under the screen of the table-cloth he thrust his own hand across and met a firm grip of woman's fingers that sent another wave of warmth through him.

"What will Shorty say?" was the thought that flashed whimsically through his mind as he withdrew his hand. He glanced almost jealously at the faces of Von Schroeder and

Jones, and wondered if they had not divined the remark-
ableness and deliciousness of this woman who sat beside him.

He was aroused by her voice, and realized that she had
been speaking for some moments.

"So, you see, Arizona Bill is a white Indian," she was saying. "And Big Olaf is a bear-wrestler, a king of the snows, a
mighty savage. He can out-travel and out-endure an Indian,
and he's never known any other life than that of the wild and
the frost."

"Who's that?" Captain Consadine broke in from across
the table.

"Big Olaf," she answered. "I was just telling Mr. Bellew
what a traveler he is."

"You're right," the captain's voice boomed. "Big Olaf is
the greatest traveler in the Yukon. I'd back him against Old
Nick himself for snow-bucking and ice-travel. He brought in
the government despatches in 1895, and he did it after two
couriers were frozen on Chilkoot and the third drowned in
the open water of Thirty Mile."

Smoke had traveled in a leisurely fashion up to Mono
Creek, fearing to tire his dogs before the big race. Also, he
had familiarized himself with every mile of the trail and
located his relay camps. So many men had entered the race
that the hundred and ten miles of its course were almost a
continuous village. Relay camps were everywhere along the
trail. Von Schroeder, who had gone in purely for the sport,
had no less than eleven dog-teams — a fresh one for every ten
miles. Arizona Bill had been forced to content himself with
eight teams. Big Olaf had seven, which was the complement
of Smoke. In addition, over two score of other men were in
the running. Not every day, even in the golden north, was a
million dollars the prize for a dog-race. The country had

been swept of dogs, and their prices had doubled and quad-
rupled in the course of the frantic speculation.

Number Three below Discovery was ten miles up Mono
Creek from its mouth. The remaining hundred miles was to
be run on the frozen breast of the Yukon. On Number Three
itself were fifty tents and over three hundred dogs. The old
stakes, blazed and scrawled sixty days before by Cyrus Johnson, still stood, and every man had gone over the boundaries
of the claim again and again, for the race with the dogs was
to be preceded by a foot and obstacle race. Each man had to
relocate the claim for himself, and this meant that he must
place two center-stakes and four corner-stakes and cross the
creek twice, before he could start for Dawson with his dogs.

Furthermore, there were to be no "sooners." Not until the
stroke of midnight of Friday night was the claim open for
relocation, and not until the stroke of midnight could a man
plant a stake. This was the ruling of the gold commissioner
at Dawson, and Captain Consadine had sent up a squad of
mounted police to enforce it. Discussion had arisen about
the difference between sun-time and police-time, but Consadine had sent forth his fiat that police-time went, and,
further, that it was the watch of Lieutenant Pollock that
went.

The Mono trail ran along the level creek-bed, and, less
than two feet in width, was like a groove, walled on either
side by the snowfall of months. The problem of how forty-
odd sleds and three hundred dogs were to start in so narrow
a course was in everybody's mind.

"Huh!" said Shorty. "It's goin' to be the gosh-dangdest
mix-up that ever was. I can't see no way out, Smoke, except
main strength an' sweat an' to plow through. If the whole
creek was glare-ice they ain't room for a dozen teams
abreast. I got a hunch right now they's goin' to be a heap of

scrappin' before they get strung out. An' if any of it comes our way, you got to let me do the punchin'.''

Smoke squared his shoulders and laughed non-committally.

"No, you don't!" his partner cried in alarm. "No matter what happens, you don't dast hit. You can't handle dogs a hundred miles with a busted knuckle, an' that's what'll happen if you land on somebody's jaw."

Smoke nodded his head. "You're right, Shorty. I couldn't risk the chance."

"An' just remember," Shorty went on, "that I got to do all the shovin' for them first ten miles, an' you got to take it easy as you can. I'll sure jerk you through to the Yukon. After that it's up to you an' the dogs. Say, what d'ye think Schroeder's scheme is? He's got his first team a quarter of a mile down the creek, an' he'll know it by a green lantern. But we got him skinned. Me for the red flare every time."

The day had been clear and cold, but a blanket of cloud formed across the face of the sky, and the night came on warm and dark, with the hint of snow impending. The thermometer registered fifteen below zero, and in the Klondike winter fifteen below is esteemed very warm.

At a few minutes before midnight, leaving Shorty with the dogs five hundred yards down the creek, Smoke joined the racers on Number Three. There were forty-five of them waiting the start for the thousand thousand dollars Cyrus Johnson had left lying in the frozen gravel. Each man carried six stakes and a heavy wooden mallet, and was clad in a smock-like parka of heavy cotton drill.

Lieutenant Pollock, in a big bearskin coat, looked at his watch by the light of a fire. It lacked a minute of midnight. "Make ready," he said, as he raised a revolver in his right hand and watched the second-hand tick around.

Forty-five hoods were thrown back from the parkas, forty-five pairs of hands were unmittened, and forty-five pairs of moccasins pressed tensely into the packed snow. Also, forty-five stakes were thrust into the snow, and the same number of mallets lifted in the air.

The shot rang out, and the mallets fell. Cyrus Johnson's right to the million had expired.

Smoke drove in his stake and was away with the leading dozen. Fires had been lighted at the corners, and by each fire stood a policeman, list in hand, checking off the names of the runners. A man was supposed to call out his name and show his face. There was to be no staking by proxy while the real racer was off and away down the creek.

At the first corner, beside Smoke's stake, Von Schroeder placed his. The mallets struck at the same instant. As they hammered, more arrived from behind and with such impetuosity as to get in one another's way and cause jostling and shoving. Squirming through the press and calling his name to the policeman, Smoke saw the baron, struck in collision by one of the rushers, hurled clean off his feet into the snow. But Smoke did not wait. Others were still ahead of him. By the light of the vanishing fire, he was certain that he saw the back, hugely looming, of Big Olaf, and at the southwestern corner Big Olaf and he drove their stakes side by side.

It was no light work, this preliminary obstacle race. The boundaries of the claim totaled nearly a mile, and most of it was over the uneven surface of a snow-covered, niggerhead flat. All about Smoke men tripped and fell, and several times he pitched forward himself, jarringly, on hands and feet. Once, Big Olaf fell so immediately in front of him as to bring him down on top.

The upper center-stake was driven by the edge of the bank, and down the bank the racers plunged, across the frozen creek-bed, and up the other side. Here, as Smoke clambered, a hand gripped his ankle and jerked him back. In the flickering light of a distant fire, it was impossible to see who had played the trick. But Arizona Bill, who had been treated similarly, rose to his feet and drove his fist with a crunch into the offender's face. Smoke saw and heard as he was scrambling to his feet, but before he could make another lunge for the bank a fist dropped him half stunned into the snow. He staggered up, located the man, half swung a hook for his jaw, then remembered Shorty's warning and refrained. The next moment, struck below the knees by a hurtling body, he went down again.

It was a foretaste of what would happen when the men reached their sleds. Men were pouring over the other bank and piling into the jam. They swarmed up the bank in bunches, and in bunches were dragged back by their impatient fellows. More blows were struck, curses rose from the panting chests of those who still had wind to spare, and Smoke, curiously visioning the face of Joy Gastell, hoped that the mallets would not be brought into play. Overthrown, trod upon, groping in the snow for his lost stakes, he at last crawled out of the crush and attacked the bank farther along. Others were doing this, and it was his luck to have many men in advance of him in the race for the northwestern corner.

Reaching the fourth corner, he tripped headlong, and in the sprawling fall lost his remaining stake. For five minutes he groped in the darkness before he found it, and all the time the panting runners were passing him. From the last corner to the creek he began overtaking men for whom the mile run had been too much. In the creek itself bedlam had broken loose. A dozen sleds were piled up and overturned, and nearly a hundred dogs were locked in combat. Among them men struggled, tearing the tangled animals apart, or beating them apart with clubs.

Leaping down the bank beyond the glutted passage, he gained the hard-footing of the sled-trail and made better time. Here, in packed harbors beside the narrow trail, sleds and men waited for runners that were still behind. From the rear came the whine and rush of dogs, and Smoke had barely time to leap aside into the deep snow. A sled tore past, and he made out the man kneeling and shouting madly. Scarcely was it by when it stopped with a crash of battle. The excited dogs of a harbored sled, resenting the passing animals, had got out of hand and sprung upon them.

Smoke plunged around and by. He could see the green lantern of Von Schroeder and, just below it, the red flare that marked his own team. Two men were guarding Von Schroeder's dogs, with short clubs interposed between them and the trail.

"Come on, you Smoke! Come on, you Smoke!" he could hear Shorty calling anxiously.

"Coming!" he gasped.

By the red flare, he could see the snow torn up and trampled, and from the way his partner breathed he knew a battle had been fought. He staggered to the sled, and, in the moment he was falling on it, Shorty's whip snapped as he yelled:

"Mush! you devils! Mush!"

The dogs sprang into the breast-bands, and the sled jerked abruptly ahead. They were big animals — Hanson's prize team of Hudson Bays — and Smoke had selected them for the first stage, which included the ten miles of Mono, the heavy going of the cut-off across the flat at the mouth, and the first ten miles of the Yukon stretch.

"How many are ahead?" he asked.

"You shut up an' save your wind," Shorty answered. "Hi! you brutes! Hit her up! Hit her up!"

He was running behind the sled, towing on a short rope. Smoke could not see him; nor could he see the sled on which he lay full length. The fires had been left in the rear, and they were tearing through a wall of blackness as fast as the dogs could spring into it. This blackness was almost sticky, so nearly did it take on the seeming of substance.

Smoke felt the sled heel up on one runner as it rounded an invisible curve, and from ahead came the snarls of beasts and the oaths of men. This was known afterward as the Barnes-Slocum jam. It was the teams of those two men which first collided, and into it, at full career, piled Smoke's seven big fighters. Scarcely more than semi-domesticated wolves, the excitement of that night on Mono Creek had sent every dog fighting mad. The Klondike dogs, driven without reins, cannot be stopped except by voice, so that there was no stopping this glut of struggle that heaped itself between the narrow rims of the creek. From behind, sled after sled hurled into the turmoil. Men who had their teams merely extricated were overwhelmed by fresh avalanches of dogs — each animal well fed, well rested, and ripe for battle.

"It's knock down an' drag out an' plow through!" Shorty yelled in his partner's ear. "An' watch out for your knuckles! You drag dogs out an' let me do the punchin'!"

What happened in the next half-hour Smoke never distinctly remembered. At the end he emerged exhausted, sobbing for breath, his jaw sore from a fist-blow, his shoulder aching from the bruise of a club, the blood running warmly down one leg from the rip of a dog's fangs, and both sleeves of his parka torn to shreds. As in a dream, while the battle still raged behind, he helped Shorty reharness the dogs. One, dying, they cut from the traces, and in the darkness they felt their way to the repair of the disrupted harness.

"Now you lie down an' get your wind back," Shorty commanded.

And through the darkness the dogs sped, with unabated strength, down Mono Creek, across the long cut-off, and to the Yukon. Here, at the junction with the main river-trail, somebody had lighted a fire, and here Shorty said good-by. By the light of the fire, as the sled leaped behind the flying dogs, Smoke caught another of the unforgettable pictures of the Northland. It was of Shorty, swaying and sinking down limply in the snow, yelling his parting encouragement, one eye blackened and closed, knuckles bruised and broken, and one arm, ripped and fang-torn, gushing forth a steady stream of blood.

"How many ahead?" Smoke asked, as he dropped his tired Hudson Bays and sprang upon the waiting sled at the first relay-station.

"I counted eleven," the man called after him, for he was already away, behind the leaping dogs.

Fifteen miles they were to carry him on the next stage, which would fetch him to the mouth of White River. There were nine of them, but they composed his weakest team. The twenty-five miles between White River and Sixty Mile he had broken into two stages because of ice-jams, and here two of his heaviest, toughest teams were stationed.

He lay on the sled at full length, face down, holding on with both hands. Whenever the dogs slacked from topmost speed he rose to his knees, and, yelling and urging, clinging precariously with one hand, threw his whip into them. Poor team that it was, he passed two sleds before White River was reached. Here, at the freeze-up, a jam had piled a barrier, allowing the open water that formed for half a mile below to freeze smoothly. This smooth stretch enabled the racers to make flying exchanges of sleds, and down all the course they had placed their relays below the jams.

Over the jam and out onto the smooth, Smoke tore along, calling loudly, "Billy! Billy!"

Billy heard and answered, and by the light of the many fires on the ice, Smoke saw a sled swing in from the side and come abreast. Its dogs were fresh and overhauled his. As the sleds swerved toward each other he leaped across, and Billy promptly rolled off.

"Where's Big Olaf?" Smoke cried.

"Leading!" Billy's voice answered; and the fires were left behind, and Smoke was again flying through the wall of darkness.

In the jams of that relay, where the way led across a chaos of up-ended ice-cakes, and where Smoke slipped off the forward end of the sled and with a haul-rope toiled behind the wheel-dog, he passed three sleds. Accidents had happened, and he could hear the men cutting out dogs and mending harnesses.

Among the jams of the next short relay into Sixty Mile, he passed two more teams. And that he might know adequately what had happened to them, one of his own dogs wrenched a shoulder, was unable to keep up, and was dragged in the harness. Its teammates, angered, fell upon it with their fangs, and Smoke was forced to club them off with the heavy butt of his whip. As he cut the injured animal out, he heard the whining cries of dogs behind him and the voice of a man that was familiar. It was Von Schroeder. Smoke called a warning to prevent a rear-end collision, and the baron, hawing his animals and swinging on the gee-pole, went by a dozen feet to the side. Yet so impenetrable was the blackness that Smoke heard him pass but did not see him.

On the smooth stretch of ice beside the trading-post at Sixty Mile, Smoke overtook two more sleds. All had just changed teams, and for five minutes they ran abreast, each man on his knees and pouring whip and voice into the maddened dogs. But Smoke had studied out that portion of the trail, and now marked the tall pine on the bank that showed faintly in the light of the many fires. Below that pine was not merely darkness, but an abrupt cessation of the smooth stretch. There the trail, he knew, narrowed to a single sled-width. Leaning out ahead, he caught the haul-rope and drew his leaping sled up to the wheel-dog. He caught the animal by the hind legs and threw it. With a snarl of rage it tried to slash him with its fangs, but was dragged on by the rest of the team. Its body proved an efficient brake, and the two other teams, still abreast, dashed ahead into the darkness for the narrow way.

Smoke heard the crash and uproar of their collision, released his wheeler, sprang to the gee-pole, and urged his team to the right into the soft snow where the straining animals wallowed to their necks. It was exhausting work, but he won by the tangled teams and gained the hard-packed trail beyond.

On the relay out of Sixty Mile, Smoke had next to his poorest team, and though the going was good, he had set it a short fifteen miles. Two more teams would bring him into Dawson and to the gold-recorder's office, and Smoke had selected his best animals for the last two stretches. Sitka Charley himself waited with the eight Malemutes that would jerk Smoke along for twenty miles, and for the finish, with a fifteen-mile run, was his own team — the team he had had all winter and which had been with him in the search for Surprise Lake.

The two men he had left entangled at Sixty Mile failed to overtake him, and, on the other hand, his team failed to overtake any of the three that still led. His animals were willing though they lacked stamina and speed, and little urging was needed to keep them jumping into it at their best. There was nothing for Smoke to do but to lie face downward and hold on. Now and again he would plunge out of the darkness into the circle of light about a blazing fire, catch a glimpse of furred men standing by harnessed and waiting dogs, and plunge into the darkness again. Mile after mile, with only the grind and jar of the runners in his ears, he sped on. Almost automatically he kept his place as the sled bumped ahead or half lifted and heeled on the swings and swerves of the bends.

The gray twilight of the morning was breaking as he exchanged his weary dogs for eight fresh Malemutes. Lighter animals than the Hudson Bays, they were capable of greater speed, and they ran with the supple tirelessness of true wolves. Sitka Charley called out the order of the teams ahead. Big Olaf led, Arizona Bill was Second, and Von Schroeder third. These were the three best men in the country. In fact, ere Smoke had left Dawson, the popular betting had placed them in that order. While they were racing for a million, at least half a million had been staked by others on the outcome of the race. No one had bet on Smoke, who despite his several known exploits, was still accounted a chekako with much to learn.

As daylight strengthened, Smoke caught sight of a sled ahead, and, in half an hour, his own lead-dog was leaping at its tail. Not until the man turned his head to exchange greetings, did Smoke recognize him as Arizona Bill. Von Schroeder had evidently passed him. The trail, hard-packed, ran too narrowly through the soft snow, and for another half-hour Smoke was forced to stay in the rear. Then they topped an ice-jam and struck a smooth stretch below, where were a number of relay-camps and where the snow was packed widely. On his knees, swinging his whip and yelling, Smoke drew abreast of Arizona Bill, then pulled ahead.

Bill dropped behind very slowly, though when the last relay-station was in sight he was fully half a mile in the rear. Ahead, bunched together, Smoke could see Big Olaf and Von Schroeder. Again Smoke arose to his knees, and he lifted his jaded dogs into a burst of speed such as a man only can who has the proper instinct for dog-driving. He drew up close to the tail of Von Schroeder's sled, and in this order the three sleds dashed out on the smooth going below a jam, where many men and many dogs waited. Dawson was fifteen miles away.

Von Schroeder, with his ten-mile relays, had changed five miles back and would change five miles ahead. So he held on, keeping his dogs at full leap. Big Olaf and Smoke made flying changes, and their fresh teams immediately regained what had been lost to the baron. Big Olaf led past, and Smoke followed into the narrow trail beyond.

"Still good, but not so good," Smoke paraphrased Spencer to himself.

Of Von Schroeder, now behind, he had no fear; but ahead was the greatest dog-driver in the country. To pass him seemed impossible. Again and again, many times, Smoke forced his leader to the other's sled-tail, and each time Big Olaf let out another link and drew away. Smoke contented himself with taking the pace, and hung on grimly. The race was not lost until one or the other won, and in fifteen miles many things could happen.

Three miles from Dawson something did happen. To Smoke's surprise, Big Olaf rose up and with oaths and leather proceeded to fetch out the last ounce of effort in his animals. It was a spurt that should have been reserved for the last hundred yards instead of being begun three miles from the finish. Sheer dog-killing that it was, Smoke followed. His own team was superb. No dogs on the Yukon had had harder work or were in better condition. Besides, Smoke had toiled with them, and eaten and bedded with them, and he knew each dog as an individual and how best to win in to the animal's intelligence and extract its last shred of willingness.

They topped a small jam and struck the smooth going below. Big Olaf was barely fifty feet ahead. A sled shot out from the side and drew in toward him, and Smoke understood Big Olaf's terrific spurt. He had tried to gain a lead for the change. This fresh team that waited to jerk him down the home-stretch had been a private surprise of his. Even the men who had backed him to win had no knowledge of it.

Smoke strove desperately to pass during the exchange of sleds. Lifting his dogs to the effort, he ate up the intervening fifty feet. With urging and pouring of leather, he went to the side and on until his head-dog was jumping abreast of Big Olaf's wheeler. On the other side, abreast, was the relay sled. At the speed they were going, Big Olaf did not dare try the flying leap. If he missed and fell off, Smoke would be in the lead, and the race would be lost.

Big Olaf tried to spurt ahead, and he lifted his dogs magnificently, but Smoke's leader still continued to jump beside Big Olaf's wheeler. For half a mile the three sleds tore and

bounced along side by side. The smooth stretch was nearing
its end when Big Olaf took the chance. As the flying sleds
swerved toward each other, he leaped, and the instant he
struck he was on his knees, with whip and voice spurting the
fresh team. The smooth stretch pinched out into the narrow
trail, and he jumped his dogs ahead and into it with a lead
of barely a yard.

A man was not beaten until he was beaten, was Smoke's
conclusion, and drive no matter how, Big Olaf failed to
shake him off. No team Smoke had driven that night could
have stood such a killing pace and kept up with fresh dogs —
no team save this one. Nevertheless, the pace *was* killing it,
and as they began to round the bluff at Klondike City, he
could feel the pitch of strength going out of his animals.
Almost imperceptibly they lagged behind, and foot by foot
Big Olaf drew away until he led by a score of yards.

A great cheer went up from the population of Klondike
City assembled on the ice. Here the Klondike entered the
Yukon, and half a mile away, across the Klondike, on the
north bank, stood Dawson. An outburst of madder cheering
arose, and Smoke caught a glimpse of a sled shooting out to
him. He recognized the splendid animals that drew it. They
were Joy Gastell's. And Joy Gastell drove them. The hood of
her squirrel-skin parka was tossed back, revealing the
cameo-like oval of her face outlined against her heavily-
massed hair. Mittens had been discarded, and with bare
hands she clung to whip and sled.

"Jump!" she cried, as her leader snarled at Smoke's.

Smoke struck the sled behind her. It rocked violently
from the impact of his body, but she was full up on her knees
and swinging the whip.

"Hi! You. Mush on! Chook! Chook!" she was crying, and

the dogs whined and yelped in eagerness of desire and effort to overtake Big Olaf.

And then, as the lead-dog caught the tail of Big Olaf's sled, and yard by yard drew up abreast, the great crowd on the Dawson bank went mad. It *was* a great crowd, for the men had dropped their tools on all the creeks and come down to see the outcome of the race, and a dead heat at the end of a hundred and ten miles justified any madness.

"When you're in the lead I'm going to drop off!" Joy cried out over her shoulder.

Smoke tried to protest.

"And watch out for the dip curve halfway up the bank," she warned.

Dog by dog, separated by half a dozen feet, the two teams were running abreast. Big Olaf, with whip and voice, held his own for a minute. Then, slowly, an inch at a time, Joy's leader began to forge past.

"Get ready!" she cried to Smoke. "I'm going to leave you in a minute. Get the whip."

And as he shifted his hand to clutch the whip, they heard Big Olaf roar a warning, but too late. His lead dog, incensed at being passed, swerved in to the attack. His fangs struck Joy's leader on the flank. The rival teams flew at one another's throats. The sleds overran the fighting brutes and capsized. Smoke struggled to his feet and tried to lift Joy up. But she thrust him from her, crying,

"Go!"

On foot, already fifty feet in advance, was Big Olaf, still intent on finishing the race. Smoke obeyed, and when the two men reached the foot of the Dawson bank, he was at the other's heels. But up the bank Big Olaf lifted his body hugely, regaining a dozen feet.

Five blocks down the main street was the gold-recorder's office. The street was packed as for the witnessing of a parade. Not so easily this time did Smoke gain to his giant rival, and when he did he was unable to pass. Side by side they ran along the narrow aisle between the solid walls of cheering men. Now one, now the other, with great convulsive jerks, gained an inch or so, only to lose it immediately after.

If the pace had been a killing one for their dogs, the one they now set themselves was no less so. But they were racing for a million dollars and greatest honor in the Yukon country. The only outside impression that came to Smoke on that last mad stretch was one of astonishment that there should be so many people in the Klondike. He had never seen them all at once before.

He felt himself involuntarily lag, and Big Olaf sprang a full stride in the lead. To Smoke it seemed that his heart would burst, while he had lost all consciousness of his legs. He knew they were flying under him, but he did not know how he continued to make them fly, nor how he put even greater pressure of will upon them and compelled them again to carry him to his giant competitor's side.

The open door of the recorder's office appeared ahead of them. Both men had made a final, futile spurt. Neither could draw away from the other, and side by side they hit the doorway, collided violently, and fell headlong on the office floor.

They sat up, but were too exhausted to rise. Big Olaf, the sweat pouring from him, breathing with tremendous, painful gasps, pawed the air and vainly tried to speak. Then he reached out his hand with unmistakable meaning; Smoke extended his, and they shook.

"It's a dead heat," Smoke could hear the recorder saying,

but it was as if in a dream, and the voice was very thin and very far away. "And all I can say is that you both win. You'll have to divide the claim between you. You're partners."

Their two arms pumped up and down as they ratified the decision. Big Olaf nodded his head with great emphasis, and spluttered. At last he got it out.

"You damn chekako," was what he said, but in the saying of it was admiration. "I don't know how you done it, but you did."

Outside, the great crowd was noisily massed, while the office was packing and jamming. Smoke and Big Olaf essayed to rise, and each helped the other to his feet. Smoke found his legs weak under him, and staggered drunkenly. Big Olaf tottered toward him.

"I'm sorry my dogs jumped yours."

"It couldn't be helped," Smoke panted back. "I heard you yell."

"Say," Big Olaf went on with shining eyes. "That girl — one damn fine girl, eh?"

"One damn fine girl," Smoke agreed.

**14** OLD SAN FRANCISCO and Oakland had their share of trans-bay sports rivalries. None ever equaled the event that, according to Jack London, occurred one year at the annual bricklayers' athletic competition. With a cast of thousands of highly partisan fans, London's story describes the evolution of a disputed race into one of the most spectacular sports riots in literary history.

This account of games played and judged under highly dubious sporting ethics pokes broad, Hogarthian fun at the violent loyalties and latent hostilities of mass spectator sport. At the same time, it satirizes the "win at any price" philosophy which has come to dominate so much of contemporary sport in America, afflicting players and fans alike with the same kind of ruthless, gladitorial enthusiasm which London lampoons here.

The line between organized sport and open battle, London warns us, is as fine as the line between civilized man and his savage ancestor. See if you can tell the difference.

*"Unsportsmanlike Conduct: Winner Take Nothing"*
*is reprinted from* Valley of the Moon.
*Copyright 1913 by The Macmillan Company,*
*Chapter IV.*

# Unsportsmanlike Conduct: Winner Take Nothing

AFTER DINNER THERE were two dances in the pavilion, and then the band led the way to the race track for the games. The dancers followed, and all through the grounds the picnic parties left their tables to join in. Five thousand packed the grassy slopes of the amphitheater and swarmed inside the race track. Here, first of the events, the men were lining up for a tug of war. The contest was between the Oakland Bricklayers and the San Francisco Bricklayers, and the picked braves, huge and heavy, were taking their positions along the rope. They kicked heel-holds in the soft earth, rubbed their hands with the soil from underfoot, and laughed and joked with the crowd that surged about them.

The judges and watchers struggled vainly to keep back this crowd of relatives and friends. The Celtic blood was up, and the Celtic faction spirit ran high. The air was filled with cries of cheer, advice, warning, and threat. Many elected to leave the side of their own team and go to the side of the other team with the intention of circumventing foul play. There were as many women as men among the jostling supporters. The dust from the trampling, scuffling feet rose in the air, and Mary gasped and coughed and begged Bert to take her away. But he, the imp in him elated with the prospect of trouble, insisted on urging in closer. Saxon clung to Billy, who slowly and methodically elbowed and shouldered a way for her.

"No place for a girl," he grumbled, looking down at her with a masked expression of absent-mindedness, while his elbow powerfully crushed on the ribs of a big Irishman who gave room. "Thing'll break loose when they start pullin'. They's been too much drink, an' you know what the Micks are for a rough house."

Saxon was very much out of place among these large-bodied men and women. She seemed very small and child-like, delicate and fragile, a creature from another race. Only Billy's skilled bulk and muscle saved her. He was continually glancing from face to face of the women and always returning to study her face, nor was she unaware of the contrast he was making.

Some excitement occurred a score of feet away from them, and to the sound of exclamations and blows a surge ran through the crowd. A large man, wedged sidewise in the jam, was shoved against Saxon, crushing her closely against Billy, who reached across to the man's shoulder with a massive thrust that was not so slow as usual. An involuntary grunt came from the victim, who turned his head, showing sun-reddened blond skin and unmistakable angry Irish eyes.

"What's eatin' yeh?" he snarled.

"Get off your foot; you're standin' on it," was Billy's contemptuous reply, emphasized by an increase of thrust.

The Irishman grunted again and made a frantic struggle to twist his body around, but the wedging bodies on either side held him in a vise.

"I'll break yer ugly face for yeh in a minute," he announced in wrath-thick tones.

Then his own face underwent transformation. The snarl left the lips, and the angry eyes grew genial.

"An' sure an' it's yerself," he said. "I didn't know it was

yeh a-shovin'. I seen yeh lick the Terrible Swede, if yeh *was* robbed on the decision."

"No, you didn't, Bo," Billy answered pleasantly. "You saw me take a good beatin' that night. The decision was all right."

The Irishman was now beaming. He had endeavored to pay a compliment with a lie, and the prompt repudiation of the lie served only to increase his hero-worship.

"Sure, an' a bad beatin' it was," he acknowledged, "but yeh showed the grit of a bunch of wildcats. Soon as I can get me arm free I'm goin' to shake yeh by the hand an' help yeh aise yer young lady."

Frustrated in the struggle to get the crowd back, the referee fired his revolver in the air, and the tug-of-war was on. Pandemonium broke loose. Saxon, protected by the two big men, was near enough to the front to see much that ensued. The men on the rope pulled and strained till their faces were red with effort and their joints crackled. The rope was new, and, as their hands slipped, their wives and daughters sprang in, scooping up the earth in double handfuls and pouring it on the rope and the hands of their men to give them better grip.

A stout, middle-aged woman, carried beyond herself by the passion of the contest, seized the rope and pulled beside her husband, encouraged him with loud cries. A watcher from the opposing team dragged her screaming away and was dropped like a steer by an ear-blow from a partisan from the woman's team. He, in turn, went down, and brawny women joined with their men in the battle. Vainly the judges and watchers begged, pleaded, yelled, and swung with their fists. Men, as well as women, were springing in to the rope and pulling. No longer was it team against team, but all

Oakland against all San Francisco, festooned with a free-for-all fight. Hands overlaid hands two and three deep in the struggle to grasp the rope. And hands that found no holds, doubled into bunches of knuckles that impacted on the jaws of the watchers who strove to tear hand-holds from the rope.

Bert yelped with joy, while Mary clung to him, mad with fear. Close to the rope the fighters were going down and being trampled. The dust arose in clouds, while from beyond, all around, unable to get into the battle, could be heard the shrill and impotent rage-screams and rage-yells of women and men.

"Dirty work, dirty work," Billy muttered over and over; and, though he saw much that occurred, assisted by the friendly Irishman he was coolly and safely working Saxon back out of the melee.

At last the break came. The losing team, accompanied by its host of volunteers, was dragged in a rush over the ground and disappeared under the avalanche of battling forms of the onlookers.

Leaving Saxon under the protection of the Irishman in an outer eddy of calm, Billy plunged back into the mix-up. Several minutes later he emerged with the missing couple — Bert bleeding from a blow on the ear, but hilarious, and Mary rumpled and hysterical.

"This ain't sport," she kept repeating. "It's a shame, a dirty shame."

"We got to get outa this," Billy said. "The fun's only commenced."

"Aw, wait," Bert begged. "It's worth eight dollars. It's cheap at any price. I ain't seen so many black eyes and bloody noses in a month of Sundays."

"Well, go on back an' enjoy yourself," Billy commended. "I'll take the girls up there on the side hill where we can look on. But I won't give much for your good looks if some of them Micks lands on you."

The trouble was over in an amazingly short time, for from the judges' stand beside the track the announcer was bellowing the start of the boys' foot-race; and Bert, disappointed, joined Billy and the two girls on the hillside looking down upon the track.

There were boys' races and girls' races, races of young women and old women, of fat men and fat women, sack races and three-legged races, and the contestants strove around the small track through a Bedlam of cheering supporters. The tug-of-war was already forgotten, and good nature reigned again.

Five young men toed the mark, crouching with fingertips to the ground and waiting the starter's revolver-shot. Three were in their stocking-feet, and the remaining two wore spiked running-shoes.

"Young men's race," Bert read from the program. "An' only one prize — twenty-five dollars. See the red-head with the spikes — the one next to the outside. San Francisco's set on him winning. He's their crack, an' there's a lot of bets up."

"Who's goin' to win?" Mary deferred to Billy's superior athletic knowledge.

"How can I tell?" he answered. "I never saw any of 'em before. But they all look good to me. May the best one win, that's all."

The revolver was fired, and the five runners were off and away. Three were outdistanced at the start. Red-head led, with a black-haired young man at his shoulder, and it was plain that the race lay between these two. Half-way around, the black-haired one took the lead in a spurt that was intended to last to the finish. Ten feet he gained, nor could Red-head cut down an inch.

"The boy's a streak," Billy commented. "He ain't tryin' his hardest, an' Red-head's just bustin' himself."

Still ten feet in the lead, the black-haired one breasted the tape in a hubbub of cheers. Yet yells of disapproval could be distinguished. Bert hugged himself with joy.

"Mm-mm," he gloated. "Ain't Frisco sore? Watch out for fireworks now. See! He's bein' challenged. The judges ain't payin' him the money. An' he's got a gang behind him. Oh! Oh! Oh! Ain't had so much fun since my old woman broke her leg!"

"Why don't they pay him, Billy?" Saxon asked. "He won."

"The Frisco bunch is challengin' him for a professional," Billy elucidated. "That's what they're all beefin' about. But it ain't right. They all ran for that money, so they're all professional."

The crowd surged and argued and roared in front of the judges' stand. The stand was a rickety, two-story affair, the second story open at the front, and here the judges could be seen debating as heatedly as the crowd beneath them.

"There she starts!" Bert cried. "Oh, you rough-house!"

The black-haired racer, backed by a dozen supporters, was climbing the outside stairs to the judges.

"The purse-holder's his friend," Billy said. "See, he's paid him, an' some of the judges is willin' an' some are beefin'. An' now that other gang's going up — they're Red-head's." He turned to Saxon with a reassuring smile. "We're well out of it this time. There's goin' to be rough stuff down there in a minute."

"The judges are tryin' to make him give the money back," Bert explained. "An' if he don't the other gang'll take it away from him. See! They're reachin' for it now."

High above his head, the winner held the roll of paper containing the twenty-five silver dollars. His gang, around him, was shouldering back those who tried to seize the money. No blows had been struck yet, but the struggle increased until the frail structure shook and swayed. From the crowd beneath the winner was variously addressed: "Give it back, you dog!" "Hang on to it, Tim!" "You won fair, Timmy!" "Give it back, you dirty robber!" Abuse unprintable as well as friendly advice was hurled at him.

The struggle grew more violent. Tim's supporters strove to hold him off the floor so that his hand would still be above the grasping hands that shot up. Once, for an instant, his arm was jerked down. Again it went up. But evidently the paper had broken, and with a last desperate effort, before he went down, Tim flung the coin out in a silvery shower upon the heads of the crowd beneath. Then ensued a weary period of arguing and quarreling.

"I wish they'd finish, so as we could get back to the dancin'," Mary complained. "This ain't no fun."

Slowly and painfully the judges' stand was cleared, and an announcer, stepping to the front of the stand, spread his arms appealing for silence. The angry clamor died down.

"The judges have decided," he shouted, "that this day of good fellowship an' brotherhood —"

"Hear! Hear!" Many of the cooler heads applauded. "That's the stuff!" "No fightin'!" "No hard feelin's!"

"An' therefore," the announcer became audible again, "the judges have decided to put up another purse of twenty-five dollars an' run the race over again!"

"An' Tim?" bellowed scores of throats. "What about Tim?" "He's been robbed!" "The judges is rotten!"

Again the announcer stilled the tumult with his arm appeal.

"The judges have decided, for the sake of good feelin', that Timothy McManus will also run. If he wins, the money's his."

"Now wouldn't that jar you?" Billy grumbled disgustedly. "If Tim's eligible now, he was eligible the first time. An' if he was eligible the first time, then the money was his."

"Red-head'll bust himself wide open this time," Bert jubilated.

"An' so will Tim," Billy rejoined. "You can bet he's mad clean through, and he'll let out the links he was holdin' in last time."

Another quarter of an hour was spent in clearing the track of the excited crowd, and this time only Tim and Red-head toed the mark. The other three young men had abandoned the contest.

The leap of Tim, at the report of the revolver, put him a clean yard in the lead.

"I guess he's professional, all right, all right," Billy remarked. "An' just look at him go!"

Half-way around, Tim led by fifty feet, and, running swiftly, maintaining the same lead, he came down the home-stretch an easy winner. When directly beneath the group on the hillside, the incredible and unthinkable happened. Standing close to the inside edge of the track was a dapper young man with a light switch cane. He was distinctly out of place in such a gathering, for upon him was no earmark of the working class. Afterward, Bert was of the opinion that he looked like a swell dancing master, while Billy called him "the dude."

So far as Timothy McManus was concerned, the dapper young man was destiny; for as Tim passed him, the young man, with utmost deliberation, thrust his cane between Tim's flying legs. Tim sailed through the air in a headlong pitch, struck spread-eagled on his face, and plowed along in a cloud of dust.

There was an instant of vast and gasping silence. The young man, too, seemed petrified by the ghastliness of his deed. It took an appreciable interval of time for him, as well as for the onlookers, to realize what he had done. They recovered first, and from a thousand throats the wild Irish yell went up. Red-head won the race without a cheer. The storm center had shifted to the young man with the cane. After the yell, he had one moment of indecision; then he turned and darted up the track.

"Go it, sport!" Bert cheered, waving his hat in the air. "You're the goods for me! Who'd a-thought it? Who'd a-thought it? Say! — wouldn't it now? Just wouldn't it?"

"Phew! He's a streak himself," Billy admired. "But what did he do it for? He's no bricklayer."

Like a frightened rabbit, the mad roar at his heels, the young man tore up the track to an open space on the hillside, up which he clawed and disappeared among the trees. Beside him toiled a hundred vengeful runners.

"It's too bad he's missing the rest of it," Billy said. "Look at 'em goin' to it."

Bert was beside himself. He leaped up and down and cried continuously:

"Look at 'em! Look at 'em! Look at 'em!"

The Oakland faction was outraged. Twice had its favorite runner been jobbed out of the race. This last was only another vile trick of the Frisco faction. So Oakland doubled its brawny fists and swung into San Francisco for blood. And

San Francisco, consciously innocent, was no less willing to join issues. To be charged with such a crime was no less monstrous than the crime itself. Besides, for too many tedious hours had the Irish heroically suppressed themselves. Five thousands of them exploded into joyous battle. The women joined with them. The whole amphitheater was filled with the conflict. There were rallies, retreats, charges, and counter-charges. Weaker groups were forced fighting up the hillsides. Other groups, bested, fled among the trees to carry on guerrilla warfare, emerging in sudden dashes to overwhelm isolated enemies. Half a dozen special policemen, hired by the Weasel Park management, received an impartial trouncing from both sides.

"Nobody's the friend of a policeman," Bert chortled, dabbing his handkerchief to his injured ear, which still bled.

The bushes crackled behind him, and he sprang aside to let the locked forms of two men go by, rolling over and over down the hill, each striking when uppermost, and followed by a screaming woman who rained blows on the one who was patently not of her clan.

The judges, in the second story of the stand, valiantly withstood a fierce assault until the frail structure toppled to the ground in splinters.

"What's that woman doing?" Saxon asked, calling attention to an elderly woman beneath them on the track, who had sat down and was pulling from her foot an elastic-sided shoe of generous dimensions.

"Goin' swimming," Bert chuckled, as the stocking followed.

They watched, fascinated. The shoe was pulled on again over the bare foot. Then the woman slipped a rock the size of her fist into the stocking, and, brandishing this ancient and horrible weapon, lumbered into the nearest fray.

"Oh! — Oh! — Oh!" Bert screamed, with every blow she struck. "Hey, old flannel-mouth! Watch out! You'll get yours in a second. Oh! Oh! A peach! Did you see it? Hurray for the old lady! Look at her tearin' into 'em! Watch out old girl! . . . Ah-h-h."

His voice died away regretfully, as the one with the stocking, whose hair had been clutched from behind by another Amazon, was whirled about in a dizzy semicircle.

Vainly Mary clung to his arm, shaking him back and forth and remonstrating.

"Can't you be sensible?" she cried. "It's awful! I tell you it's awful!"

But Bert was irrepressible.

"Go it, old girl!" he encouraged. "You win! Me for you every time! Now's your chance! Swat! Oh! My! A peach! A peach!"

"It's the biggest rough-house I ever saw," Bill confided to Saxon. "It sure takes the Micks to mix it. But what did that dude wanta do it for? That's what gets me. He wasn't a bricklayer — not even a workingman — just a regular sissy dude that didn't know a livin' soul in the grounds. But if he wanted to raise a rough-house he certainly done it. Look at 'em. They're fightin' everywhere."

He broke into sudden laughter, so hearty that the tears came into his eyes.

"What is it?" Saxon asked, anxious not to miss anything.

"It's that dude," Billy explained between gusts. "What did he wanta do it for? That's what gets my goat. What'd he wanta do it for?"

There was more crashing in the brush, and two women erupted upon the scene, one in flight, the other pursuing. Almost ere they could realize it, the little group found itself merged in the astounding conflict that covered, if not the face of creation, at least all the visible landscape of Weasel Park.

The fleeing woman stumbled in rounding the end of a picnic bench, and would have been caught had she not seized Mary's arm to recover balance, and then flung Mary full into the arms of the woman who pursued. This woman, largely built, middle-aged, and too irate to comprehend, clutched Mary's hair by one hand and lifted the other to smack her. Before the blow could fall, Billy had seized both the woman's wrists.

"Come on, old girl, cut it out," he said appeasingly. "You're in wrong. She ain't done nothin'."

Then the woman did a strange thing. Making no resistance, but maintaining her hold on the girl's hair, she stood still and calmly began to scream. The scream was hideously compounded of fright and fear. Yet in her face was neither fright nor fear. She regarded Billy coolly and appraisingly, as if to see how he took it — her scream merely the cry to the clan for help.

"Aw, shut up, you battleax!" Bert vociferated, trying to drag her off by the shoulders.

The result was that the four rocked back and forth, while the woman calmly went on screaming. The scream became touched with triumph as more crashing was heard in the brush.

Saxon saw Billy's slow eyes glint suddenly to the hardness of steel, and at the same time she saw him put pressure on his wrist-holds. The woman released her grip on Mary and was shoved back and free. Then the first man of the rescue was upon them. He did not pause to inquire into the merits of the affair. It was sufficient that he saw the woman reeling away from Billy and screaming with pain that was largely feigned.

"It's all a mistake," Billy cried hurriedly. "We apologize, sport —"

The Irishman swung ponderously. Billy ducked, cutting his apology short, and as the sledge-like fist passed over his head, he drove his left to the other's jaw. The big Irishman toppled over sidewise and sprawled on the edge of the slope. Half-scrambled back to his feet and out of balance, he was caught by Bert's fist, and this time went clawing down the slope that was slippery with short, dry grass.

Bert was redoubtable. "That for you, old girl — my compliments," was his cry, as he shoved the woman over the edge on to the treacherous slope. Three more men were emerging from the brush.

In the meantime, Billy had put Saxon in behind the protection of the picnic table. Mary, who was hysterical, had evinced a desire to cling to him, and he had sent her sliding across the top of the table to Saxon.

"Come on you flannel-mouths!" Bert yelled at the newcomers, himself swept away by passion, his black eyes flashing wildly, his dark face inflamed by the too-ready blood. "Come on, you cheap skates! Talk about Gettysburg. We'll show you all the Americans ain't dead yet!"

"Shut your trap — we don't want a scrap with the girls here," Billy growled harshly, holding his position in front of the table. He turned to the three rescuers, who were bewildered by the lack of anything visible to rescue. "Go on, sports. We don't want a row. You're in wrong. They ain't nothin' doin' in the fight line. We don't wanta fight — d'ye get me?"

They still hesitated, and Billy might have succeeded in avoiding trouble had not the man who had gone down the bank chosen that unfortunate moment to reappear, crawling groggily on hands and knees and showing a bleeding face. Again Bert reached him and sent him down-slope, and the other three, with wild yells, sprang in on Billy, who punched, shifted position, ducked and punched, and shifted again ere he struck the third time. His blows were clean and hard, scientifically delivered, with the weight of his body behind.

Saxon, looking on, saw his eyes and learned more about him. She was frightened, but clear-seeing, and she was startled by the disappearance of all depth of light and shadow in his eyes. They showed surface only — a hard, bright surface, almost glazed, devoid of all expression save deadly seriousness. Bert's eyes showed madness. The eyes of the Irishmen were angry and serious, and yet not all serious. There was a wayward gleam in them, as if they enjoyed the fracas. But in Billy's eyes was no enjoyment. It was as if he had certain work to do and had doggedly settled down to do it.

Scarcely more expression did she note in the face, though there was nothing in common between it and the one she had seen all day. The boyishness had vanished. This face was mature in a terrifying, ageless way. There was no anger in it. Nor was it even pitiless. It seemed to have glazed as hard and passionless as his eyes. Something came to her of her wonderful mother's tales of the ancient Saxons, and he seemed to her one of those Saxons, and she caught a glimpse, on the wall of her consciousness, of a long, dark boat, with a prow like the beak of a bird of prey, and of huge, half-naked men, wing-helmeted, and one of their faces, it seemed to her, was his face. She did not reason this. She felt it, and visioned it as by an unthinkable clairvoyance, and gasped, for the flurry of war was over. It had lasted only seconds. Bert was dancing on the edge of the slippery slope and mocking the vanquished who had slid impotently to the bottom. But Billy took charge.

"Come on, you girls," he commanded. "Get onto yourself, Bert. We got to get outa this. We can't fight an army."

He led the retreat, holding Saxon's arm, and Bert, giggling and jubilant, brought up the rear with an indignant Mary who protested vainly in his unheeding ears.

For a hundred yards they ran and twisted through the trees, and then, no signs of pursuit appearing, they slowed down to a dignified saunter. Bert, the trouble-seeker, pricked his ears to the muffled sound of blows and sobs, and stepped aside to investigate.

"Oh! — look what I've found!" he called.

They joined him on the edge of a dry ditch and looked down. In the bottom were two men, strays from the fight, grappled together and still fighting. They were weeping out of sheer fatigue and helplessness, and the blows they only occasionally struck were open-handed and ineffectual.

"Hey, you, sport — throw sand in his eyes," Bert counseled. "That's it, blind him an' he's your'n."

"Stop that!" Billy shouted at the man, who was following instructions. "Or I'll come down there an' beat you up myself. It's all over — d'ye get me? It's all over an' everybody's friends. Shake an' make up. The drinks are on both of you. That's right — here, gimme your hand an' I'll put you out."

They left them shaking hands and brushing each other's clothes.

"It soon will be over," Billy grinned to Saxon. "I know 'em. Fight's fun with them. An' this big scrap's made the day a howlin' success. What did I tell you? — look over at that table there."

A group of disheveled men and women, still breathing heavily, were shaking hands all around.

"Come on, let's dance," Mary pleaded, urging them in the direction of the pavilion.

All over the park the warring bricklayers were shaking
hands and making up, while the open-air bars were crowded
with the drinkers.

Saxon walked very close to Billy. She was proud of him.
He could fight, and he could avoid trouble. In all that had
occurred he had striven to avoid trouble. And, also, con-
sideration for her and Mary had been uppermost in his
mind.

"You are brave," she said to him.

"It's like takin' candy from a baby," he disclaimed. "They
only rough-house. They don't know boxin'. They're wide
open, an' all you gotta do is hit 'em. It ain't real fightin', you
know." With a troubled, boyish look in his eyes, he stared at
his bruised knuckles. "An' I'll have to drive team to-morrow
with 'em," he lamented. "Which ain't fun, I'm tellin' you,
when they stiffen up."

# 15

THE SCENE IS a remote South Sea island. The time is that long-ago era of colonial "outposts" of progress," when lonely planters and traders kept the most fragile contact with the outside world and tried to resist the temptations of going native.

Rivals in love and business, two sportsmen named Sheldon and Tudor decide to do the civilized thing and engage in a most unusual kind of hunt — a sporting stalk designed to eliminate one of them from competition.

Each man is armed with a rifle and automatic pistol. The arena of their hunt is the one mile of jungle plantation that stretches between the Berande and Balesuna rivers. The rules of the game decree that the hunters shall "start a mile apart, and advance on each other, taking advantage of cover, retreating, circling, feinting — anything and everything permissible."

So begins the most dangerous game.

*"The Most Dangerous Game"*
*(originally entitled "Modern Duelling")*
*is reprinted from* Adventure.
*Copyright 1911 by The Macmillan Company;*

# The Most Dangerous Game

**B**ARELY HAD SHELDON reached the Balesuna, when he heard the faint report of a distant rifle and knew it was the signal of Tudor, giving notice that he had reached the Berande, turned about, and was coming back. Sheldon fired his rifle into the air in answer, and in turn proceeded to advance. He moved as in a dream, absent-mindedly keeping to the open beach. The thing was so preposterous that he had to struggle to realize it, and he reviewed in his mind the conversation with Tudor, trying to find some clew to the common-sense of what he was doing. He did not want to kill Tudor. Because that man had blundered in his love-making was no reason that he, Sheldon, should take his life. Then what was it all about? True, the fellow had insulted Joan by his subsequent remarks and been knocked down for it, but because he had knocked him down was no reason that he should now try to kill him.

In this fashion, he covered a quarter of the distance between the two rivers, when it dawned upon him that Tudor was not on the beach at all. Of course not. He was advancing, according to the terms of the agreement, in the shelter of the cocoanut trees. Sheldon promptly swerved to the left to seek similar shelter, when the faint crack of a rifle came to his ears, and almost immediately the bullet, striking the hard sand a hundred feet beyond him, ricochetted and whined onward in a second flight, convincing him that preposterous and unreal as it was, it was, nevertheless, sober fact. It had been intended for him. Yet even then it was hard to believe. He glanced over the familiar landscape and at the sea, dimpling in the light but steady breeze. From the direction of Tulagi he could see the white sails of a schooner laying a tack across toward Berande. Down the beach a horse was grazing, and he idly wondered where the others were. The smoke rising from the copra-drying caught his eyes, which roved on over the barracks, the tool-houses, the boat-sheds, and the bungalow, and came to rest on Joan's little grass house in the corner of the compound.

Keeping now to the shelter of the trees, he went forward another quarter of a mile. If Tudor had advanced with equal speed, they should have come together at that point, and Sheldon concluded that the other was circling. The difficulty was to locate him. The rows of trees, running at right angles, enabled him to see along only one narrow avenue at a time. His enemy might be coming along the next avenue, or the next, to right or left. He might be a hundred feet away or half a mile. Sheldon plodded on, and decided that the old stereotyped duel was far simpler and easier than this protracted hide-and-seek affair. He, too, tried circling, in the hope of cutting the other's circle; but, without catching a glimpse of him, he finally emerged upon a fresh clearing where the young trees, waist-high, afforded little shelter and less hiding. Just as he emerged, stepping out a pace, a rifle cracked to his right, and though he did not hear the bullet in passing, the thud of it came to his ears when it struck a palm trunk farther on.

He sprang back into the protection of the larger trees. Twice he had exposed himself and been fired at, while he had failed to catch a single glimpse of his antagonist. A slow anger began to burn in him. It was deucedly unpleasant, he decided, this being peppered at; and nonsensical as it really was, it was none the less deadly serious. There was no avoiding the issue, no firing in the air and getting over with it as in the old-fashioned duel. This mutual manhunt must keep up until one got the other. And if one neglected a chance to get the other, that increased the other's chance to get him. There could be no false sentiment about it. Tudor had been a cunning devil when he proposed this sort of duel, Sheldon concluded, as he began to work along cautiously in the direction of the last shot.

When he arrived at the spot, Tudor was gone, and only his footprints remained, pointing out the course he had taken into the depths of the plantation. Once, ten minutes later, he caught a glimpse of Tudor, a hundred yards away, crossing the same avenue as himself but going in the opposite direction. His rifle half leaped to his shoulder, but the other was gone. More in whim than in hope of result, grinning to himself as he did so, Sheldon raised his automatic pistol and in two seconds sent eight shots scattering through the trees in the direction in which Tudor had disappeared. Wishing he had a shot-gun, Sheldon dropped to the ground behind a tree, slipped a fresh clip up the hollow butt of the pistol, threw a cartridge into the chamber, shoved the safety catch into place, and reloaded the empty clip.

It was but a short time after that that Tudor tried the same trick on him, the bullets pattering about him like spiteful rain, thudding into the palm trunks, or glancing off in whining ricochets. The last bullet of all, making a double ricochet from two different trees and losing most of its momentum, struck Sheldon a sharp blow on the forehead and dropped at his feet. He was partly stunned for the moment, but on investigation found no greater harm than a nasty lump that soon rose to the size of a pigeon's egg.

The hunt went on. Once, coming to the edge of the grove near the bungalow, he saw the house-boys and the cook, clustered on the back veranda and peering curiously among the trees, talking and laughing with one another in their queer falsetto voices. Another time he came upon a working gang busy at hoeing weeds. They scarcely noticed him when he came up, though they knew thoroughly well what was going on. It was no affair of theirs that the enigmatical white men should be out trying to kill each other, and whatever interest in the proceedings might be theirs, they were careful to conceal it from Sheldon. He ordered them to continue hoeing weeds in a distant and out-of-the-way corner, and went on with the pursuit of Tudor.

Tiring of the endless circling, Sheldon tried once more to advance directly on his foe, but the latter was too crafty, taking advantage of his boldness to fire a couple of shots at him and slipping away on some changed and continually changing course. For an hour, they dodged and turned and twisted back and forth and around and hunted each other among the orderly palms. They caught fleeting glimpses of each other and chanced flying shots which were without result. On a grassy shelter behind a tree, Sheldon came upon where Tudor had rested and smoked a cigarette. The pressed grass showed where he had sat. To one side lay the cigarette stump and the charred match which had lighted it. In front lay a scattering of bright metallic fragments. Sheldon recognized their significance. Tudor was notching his steel-jacketed bullets, or cutting them blunt, so that they would spread on striking — in short, he was making them into the vicious dumdum prohibited in modern warfare. Sheldon knew now what would happen to him if a bullet struck his body. It would leave a tiny hole where it entered, but the hole where it emerged would be the size of a saucer.

He decided to give up the pursuit, and lay down in the grass, protected right and left by the row of palms, with, on either hand, the long avenue extending. This he could watch. Tudor would have to come to him or else there would be no termination of the affair. He wiped the sweat from his face and tied the handkerchief around his neck to keep off the stinging gnats that lurked in the grass. Never had he felt so great a disgust for the thing called "adventure." Joan had been bad enough, with her Baden-Powell and long-barrelled Colt's; but here was this newcomer, also looking for adventure and finding it in no other way than by lugging a peace-loving planter into an absurd and preposterous bush-whacking duel. If ever adventure was well damned, it was by Sheldon, sweating in the windless grass and fighting gnats, the while he kept close watch up and down the avenue.

Then Tudor came. Sheldon happened to be looking in his direction at the moment he came into view, peering quickly up and down the avenue before he stepped into the open. Midway he stopped, as if debating what course to pursue. He made a splendid mark, facing his concealed enemy at two hundred yards' distance. Sheldon aimed at the centre of his chest, then deliberately shifted the aim to his right shoulder, and, with the thought, "that will put him out of business," pulled the trigger. The bullet, driving with momentum sufficient to perforate a man's body a mile distant, struck Tudor with such force as to pivot him, whirling him half around by the shock of its impact and knocking him down.

"Hope I haven't killed the beggar," Sheldon muttered aloud, springing to his feet and running forward.

A hundred feet away, all anxiety on that score was relieved by Tudor, who made shift with his left hand and from his automatic pistol hurled a rain of bullets all around Sheldon. The latter dodged behind a palm trunk, counting the shots, and when the eighth had been fired, he rushed in on the wounded man. He kicked the pistol out of the other's hand and then sat down on him in order to keep him down.

"Be quiet," he said. "I've got you, so there's no use struggling."

Tudor still attempted to struggle and to throw him off.

"Keep quiet, I tell you," Sheldon commanded. "I'm satisfied with the outcome, and you've got to be. So you might as well give in and call this affair closed."

Tudor reluctantly relaxed.

"Rather funny, isn't it, these modern duels?" Sheldon grinned down at him as he removed his weight. "Not a bit dignified. If you'd struggled a moment longer, I'd have rubbed your face in the earth. I've a good mind to do it anyway, just to teach you that duelling has gone out of fashion. Now, let us see to your injuries."

"You only got me that last," Tudor grunted sullenly, "lying in ambush like —"

"Like a wild Indian. Precisely. You've caught the idea, old man." Sheldon ceased his mocking and stood up. "You lie there quietly until I send back some of the boys to carry you in. You're not seriously hurt, and it's lucky for you I didn't follow your example. If you had been struck with one of your own bullets, a carriage and pair would have been none too large to drive through the hole it would have made. As it is, you're drilled clean — a nice little perforation. All you need is antiseptic washing and dressing and you'll be around in a month. Now take it easy, and I'll send a stretcher for you."